Wrong time, and possibly the wrong man.

But as if her arms weren't controlled by her brain, Annie reached around his back and drew him to her.

His back muscles tightened beneath her touch and he drew in a ragged breath. Tombi stilled, as if warring with his sexual desire and his duty in the world outside the tent.

Annie wanted him desperately, just for a few minutes, a little slice of time. She saw how much he gave to the others, how they looked up to him. Didn't he deserve a few minutes of happiness for himself?

Didn't she?

Who knew what dangers the night and the hunt might bring?

BAYOU SHADOW HUNTER

DEBBIE HERBERT

First Published in Great Britain 2016
By Mills & Boon, an imprint of HarperCollins*Publishers*
1 London Bridge Street, London, SE1 9GF

© 2016 Debbie Herbert

ISBN: 978-0-263-92166-3

89-0316

Our policy is to use papers that are natural, renewable and recyclable products and made from wood grown in sustainable forests. The logging and manufacturing processes conform to the legal environmental regulations of the country of origin.

Printed and bound in Spain
by CPI, Barcelona

Debbie Herbert writes paranormal romance novels reflecting her belief that love, like magic, casts its own spell of enchantment. She's always been fascinated by magic, romance and gothic stories. Married and living in Alabama, she roots for the Crimson Tide football team. Her oldest son, like many of her characters, has autism. Her youngest son is in the US Army. A past Maggie Award finalist in both young-adult and paranormal romance, she's a member of the Georgia Romance Writers of America.

Chapter 1

"Thunder Moon comin' tonight. Yer life is fixin' to change."

Grandma Tia called the August full moon "Thunder Moon" and proclaimed it a time of enchantment. Annie had to admit tonight *did* appear magical and mysterious. The forest beckoned with its thick canopy of trees draped in long tendrils of Spanish moss that fluttered in the sea breeze with a silver shimmer like a living veil of secrecy.

And so they had burned tiny scraps of paper where they'd written what they wanted purged from their lives. As she'd done every month for most of her life, Annie had written only one thing. The same thing. She held the paper to candle flame, watching it catch fire and curl in on itself before the wind carried it away. It splintered into tiny embers that flickered like fireflies before turning to ash.

Annie sat on the bed, hugging her knees to her chest and staring out the window, pondering her grandma's words.

She could use some change. Lots of it. If only she could get rid of… No. No point agonizing over that, when she was so close to sleep.

A green glow skittered erratically in the swampy darkness.

Very pretty. Annie turned away from the bedroom window, yawned and slipped into bed, pulling a thin cotton sheet over her head like a cocoon.

Wait a minute… She jerked to a sitting position and peered out the window across the room. Each glass pane framed squares of refracted moonbeams piercing through tumbles of tree limbs. A patchwork quilt of the macabre.

But on second glance, no green, glowing orbs of light dotted the night's landscape. Must have been a trick of the eye or the flash of a dream. Perhaps it was merely that Grandma had planted the suggestion of something magical happening tonight when they had gone outside after dinner and held a brief lunar ritual. Full moons represented death and change, a time for powerful magic.

A ball of light again materialized at the tree line, not more than twenty feet from their cottage. It burned blue at the center and green at the edges. Annie instinctively touched the silver cross nestled in the hollow of her throat, palm flattening above the rapid thumping of her heart.

A teal stream of light broke away from the orb, forming a tail like a comet hurtling across the night sky. The pixilated specks of color were magical as fairy dust, coalescing into the shape of an arm, beckoning her closer.

Dare she?

Annie scrambled off the bed, feet touching the rough-hewn pine floorboard, still sun-warmed from the day's ferocious heat. She raced to the back door and slid into flip-flops she kept at the entry. Hand on the door, she paused and glanced to her left. Grandma's bedroom door was open, and her deep, labored breathing wafted across the cottage. Annie softly tiptoed to the room and peeked inside.

Grandma Tia's hair was wrapped in a satin cloth that nestled against a white pillowcase. Her lined face was relaxed in a way only produced by sweet dreams. The weight and worry of time and life's sorrows laid aside in a few hours of respite.

She wouldn't rouse her from slumber. Grandma Tia's heart condition meant she needed rest. Annie's eyes rested on the red flannel gris-gris bag hung on the bedpost. Which reminded her to grab her own mojo bag. She hurried back to her bedroom, retrieved it from beneath the pillow and tied it to the drawstring of her pajama bottoms. Just in case. A quick glance out the window confirmed the green light still hovered a few feet above ground.

Despite the late hour, humidity cocooned her body in a damp embrace the moment she stepped outside. To top it off, the light had disappeared again. She sat on the concrete porch steps and lifted her hair off the back of her sticky nape, waiting and watching.

Probably nothing but swamp gas. The night buzzed with a battalion of insects, and she cocked her head to one side, listening, actively expanding her energy outward to pick up even the subtlest of sound—the wind swirling clumps of sand, the hoot of an owl far away—all against the eternal ebb and flow of the distant ocean tide.

What was she doing out here? Normally, she wouldn't think of investigating something alone, but, like a cat, curiosity overrode her fear.

Something prickled her skin. The air danced with a faint tinkling—like the fading echo of tiny bells rung from deep within the forest. Annie closed her eyes, gathering the vibration of musical notes, assimilating a pattern: *one*, two, two, *three*, two, two, *five*, two, two.

Melodic patterns had called to her since kindergarten when a teacher handed out metal triangles and wands. She'd pinged the base, and the ringing vibration had shivered down her spine. A living pulse that had been a first clue of her gift, her curse, her fate. Other kids had banged away on the triangles until the pureness of the music changed to an unbearable din, and she'd run out of the classroom.

She'd been running ever since.

But tonight's high-pitched bell notes made her feet itch to dance and throw her arms open to embrace the night. It had a certain symmetry and lyrical quality that charmed. It drew her, tugged at her soul…

Annie opened her eyes. More than a dozen orbs of light danced in the distant darkness. They were a rainbow of colors and sizes and varied in brightness.

That was where the music came from.

They called her, beckoned her to draw near. She rose unsteadily to her feet, light-headed with awe, and slowly stepped away from the cottage. The lights bobbed and darted behind and between the oaks. All at once, the orbs disappeared, as if someone had turned off a switch. Annie ran toward the woods. For once she ran *to* the music instead of *away* from its source.

Wait for me. Don't leave me behind.

As if hearing the unspoken words, a bluish-green orb flashed. A spectacular, southern aurora borealis. It was the first, lone light she'd seen from the bedroom window, as distinctive and individual as a human form. She ran across the yard, plunged into the woods, down a narrow trail littered with pinecones and broken twigs. Black night, thick with heat, pressed around her body, yet she stumbled forward, ever deeper. More lights bobbled ahead, just beyond reach. Mosquitoes buzzed her ears and nipped her arms and chest. The sulfur smell of swampland grew more pungent and sharp.

Annie didn't care. The blue light glowed like a lantern against the darkness, and the crystalline notes played from its burning core. Low-lying branches scraped her arms and face, and her legs grew wooden with exhaustion as on she walked, following ever deeper.

A clearing opened onto a muddy bank, and Annie pulled up short at the sight of a brackish pond. Mud gooshed over her sandals and between her toes. The slimy sensation worked like a face slap. Blackness shadowed the night as a cloud passed over the moon, and the glowing orbs vanished once more. The music stopped, and silence gathered, dense and foreboding.

"Umm…hello? Anybody out there?" She didn't know whether she felt more foolish or frightened. She lifted one foot out of the goo and almost lost a sandal. "Terrific. This is just great."

Screeching erupted—as if a parliament of enraged owls or a volt of vultures were descending on her for interloping on their territory. Annie clamped hands over ears and squeezed her fingertips over the ear canals, but the noise and pressure felt like a bomber plane taking off inside her brain. Turning blindly, she ran, desperate to escape the sound attack.

What the hell is this? Where is it coming from? It was like a combination of an animal screech, a howl of pain, shattering glass and a jarring, jumbled chorus of dissonant chords, as if someone were banging an untuned piano.

Silence crashed the darkness. Annie leaned her back against an oak tree and hunched down, panting. Relieved the noise had stopped but expecting it to return any moment, her body was coiled and tense. She grimaced at the stitch in her side and tried to regulate her breathing to a slower pace. *Calm down. Think.*

She tilted her head upward, rough bark grazing her scalp. The moon glowed, laced with a web of black thread from the treetops. The sky held a thin promise of dawn, evidenced only by a violet-hued line in the east that graduated to black by degrees.

Great. So she knew where east lay. But that was the extent of her internal compass. And it didn't help her figure out how to get back to the cottage. Best to stay right where she was and wait for daylight. If she was lucky, someone, maybe a hunter, would be along, or she would recognize some landmark once the sun emerged.

How could she have been so stupid as to trot off at night into the bayou after a will-o'-the-wisp or whatever that light was? She shuddered. Focus. Right now there were rattlers and water moccasins and gators to worry about. And who knew what other cursed creatures roamed the land.

She swatted at a mosquito nipping her arm. Hmm. Could snakes climb trees? A glance upward revealed that seeking higher ground was a non-option. The nearest limb was several feet above her standing height. When she recouped her strength, perhaps she should search for a stone or stick just in case...

"Help me!"

The deep baritone voice rumbled along her spine.

Annie scrambled to her feet and searched the shadows. "Who's there?"

Silence. Okay, she was going to be that person in the headline news who was lost in the woods and found days later, a nutcase raving about swamp monsters and Big Foot and saying she'd been carted away by aliens on their UFO.

Nothing's out there.

"Please."

The anguish in that word was too tortured not to be real. Annie shivered despite the heat and sweat coating her body. Ignoring someone else's pain went against all her healing instincts. "Where are you? *Who* are you?"

An orb manifested not ten feet from where she stood. No warning, no gathering of light, no sound. One second before loomed a dark void, and in a clock's single tick, the orb absorbed the space.

The blue-green light swirled and pulsed like a breathing, living thing. The same orb she'd seen first from her bedroom window.

So the question was no longer where or who but "*What* are you?" she whispered.

"The shadows trapped me."

The voice rumbled in her gut, vibrating in her being. "You're...trapped in the light?" she asked haltingly.

"My heart beats within. Look."

At the core of the blue light shone a concentrated mass of teal that swelled and contracted. In, out, in, out, pulsing with the cosmic rhythm of life.

A heart.

Not the flowers-and-lace, cupid sort drawn by five-year-olds, but the it's-alive-and-it's-real-and-it-beats kind. Annie's breath hitched, and she took an unsteady step backward. She couldn't stop staring at the fist-sized gelatinous mass of muscle that pumped and wobbled.

"I need out," the low-timbered voice pleaded. "Help me get out."

She shook her head violently, her own heart pounding a song of fear. "I don't know how." And even if she did, no way was she freeing...whatever it was. Not until she knew its true nature.

"My name is Bo," it said. "Find Tombi and tell him I

live. He's in grave danger. Trust no one within the circle. I was betrayed. And if he was ever my true friend, he needs to find that betrayer. I can't be released until then."

"I don't know this Tombi person," she protested.

"He's coming now. Tell him to beware."

Annie swung her head in all directions but saw and sensed nothing in the shadows. "Why don't you tell him yourself?"

"He can't hear me, witch. No one ever has but you."

"Oh," she breathed. "That's why you brought me here." It...Bo...either knew her grandma or of her reputation. "I think you want my grandmother, not me. I'm only here on a visit and—"

"Warn him."

The light shifted, swirling in individuated sparkles and growing smaller, denser.

"Wait," she called out sharply. "Where are you going?"

But it had vanished.

A man slipped into her presence, silent as a windless sky. He leaned against a cypress, arms folded, face and body as unyielding and hard as the ancient tree. Eyes and hair were black as the night, and the only lightness on his figure was a golden sheen on his face and arms.

Friend or foe?

Silence blanketed her mind. A condition she normally welcomed, but not now. Where was her accursed ability when she needed it? Not the slightest syllable of sound surrounded the man.

"Who are you?" she asked, hoping her voice didn't portray fear.

He stepped closer, and she willed her feet to remain rooted to the ground, to cloak the fear.

"Who are *you*?" His voice was deep, sharp-edged with suspicion.

She'd been wrong. The golden sheen of his skin wasn't the only thing that stood out in the darkness. The man's eyes radiated a copper glint like an encapsulated sun with rays. His teeth were white and sharp.

He didn't wait for an answer. "Who were you talking to? There's no one else out here but us."

"I was talking to myself," she lied. No sense exposing herself to ridicule.

"Roaming the woods alone at night and talking to yourself?" He scowled. "You must be crazy."

Despite the scowl and rough tone, the icy touch of fear at the base of her spine thawed a bit. This stranger could think what he wanted about her mental health and lecture her ad nauseam about the idiotic decision to follow the wisp. At least he wasn't attacking her. If he meant harm, he could have lunged forward and grabbed her by now.

"Yes." Annie agreed. "I'm totally off my rocker." Wouldn't be the first time someone thought that. "How about being a good Boy Scout and help me find my way home?"

"First, tell me your name and why you're out here."

"Fine. My name's Annie Matthews, and I saw a strange light from my bedroom window. Like an idiot, I decided to check it out. Now, can you please get me out of here?"

He stared, those strange copper rays in his irises warming her insides. Abruptly, he turned his back and stepped away.

What a jerk. Annie's lips tightened to a pinched line. "Hey—wait a minute. Are you going to help me or not?"

The man didn't even look back but motioned with an arm for her to follow.

She let out a huge sigh. Jerk or not, her best bet was to follow him out of the swamp. Annie stumbled after him and onto the barest sliver of a trail. The narrow footpath was canopied by pines and oaks, obscuring the full-moon light. Her toe caught under a tree root, and she pitched forward, free-falling. She braced herself for the impact of packed dirt to face.

Strong arms grabbed the sides of her waist, and her chest bumped solid flesh. Annie raised her chin and stared deeply into the brown eyes. "Th-thank you," she whispered. His hands above her hips held fast, steadying her—burning her. Annie's hands rested lightly on his chest, and she couldn't move or speak.

A low, thudding bass note, a drumbeat, pounded in her ears. Was it from her heart beating faster, or was sound escaping his controlled aura?

"I forget you can't see like me." He took one of her hands in his. "Stay close."

Before she could object or ask what his remark meant, he pulled her forward.

She should be terrified alone in the woods with a stranger.

But for the first time since hearing the voice inside the wisp, Annie felt safe.

The narrow trail of dense shrubs and overarching tree limbs gave way to a wider, more open trail illuminated by the Thunder Moon. It was as if he were leading her down a silent passage that exited a nightmare.

At the edge of the tree line lay an open field. Weeds and brambles rippled, silver-tipped from moonbeams and glistening like drops of water dancing on waves. A glow flickered in Grandma Tia's cottage, a lighthouse beam signaling home.

Annie glanced at the man's chiseled profile. Harsh, fierce even. *Handsome* seemed too pretty a word to describe him. He was powerful, a force of the night.

"Beyond this field is a dirt road that leads to County Road 143. Know where you are now?"

She laughed, giddy with relief, and pointed to the cottage. "Of course. That's my grandma's house. Her name's Tia Henrietta. Maybe you've met her before?"

"The witch in the woods?" Surprise flickered in his eyes. "I should have guessed. Are you one, as well?"

She tugged her hand away from his. "No more than you."

His hand reached out and stroked the red flannel mojo pouch belted at her waist. "What magic is this?"

"Gris-gris bags. My grandma makes them. For protection."

"Didn't work, huh?"

"Sure it did. It brought you to me, and then you brought me home."

His lips curled. "I don't know what kind of magic your grandmother claims to have, but that pouch didn't help you when the will-o'-the-wisp conjured you into the woods."

"What do you know of them?" she asked, burning with curiosity now the danger had passed.

He ignored her question. "So you followed this light. What happened next?"

She bit her lip. "Looks like I'm the one doing all the talking. How about I tell you one thing, then you tell me one thing?"

He nodded. "Deal."

"Okay, then. The light disappeared a few minutes. When it came back, something inside it spoke." Annie took a deep breath. This wasn't easy to talk about. This was partly what alienated her from everyone. The crazy sticker on her forehead.

But the man didn't flinch. "What did it say?"

Annie hedged. Once again, she was doing most of the talking. "Tell me your name."

"Tombi. Tombi Silver."

She inhaled sharply, and his eyes narrowed.

"What is it?" he demanded.

"The voice. It mentioned you by name."

He leaned in and grabbed her arms, not bruising-hard, but enough so that she couldn't run away. "What. Did. It. Say?"

What the hell. This wouldn't be the first time she'd been used as a conduit for messages. Best to relay it and get on with her life. Otherwise, the wisp or spirit, or whatever that thing was, would keep appearing in some form or another until it had its way.

"It said you were in great danger and to trust no one, not even in your inner circle. That there's a betrayer in your ranks, and if you were ever his true friend you need to find the betrayer, so he can be released."

She didn't think it possible the man—Tombi—could look fiercer, but he did. He let go of her and shook his head.

"No. I don't believe you."

Annie hitched her shoulders and raised her palms. "Fine. But that's what the thing told me."

"Did it have a name?"

"Bo."

Ringing flooded Tombi's ears. *There's worse things than witches. Much worse.*

"What did Bo say?"

Annie recoiled, and he realized he was shouting. With great effort, he lowered his voice. "Tell me what he said."

"He's trapped inside a wisp and wants you to free him."

Guilt and anger heaved in his stomach. "I've been trying to find him for weeks. Why didn't he come to me? I was his best friend."

Bo. His blood brother and childhood comrade. Always reliable. Always quick with the jokes and the laughter. And the only man who could make Tallulah laugh. His sister hadn't smiled in months. Not since Bo died. Sometimes he wondered if she ever would again.

"*Was* your best friend?" Annie's eyes rounded. "What happened to him?"

Tombi gritted his teeth. Oh, she looked innocent enough. Standing there in her flower-print T-shirt and drawstring pajama shorts. Brown hair tumbling in waves down to her hips. At first glance, she'd appeared a mere slip of a girl—skinny and all legs.

His eyes shifted to the fullness of her breasts and slight swelling of her hips. Definitely a woman. A very sexy woman. Not that it mattered. Evil spirits roamed in many guises.

"He died. Snakebite." He watched her closely, checking for signs of guilt or glee.

She shuddered. "That's horrible."

"Died right where I found you tonight."

Annie crossed her arms and looked downward apprehensively. "I hate snakes. Was it a rattler or a water moccasin?"

"Rattler. He died alone out there in the woods." How many times had he imagined Bo's horrible death? Imagined him feeling the rapid, burning spread of venom in his veins, knowing he was doomed.

Tombi drew a rasping breath. "He shouldn't have had to die alone."

"Nobody should," she agreed. "How—how did he get trapped in a wisp?"

"You really don't know?" he asked sharply.

"No." She squared her shoulders. "I've only been out here a few weeks visiting my grandma. Lots of weirdness down here, even more than usual this summer. Stuff I've never seen before. Or heard."

"About what you heard…what did Bo say exactly?"

"I told you. There's a betrayer in your ranks. He wanted me to warn you of danger."

A likely story. Wasn't that the way evil sank its fangs into people? It insinuated and manipulated fear and mistrust where none existed. Until you became paranoid and relied only on your own wits for survival. He'd seen it so many times over the past few years.

"I don't believe you."

She shrugged. "Suit yourself. Don't shoot me, I'm just the messenger."

"You always go around hearing voices?" he sneered.

"Yes."

Her quick, short response surprised him. "You do?"

"You already think I'm a witch, so—what the hell—yes, I hear things. Not voices usually. I hear music around people."

"Music?" He snorted. What kind of strange magic was this?

Her lips compressed in a thin line. "It's what drew me to the woods tonight. I heard the most beautiful music—it sounded like fairy bells."

Tombi considered Annie's words. "Did you smell anything?"

"Hmm? No. Not unless you count the constant smell of the ocean. Do the wisps have a certain smell?"

"They can. Will-o'-wisps appeal to different people differently ways." With him, they tried to mask their foul odor under the clean, sweet scent of balsam fir. He'd learned not to be drawn in by it.

"Your turn," she said, casting him a curious look. "What are *you* doing running around the woods in the middle of the night?"

"Chasing shadows." A half-truth.

Annie scowled. "Not fair. I answered your questions."

As if there were anything fair about life.

The silhouette of an old woman appeared at the cottage window. Impossible to see her facial expression from this distance, but the prickling of his forearm skin alerted Tombi that she watched. Somehow, through distance and darkness, the old lady's eyes clamped upon them.

Witch.

And this Annie girl was Tia Henrietta's direct descendant. She was a perfect target for the dark spirit ruler and his host of creatures, potentially more valuable than a normal human who possessed no sensory power whatsoever. Had she been tainted yet by evil? Despite her scowl and crossed arms, she looked as harmless as a kitten with her big, wide eyes and skinny arms and legs.

Don't be fooled by appearances. Tombi met her challenge with evasion. "There's evil and dark shadows in the bayou that you've never imagined. If you're not part of it, best you don't learn."

She cocked her head to one side and stilled, as if listening to something he couldn't hear.

"What is it?" Tombi asked sharply. "Do you hear something?"

She nodded. "It's faint, but distinct."

Could this girl really hear others' auras? Tombi shifted his feet and concentrated on containing his energy. The only sound in the night was the constant rolling of distant waves and the eternal screech of insects.

"It's gone now," Annie said. "But I heard your aura. Finally. I've never run across someone that I couldn't."

An undertow of intrigue tugged his mind. "Well? What do I sound like to you?"

"Drumming. A deep bass note. Steady as a heartbeat."

He studied the delicate features of her face, the heart-shaped chin, small nose and wide brown eyes beneath arched brows. Air charged between them, an unexpected sexual energy that rolled over him. The jackhammer beating of his heart exploded through his normal wall of self-control. The darkening of Annie's brown eyes said she heard it. Her gaze dropped to his lips, and Tombi leaned in…

"Annie?"

The old lady's voice cut through the night. It felt like ice water dousing his fevered skin. At the cottage, Annie's grandmother leaned her considerable girth half out of the window.

"Whatcha doin' out there? Who's that with ya?" she yelled.

Soft, moist heat brushed his left jaw. Startled, his gaze returned to Annie.

"Thank you for bringing me home." Her voice was breathless, and her hair was tousled and wild. She stretched up on tiptoes and planted another quick, chaste kiss on his cheek. "I have to go now."

Annie ran through the moon-silvered field, and he followed her slight figure until she entered the cottage. Bemused, he lifted a hand and traced his chin and jaw where her lips had momentarily caressed his skin. The memory of those quick kisses left him feeling anything but chaste. Why had she kissed him?

The light in the cottage blinked out, but Tombi lingered, reluctant to resume his hunt. For a small interlude, Annie had pricked through his armor, had touched something deep inside.

Bewitched him.

Chapter 2

Why had she kissed him?

True, he'd saved her from spending the night in the swamp, but he'd been evasive. Even accused her of being a witch.

But she'd been irresistibly pulled to his masculine strength, in a way she'd never experienced before. Kissing strangers was a novelty. Best to place the blame on the Thunder Moon and forget it ever happened. With a deep sigh, Annie shook off the question. It was done. Over. She might never see Tombi again. And she certainly would never go back into the night woods chasing will-o'-the-wisps.

Filled with resolve, she returned to preparing a new batch of mojo bags designed for attracting the opposite sex. Grandma Tia had awoken this morning declaring they would be in demand today, and supplies were getting low. Annie crushed lovage leaves with a mortar and pestle, releasing its unique lime and celery fragrance.

The cramped kitchen could almost be mistaken for one set in medieval times. Dried herbs from their garden hung from the ceiling. The countertops were wooden, as were the floors, table and cabinets. On the pine table, Annie had spread out over a dozen pink flannel mojo bags and mason jars filled with dried flowers and spices.

She emptied the freshly ground lovage into a new jar, humming contentedly. Next, she took a pinch of powdered substance from each jar and placed it in the bags, along with a sprinkle of salt and a tiny magnet. The base ingredients were set. Her grandma would personalize each bag as needed.

The murmur of conversation from the living room grew louder. Grandma Tia's voice was low and calm, in contrast to the other woman's high-pitched agitation.

"That hussy knew Jeb was my man, and it didn't make no bit a difference to her."

Every syllable of the woman's words buzzed like angry bees in Annie's ears. She hummed louder to block the buzzing and opened the pantry, which was lined with shelves of different-colored mojo bags, stones, nails, oils, graveyard dirt and hunks of dirt-dauber nests. A few murky jars were filled with liquid the color of swamp water, and she shuddered to think of what unsavory ingredients her grandma used in other kinds of spells.

Tia Henrietta popped her head in the door. "I need that there—"

Annie plucked two items from the shelf and held them out. "Here's twine and a vial of Stay Me oil. You need to add these to one of the pink bags for a Taking-Back-Yer-Man spell. Right?"

"You a quick learner, child." Grandma Tia gave a broad wink before closing the door behind her.

Annie shook her head in bemusement. It wasn't too hard

to learn the hoodoo basics. Grandma Tia had explained there were certain common spells: one for getting back a lover (mostly female customers), another for gambling luck (mostly men) and another for revenge or blocking enemies (popular with both sexes). That was in addition to using the all-purpose good-luck charms and cleansing waters she concocted.

The front door slammed shut, and Annie watched the wronged woman march to her sedan, tightly clenching the mojo bag in her right fist. The hapless Jeb didn't stand a chance against her determination to cure him of his wandering ways. What a relief Grandma hadn't insisted she join them for the consultation. Lately, Grandma Tia had been making her meet customers, saying she needed to come out of her shell. But she'd given her a break today and let her putter about the kitchen, allowing her to get her bearings after last night.

The teakettle whistled, and Annie poured steaming water into two mugs and carried them on a tray into the living room.

Her grandma was sprawled on the sofa, head in her hands.

"What's wrong?" Annie hurried forward and set the mugs on the coffee table.

Tia brought her hands down and smiled wanly. "Nothing. I'll be just fine after tea."

"It's your heart, isn't it?" Annie asked, helping her sit up and placing a pillow behind her back.

"Cain't expect it to last forever." Grandma Tia mixed a dollop of honey into the hawthorn-berry tea. "This will revive me right nice."

But one day it wouldn't. Annie nervously adjusted the pillow.

As if reading her mind, Tia spoke again. "Don't you

worry 'bout me. I'm ready to meet my maker anytime He calls."

What would she do without her grandma? Her real home was here in Bayou La Siryna, always had been. Here she wasn't surrounded by people and their constant cacophony of sound and music. Unwanted sounds she'd never learned to mute or tune out. And if Grandma Tia died, there went all hope of learning to control it.

Annie sat on the couch, legs crossed, and sipped coffee. None of that slimy grass-tasting herbal tea for her. Her right leg jittered in rhythm with the tumbled whirling of her brain.

"Ain't hard to guess what yer thinkin'."

Annie cursed the guilty flush that heated her face. No use denying her one-track wish. "I can't believe there's nothing you can do to help me. There must be something."

"Why would you be wantin' to block a gift?" Tia clicked her tongue in disapproval. "One day you gonna be thanking the blessed saints for that hearing of yers."

"It's ruining my life. Why can't you see that?" Annie set down her drink and stood, pacing the floorboards. This time guilt did more than stain her cheeks; it burned her heart. Grandma Tia probably wasn't long for this world, and Annie was impatient and snippy with the one person in the world who best understood and accepted her peculiarity.

"I'm going outside to cool off," she announced, using her last bit of self-control not to slam the door on the way out.

Cool off? What a joke. The humidity slapped her as soon as she stepped onto the porch. Annie sat down and stared at the gigantic live oaks draped with moss. Beautiful in a gothic, eerie kind of way. Burning cement cooked her butt, and she shifted her seating position.

Maybe it had been a mistake to come again this year after all. Still, she couldn't bear the thought of her grandma living alone. And Mama had wanted no part of traveling down here, saying she'd rather go to hell than come back to Alabama.

So she sent me instead. Dear mom had jumped at the chance to get her weird daughter out of the house and out of her hair.

It certainly was hot as Hades down here. And the gazillion buzzing, stinging insects in the bayou were the devil's own reward. Annie swiped at a mosquito sucking her forearm.

A whisper of song blew from the treetops and teased her ears. The plaintive, haunting beauty of it was unlike anything she'd ever heard. It was as pure as a dulcimer's plucking. The notes warbled like a bird's call and bubbled like water gurgling through rocks.

Annie half rose and then sat back down with a groan. This music was different from the will-o'-the-wisp's eerily luring tune, but she wasn't going to be fooled into returning to the woods. Tombi had claimed evil dwelled there. A dangerous place swarming with snakes and spirits. Just the thought of snakes was enough to keep her rooted to the porch.

The screen door creaked open on rusty hinges, and Grandma Tia framed the doorway.

"Somethin' calling ya to go in them woods again."

Annie narrowed her eyes. For all her savvy acumen in eking out an existence bartering mojo bags and spells for groceries and other necessities, her grandma really did have an unsettling sixth sense.

"I won't be drawn into the woods again," Annie assured her. "Once was bad enough."

"This time, you should go."

Annie snorted. "Tombi said there was evil out there. Besides, I hate snakes, and I imagine the woods are full of them."

"It's still daylight. Yer Tombi will protect ya."

"Why do you trust this stranger? You've never even met him."

Again, the fluting notes of music drifted and tempted. They chirruped and whistled like a bird in flight.

"You hear that?" Annie asked, looking toward the woods.

Tia shook her head. "Not a thing."

Annie stood and lightly brushed the rear of her jeans. Gritty sand and red clay dust permeated every surface outdoors. "You think Tombi's out there now?"

Tia's eyes danced. "He been out there most of the day, hoping to see ya."

She couldn't stop the delicious shiver that vibrated along her spine. Annie cocked her head to the side, studying Tia. "You sure he's trustworthy?"

"I have a good feelin' 'bout him."

Still, Annie hesitated. Grandma's sixth sense wasn't infallible. She often leaned on the side of reckless and trusting.

"You want everyone to come to you. Just like you search for answers to yer problems outside of yerself." Tia patted her ample chest. "Sometimes you gots to take heart and just rise up to yer problems."

Even her old grandma thought she was gutless. Annie straightened her shoulders. "Fine. If I don't make it home tonight, send out a search party."

She marched into the woods, her posture rigid as a stone column, knowing her grandma watched. "Might as well have called me a coward," she muttered, stomping through tall weeds and red dirt. Once inside the woods, Annie leaned against a tree, closed her eyes and fully opened her senses, straining to catch the pure music she'd heard on the porch steps.

Cascading trills floated through the swamp. The same pure melody that had captured her attention from the cottage. "Here I go again," she said with a sigh, carefully making her way along a thin trail almost eclipsed by dense shrubs on either side. But daylight, and Grandma Tia's urging to follow the music, gave her a measure of confidence.

The notes grew louder, more fluid and enchanting. Annie rounded a bend and recognized the water bank where she'd drifted last evening.

A man sat on a fallen tree limb, playing some sort of reed instrument. Although his naked, broad back faced her, Annie sensed it was Tombi. She wasn't Tia Henrietta's granddaughter for nothing.

Staring at his sleek, muscled torso made her throat and mouth dry. She licked her lips and swallowed hard. She'd bet her grandma's pantry full of hoodoo charms that Tombi had women follow him everywhere. The Pied Piper of Bayou La Siryna.

The music stopped. In one fluid motion, like a dance of danger, Tombi jumped to his feet and whirled around, a dagger gleaming in his right fist. The wooden instrument he played dangled loosely in his left hand. Warrior and musician melded into one. His face was taut, and his eyes instantly fixed on her.

Whoa. Annie threw up her hands and took an involuntary step backward. For all she knew, Tombi might have deliberately summoned her with the music, luring her to him against her better judgment. She'd done the same thing following the will-o'-the-wisps last night.

Tombi slowly lowered the dagger and secured it in the

leather sheath belted at his waist, never breaking his gaze. "You came back," he said in a flat tone.

He didn't act like a man hoping to see her, as Grandma Tia had claimed.

"I had to. You never told me your story." Annie walked forward and nodded at the dagger. "You always this up-tight?"

"These woods are full of danger."

"Really? Because even my grandma thinks it's perfectly safe out here during the day."

He frowned and crossed his arms. "It used to be."

A series of scars tattooed the smooth, muscular plane of his chest and shoulders, distracting her from his unsettling response. "Have you been in knife fights?" she blurted.

Tombi grabbed the T-shirt on the log and swiftly pulled it on.

"I'm sorry." Annie was horrified at her rudeness. "I shouldn't have asked."

"I'm not ashamed of them," he said gruffly. He nodded at the log. "Sit."

Her embarrassment faded. "I don't take commands like a dog," she said, lifting her chin.

A ghost of a smile flitted the corners of his lips, so fleeting she might have dreamed it had been there. He bowed his head a fraction before he sat down, but didn't apologize.

Annie gestured to the surrounding trees. "So, what's the danger? Are the wisps malicious or something? I mean, your friend sounded sad and desperate to me—not evil."

"In real life, Bo was all that was true and good."

"And now?" she prompted.

"Remains to be seen." He studied her, eyes narrowed and unflinching.

Annie smoothed the tumble of curls away from her face. "What do you mean?"

"It's hard to tell good from evil sometimes."

"Do you see everything so black-and-white? Surely there's a dozen shades of gray in between."

"No." His jaw muscles clenched. "You're either with me or you are with Nalusa."

"Nah-loosa?" she asked, testing the unfamiliar word.

"Nalusa Falaya—it means 'long black being' in Choctaw. He's a spirit that resembles a man, but he can shapeshift into different forms."

Annie drew a circle in the dirt with the toe of her sneaker. Root working—the conjure magick of her grandma—was one thing…but this? It sounded like an old Native American tale invented to keep children close to camp and away from the dark unknown.

"You don't believe me." Tombi picked up a large stick on the ground by their feet and flung it violently. It hit a tall oak and splintered with a crack as loud as gunfire.

Annie sidled away from the heat of his anger, not wanting to be singed by his sudden wrath. "I really should head back home," she offered in a small voice.

"It's real," Tombi said harshly. "Nalusa exists. And he can change into snake form. And I believe that wasn't any ordinary snake that killed Bo. It was Nalusa."

"So, now you're out here trying to hunt this Nalusa down. For revenge." She backed away slowly, not wanting to set him off again. "Got it."

Tombi also stood. "Not just me. There's a whole tribe of us."

More people who shared his delusion? She glanced around uneasily, hoping she wasn't about to be ambushed by a group of demented, make-believe warriors.

"I know it sounds crazy, but it's true. C'mon, you saw the will-o'-the-wisps last night with your own eyes. Remember?"

Annie rubbed her arms. He certainly had her there. "Okay," she reluctantly conceded. "I admit there are things I know nothing of. I'd rather keep it that way, too."

His brow furrowed. "Whether you ignore Nalusa or not, he still exists."

"Yeah, well, I'd rather not make his acquaintance. I have enough problems as it is."

Alarm flickered in his dark eyes. "But Bo spoke to you. You have to help us."

Annie shrugged and took a step backward. The last thing she needed was to get caught up in his personal crusade for revenge. "Come, see my grandma one day. She'll do a protection spell if you like." She plastered on a smile and waved. "Nice seeing you. Thanks again for helping me find my way home last night."

Two steps and her shoulders tensed at the heavy pressure of his palms bearing down, barring an easy exit. Damn. He wasn't going to make retreat easy. Tombi guided her back around to face him.

"We need you, Annie." He swallowed. "Please."

She could tell the plea wasn't easy for Tombi. Pride and dignity announced their presence in the strong jaw and stiff posture.

"But I doubt I'll ever hear Bo again," she protested. "I have no plans to be lured back into the woods by the wisps."

"The wisps are controlled by Nalusa. But as long as you're with me, I'll protect you. I promise."

His words were deep and solemn. No doubt he would do his best to protect those on his side.

"I believe you."

"Good. Then come with me and—"

She shook her head and backed away. This wasn't her battle. "No. Sorry. I don't want to get involved."

Tombi glared at her, and his full lips compressed to a tight line. Evidently, he was a man used to getting his own way.

Too bad.

Stubborn woman.

Tombi took a deep breath to calm his temper. Somehow, he had to convince this slip of a girl to help him. Maybe… His gaze dropped to her lips. Those lips that had unexpectedly kissed him last night. Annie felt the attraction between them. He could use that to his advantage. Tombi slid his palms down her arms and urged her forward. So close their bodies almost touched.

Her brown eyes widened and darkened into black pools of desire. She raised her hands and placed them against his chest. Yes, this might be so easy. So pleasurable.

Later, he couldn't say who moved first. All he knew was that their lips met and their hands explored one another. Her fingers traced the bulge of his biceps, then kneaded the muscles along his spine.

Tombi stroked the thin shoulder blades on her back, ran his calloused fingers through her soft curls. She was so petite, so delicate. Fragile enough he wondered if it might hurt her should he release his full passion.

A tiny, whimpering moan cut through his reservations. She wanted him. Tombi lowered his hands until they cupped her ass. That cute ass that he'd watched walk away last night and that he'd pictured ever since. He squeezed, letting Annie feel his desire press against her core.

She moaned again. Or was that him this time? It didn't matter.

"Stop." Annie stepped out of his embrace and hugged her belly. "Sorry. It's just…this is too fast. I barely know you."

He stared at her, willing his heartbeat to slow and his brain to catch up to her words. "It's okay," he said, running a hand through his hair. "I understand."

"Thank you," she whispered, turning and making her way down the path.

Tombi shook his head to clear it. He was supposed to use their attraction to convince her to work with him. Somehow, he'd lost control, and Annie was slipping away from him once more. He couldn't let that happen. He—rather, his people—needed her skill in communicating with the *shilup*, the human spirits that wandered the land of the ghosts. Bo's spirit had been captured by the wisps, and remembering the plight of his trapped friend cooled his fever.

"Wait," he called to Annie's retreating figure.

She turned and gazed at him expectantly.

What could he offer her? This was his fight. Not hers. She was right to not get involved. Yet, Nalusa grew stronger every day, and they were desperate to stop his spread of power in Bayou La Siryna. Just last week, Nalusa had gone farther away from the swamp and invaded the heart and mind of one of his hunters while he was asleep in his own bed. Marcus had even entertained thoughts of suicide but wisely had called Tombi for help, recognizing that Nalusa was at the root of his despair.

Tombi scrambled to recall the bits and pieces of conversation with Annie, searching for an angle. He remembered her troubled face as she mentioned hearing other people's auras.

"What if I could help you?"

Her lips twisted with suspicion. "Help me with what?"

He approached Annie, confident of victory. "You want to control your sense of hearing. Correct?"

Her body and eyes lit up. "Really? You can help with that?"

"Really. You told me how surprised you were when we first met because you couldn't detect any sound from my aura."

"I remember."

"That's because I control my energy field most of the time. I can teach you to do the same."

"And that will help me block unwanted sound?"

He had no idea. But it seemed logical. "Absolutely," he said with conviction.

"And if I help you, you promise to protect me?"

"I do."

Annie looked down to the ground, and Tombi held his breath, awaiting her answer.

"I'm in," she said in a rush.

Chapter 3

What had she gotten herself into? She wanted a normal life, but what good was that if she was killed in the process? But she had to try. She had to trust that Tombi would protect her.

Grandma Tia had been no help, and no matter how many spells and strips of paper she burned under the full moon, nothing changed. If anything, her hearing grew stronger, more disruptive.

Tombi nodded. "Great. We begin now."

Hope bubbled through her like uncorked champagne on New Year's Eve. She was about to start a new life. Do all those things she'd longed to do: get a real job, be around people and relate normally. Simple acts most people took for granted.

He turned and beckoned her to follow.

"Where are we going?" she asked happily. No waiting for the full moon this time. Hope had arisen right here in the midafternoon sunshine. "Is there a special place for a spell? Like an energy vortex or something?" She hurried along the path.

He shot an incredulous look over his shoulder. "What are you babbling about?"

"I'm curious how you're going to do this. I think Grandma Tia never helped me because she didn't know how, though she would never admit it."

"We aren't casting any spells."

"Are you taking me to a special healer, then? Like a shaman?"

He sighed loudly and planted his feet so abruptly she plowed into his back.

He turned and steadied her. "We're going to my camp, so you can meet the other hunters. I want to know who that betrayer is. If there is one."

Annie's eyes narrowed. "So, you won't help me until I help you first."

"That's right."

Worry quickly overcame her frustration. "But what if I can't pick up anything from them?"

"You will," he said confidently. "I'm the best in the group at controlling my energy, yet you picked up the drumming."

"But it was only a drumming sound. Nothing good or bad about it," she protested.

"True, but it picked up something of my nature. A primitive beat passed down through my ancestry."

"Don't get your hopes up," she muttered, picking her way carefully through the prickly saw palmettos and dense underbrush. Tombi kept a slower pace today, albeit still a brisk one. "Tell me about these other hunters."

The more she knew going in, the less nervous she would be. Annie hated meeting new people, especially in a group situation where each aura would jumble with the others into a confusing din.

"We're down to four in the inner circle since Bo died. Me, Chulah, Hanan and my sister, Tallulah."

"So, what is it you actually *do*? How do you fight Nalusa and his shadow spirits?"

Tombi didn't answer right away. "It's something you would have to see and be a part of to really understand."

Meaning he didn't want to say any more on the subject. Great. Fine by her. The less she knew, the fewer nightmares she'd dream. She'd help him find the betrayer, and he'd help her control hearing auras. Then she could have the normal life she craved, and he could...maybe win his battle. Get revenge for his friend's death. They could both move on.

They continued until the path widened, and she spotted over two dozen tents pitched in a field. They were arranged in a circle, and in the middle of it all was a thin stream of smoke that wafted upward from a modest fire. The acrid smell of burning oak stirred her with a sense of home and cozy evenings warming by the fireplace.

"You all must be great friends," she said, picturing them telling stories in the evening by campfire, sharing a bond of fighting evil. They were all part of something bigger than themselves. For a moment, it made her own dream seem small and selfish.

And he wanted her to come into this...this tight group of friends and point the finger at one of them? Annie rubbed the unexpected chill on her arms. She wasn't sure what she feared most: being unable to recognize the betrayer, or singling out someone and facing their collective wrath.

Nobody would thank her for disrupting their alliance, that was for sure. She peeked at Tombi's stern profile, took in his long, slightly hooked nose, pronounced jaws and cheekbones, and heavy brows. What was his role in this band of hunters?

"Your name's unusual. What does it mean?" she asked abruptly, hoping to learn more about him.

"Ray of light."

Annie snorted, and he raised a brow. "What?"

She couldn't help but giggle. "You're no ray of sunshine."

He stared at her blankly before a rusty rumble of laughter escaped his mouth, as if it had been years since one last escaped. "At one time, my people worshiped the sun, so to be named after its ray is a great honor."

"What about your friend Bo? Is that a good ole Southern name as in *B-e-a-u*, short for Beauregard?"

"No. It's *B-o*, short for Bohpoli. That's Choctaw for 'thrower.'"

Would she ever hear Bo again? She shivered, remembering his plaintive pleas for help.

Although their movements were quiet and their voices low, they had attracted attention. A woman and three men solemnly filed out of the tent circle and stood in the center, awaiting their approach with unsmiling faces.

Holy hoodoo, this was going to be even tougher than she imagined.

Annie tugged the back of Tombi's T-shirt, and he frowned down at her. "What?"

"Have you told them anything about me?"

"We tell each other everything."

She groaned. "Terrific. Bet they can't wait to meet me. I wish you hadn't told them."

"There should be no secrets among my hunters. No doubts or suspicions about the man—or woman—you have to depend on for your life."

Her shoulders slumped. She couldn't argue with his

logic, although she resented the situation he'd put her in. They walked onward several minutes, not speaking.

Tombi abruptly halted and frowned her way. "You care so much what others think?"

"Of course I care." She thought of all the times people had skirted around her in school hallways or outright laughed in her face. She'd watched from the sidelines in the purgatory that was high school, unsure which she craved more—the huddling conspiracy of a group of girlfriends to share secrets and fun times with, or some cute guy to take her to dinner and a movie and whisper sweet seductions in the back of a car. "Everyone cares."

He shrugged. "Not me."

Easy for him to say—with his looks he probably had any woman he wanted. And he had a tribe of like-minded friends and family. Why should he give any thought to what was so easily granted to him?

Annie reluctantly walked beside him, trying to emulate his mask of calm. They came to a halt six feet in front of the group.

"This is Annie Matthews." Tombi gestured to the left with his hand. "This is Tallulah, Hanan and Chula."

The silence roared in her, air compressing and as stifling as a sealed coffin. They formed a firewall of mistrust and resentment, shutting her out of their circle. Annie sucked in her breath at the glittering hostility in Tallulah's obsidian eyes. Nearly as tall as her brother, she bore the same long face, chiseled features and strong chin. It shouldn't have worked for a female, and while she wasn't beautiful in a Miss America or girl-next-door kind of way, Tallulah was striking and commanded attention. Annie barely took in the stoic features of the other three men.

Tallulah put her hands on her hips. "Well?"

"W-well what?" Annie stammered. She glanced at Tombi in a silent plea for help.

"Go ahead," Tallulah challenged. "I dare you to point a finger at any one of us. You don't know—"

"Enough," Tombi cut in.

The man next to her—Chula—lightly touched Tallulah's forearm, and a whisper as tender as a lullaby brushed over Annie at the gesture.

"We already debated this last night and agreed to meet Annie. Let's get this over with." Hanan pinned Annie with a hard stare, and the whisper of sound vanished. "The sooner, the better."

Annie swallowed hard at their collective stare. Talk about being on the spot.

"It's not that easy. I have to be around you for a bit." She cast another look at Tombi. "Can we all sit together by the fire?"

Tombi nodded, and she followed him to the middle of the pitched tents, the others following in silence behind them.

In the center was a stack of firewood coated in ash. Colorful wool blankets were spread in a circle around the campfire. They each went to a blanket and sat, except Tombi. "You can have my blanket," he said, pointing to one. "I'll stand."

She sank down and crossed her feet beneath her. Annie tried to relax and open her senses, but it was difficult as the others stared at her expectantly. As if she was some kind of circus performer. She closed her eyes, more to shut out their stares than out of necessity.

The unnatural quiet unnerved her. How did they do it? They each had some type of guard up, some way of blocking their music. Her palms gripped her knees. Very well. She'd try to wait them out, see if any sound escaped.

The vibrations of a deep rumbling laugh iced down her spine. *Witch.* The word was an accusation, underlain with mirth. *Be gone, little girl.*

Annie opened her eyes and met their curious, blank stares. "Did you hear that laugh? That voice?"

No one spoke.

Tombi uncrossed his arms and sat beside her on the blanket. "What did you hear?"

She bit her lip. Had the laugh and the words come from one of the hunters, or was there something else out there? Something just beyond the ring of trees and the safety of the fire where shadows lengthened and danced?

Annie shook her head slightly and closed her eyes again. Silence blanketed her as thick and unrelenting as a stone wall. It was hopeless. Nothing else was coming through that wall.

She opened her eyes. "I don't know how y'all do it, but I'm impressed."

"Do what?" Chula asked.

"Close off your energy." Annie turned to Tombi. "Isn't that how you described it? Keeping everything closed in?"

Tallulah made an impatient *tsk* sound. "Why did you tell this girl our secrets? For all we know, she could be one of them."

"One of who?" Annie asked.

"Don't act so innocent," Tallulah snapped. "If there's someone controlled by the dark side, my guess is that it's you."

Annie rose to her feet and took in their hostile stares. "I didn't have to tell Tombi what I heard last night. I didn't ask Bo to seek me out. And I certainly don't have to take your attitude."

She stalked off. Screw them. She'd tried. Not her fault if they had some special power to resist her hearing.

Dry grass crunched in the parched soil behind her. Tombi stepped to her side and walked, matching her pace.

"I'm not going back there," she spat, "so don't try to talk me into it."

He said nothing but walked in front of her as they re-entered the narrow path. He held back branches to keep them from slapping her in the face. A snapping, crackling sound simmered in the air swirling around him, like dry brush catching fire.

"You're angry with me," Annie said. "I really did try. But your sister…" She tried to collect her temper. She still needed his help and insulting Tallulah wouldn't serve her cause. "You are going to help me. Right?"

She looked desperate, but Tombi hardened his heart. He wasn't about to give up. Not as long as Bo was trapped and not as long as Nalusa and the other shadow spirits grew and trespassed the ancient boundaries.

"Eventually," he promised. "What did you hear back there?"

"Nothing that can help you."

Tombi stopped in his tracks and folded his arms against his chest. "Might as well spit it out. I'll be out in these woods through the night anyhow."

"Do you live out here all the time?"

"Only one week out of the month, around the full moon."

Her dark eyes widened. "We believe in the power of the full moon, too."

"We?"

"My grandmother and I." She swallowed. "And others like us."

"Other witches?"

"Why must you put labels on people?" she countered.

"We're known by many names, and we all have different practices—root workers, healers, pagans and, okay, witches."

"Do they all hear as you do?"

Her full lips twisted in a scowl. "No. I'm the lucky one."

Tombi shook off his fascination with Annie and her kind. "You neatly skirted my question. What did you hear back there?"

She sighed, realizing he would interrogate until she answered his question. "A laugh. Not a funny one, but the laugh of the evil or crazy or demented. And then…the voice called me a witch and told me to go away."

Tombi considered her words. He hated knowing Nalusa knew of Annie and her gift and their connection, but Nalusa must be worried to warn her off. That was, if Annie wasn't in league with him to start with.

"So, just like that, you're giving up?"

She winced at the sharp edge of his tone. "The attitude of your sister and your friends didn't make me want to stay and try harder."

He grew hot thinking of Tallulah's antagonism. Annie didn't deserve to be treated that way. Even if he had his own suspicions, nothing would be gained by hostility.

"They can't help but be suspicious of strangers. Time and again, Nalusa has gained a foothold over people, even if only temporarily. Made them say and do things they wouldn't normally do."

Annie lifted her chin. "I can assure you that I'm in complete command of my own thoughts and actions."

"I'll help you, but you have to help me, too."

"Can't you just say some words and cure me?"

"Nothing's that easy. It's a process. It takes time to learn to control your energy."

"You say you don't trust me. That goes two ways. I

think you're dragging out everything to suit your own purposes."

"You've barely spent five minutes among us. You'll have to gain their trust."

"Or catch them unawares," she muttered.

"That would be hard to do. Our hearing may not be as sharp as yours. But we can sense energy before it senses us."

"You have to sleep sometime."

Of course. He should have realized. Tombi laid a hand on her thin shoulder, noticing his palm engulfed the side of her neck and curve of her shoulder. "Come meet us tonight. Hunt with us and spend the night."

Her eyebrows drew up. "Spend the night with you in your tent?"

An image of Annie, naked and curled up beside him, flushed his body with desire. "I can spring for a new tent and sleeping bag," he said past the dryness at the back of his throat.

"I'll think—" She came to a dead halt and tilted her head to the side, listening to a faint sound.

"Wh—"

She raised a finger to her lips to silence him. Her forehead wrinkled, and her eyes grew distant. Suddenly, Annie grabbed his arm and looked around wildly. "Let's run!"

And then he sensed it, too. Dread enveloped him like a heavy blanket. The metallic scent of blood and a whisper of decay could alone mean only one thing. Nalusa was near.

Very near. Within striking range.

Not now. Not with Annie so close. "Go without me," he urged.

She stood still, as if paralyzed, staring at him with brown eyes full of fear. "But what about you?"

"I can take care of myself." He drew out the dagger from his side. "Go!"

She hesitated.

A rustling whipped through the underbrush, unnaturally loud, drowning out birds and insects and the rumble of the sea. A sibilant hiss sent a tingle across the skin of his back and arms. Another second and Nalusa would be upon them. Tombi looked over his shoulder and pointed at Annie with his dagger. "I said, go!"

Her dark eyes were like a well of smooth, black water. And in those pupils Tombi saw a triangular head arise, a long forked tongue slithering from its mouth. The snake's copper eyes appeared to hold Annie entranced. The Medusa of the bayou.

If Bo were still alive and with him, he'd throw a dagger accurate enough to strike the snake in between the eyes. Tombi didn't trust his aim to be as accurate. He needed to be a little closer. He slowly turned to directly face Nalusa, his body a shield to protect Annie behind him. Nalusa coiled his long snake form in upon itself, his muscles rippling beneath the gray-and-brown patchwork of scales.

The striking position. His tail rose up with its rings of rattles and shook. The sound was as loud as a tumbling steel barrel full of iron pellets.

Tombi deliberately stepped toward Nalusa, every nerve flooded with adrenaline. Warring instincts battled inside. His muscles twitched to take action, to strike the enemy, yet his mind urged caution. One miscalculation and his tribe would be further reduced and without its leader.

They were within a few feet of one another. Striking distance. Tombi willed Annie to leave, but he sensed her presence behind him.

Why hadn't she run? His jaw tightened. It could be the two were in league together. She drew him to just the right place at the right time. Tombi shrugged off the disquieting notion, trying to stay focused. If he lived, he would have his answer. If he didn't…the other hunters would guess at her treachery and the trap she had plotted.

But no matter. The death match was on. He had to kill this monster before Nalusa crept past his boundaries, past the deep swamp where his ancestors had bound him many years ago. Hurricane Katrina had unleashed something; her destruction and the resulting chaos in the Deep South had made it possible for Nalusa to escape his chains and increase his power.

Now he seemed ready to inflict his evil upon the world. Now he must die.

Tombi lunged forward, aiming for the eyes. His dagger sank into the thick, muscular skin of the snake, under its throat. It was as if he could feel the pain in his own body. A bolt of agony exploded a few inches under his collarbone, a needle sharpness that quickly radiated toward his chest, as if he'd been injected with poison.

Bitten. He'd been bitten. Moaning rent the space between man and beast, and Tombi couldn't say if it was his own or Nalusa's. Blood poured from the snake's throat where Tombi's silver dagger had sunk in deep. Its black tongue whipped out, ready to strike again.

Tiny white grains and bits of dirt rained down on Nalusa's coiled body, and he jerked backward, eyes fixed somewhere past Tombi's shoulder. What was happening?

Tombi took advantage of the distraction and scrambled to his knees, but pain exploded everywhere, and his vision filled with tiny black dots. His limbs felt numb and paralyzed, and with every breath the pain spread farther, deeper. He collapsed on the hard ground. *I'm joining you, Bo.*

The image of his parents arose as he last saw them.

His father whittling his latest sculpture, his mom shucking corn. All that work, and the sculpture was taken out by the tide, by that bitch of a hurricane, Katrina.

I tried. I failed. You win, Nalusa. He could do no more.

Annie ran across the field to their cottage. Ran until her lungs burned and her chest heaved like fireplace billows. And still there wasn't enough oxygen to fuel her body's race against time. *Don't die don't die please don't die.* She'd flung the salt and consecrated earth from her mojo bag at the attacker, but it may have been too little, too late.

Tombi's unconscious body, sprawled in the red clay dirt, was as clear to her as the door to the cottage. She couldn't, wouldn't think of that—thing, not a snake and not a man. The snake form had dissolved into a thin, tall column of a creature howling with pain. Tombi's dagger had dislodged, and the creature retreated to the darkness of the woods from which it had come.

But not Tombi. She'd felt his pulse, saw the slight rise and fall of his chest. So fragile.

The door opened, and Grandma Tia descended the steps, carrying the large straw bag that held her roots and herbs for her healing home visitations.

"Hurry." Annie tried to scream, but her voice was only a puff, as light as dandelion seeds that scattered in the briny breeze.

Tia hustled over with a speed and agility Annie hadn't observed in her for years.

"Where is he?" she asked without preamble.

Annie hastily removed the shoulder strap from her grandma's bag and hoisted it over her own shoulders. "This way. He's been bitten, Grandma." She felt six years old again and seeking her grandma's comfort after other kids made fun of her. She still needed her assurance and knowledge, wanted her grandma to tell her everything was going to be okay.

"Ole devil snake got 'em, eh?" They were only midway through the field, but Tia's breathing was already labored.

"Your heart," Annie said, drawing burning air into oxygen-starved lungs. She laid a hand on Tia's shoulder. "Tell me what to do, and you can stay here."

"Ain't goin' be that easy," Tia huffed. "Gonna take both of us to set this right." She nodded at the trail. "Best keep on. Sooner I start workin', better chance he lives."

They hurried on, and Annie resumed her frantic litany. *Don't die don't die don't die.*

There. His body lay in the same spot. Annie laid his head in her lap and swept his long hair out of his eyes. Only a supernatural force could have felled such a strong man. Such a warrior. His bronze skin stretched tightly across lean, compact muscles. She wondered what had drawn him into this fight with evil, what ancient curse haunted him and his people.

Grandma Tia began humming and chanting, calling upon her Jesus and the holy saints as she pulled out herbs and protection wards from the bag—graveyard dirt, hollowed-out dirt-dauber nests, chopped swamp-alder root, strings of Dixie John root, and other bits and pieces of unidentifiable objects.

"I call on thee, archangels most high," Tia said in her firmest voice. "I call on thee, King Solomon, and thou keys of wisdom, and I call on thee, Moses, for thy power and faith. By the spirit of the Great Black Hawk, I summon thee."

Annie kept her eyes fixed on Tombi's swollen chest with its mottled skin as her grandmother continued her petitions. It could have been ten seconds or ten minutes later—Annie couldn't say—but Tia stopped and turned grave eyes on her.

"It ain't working."

Annie's fingers sank tighter into Tombi's shoulder, and she squeezed, willing him to fight. "You can't quit. Keep going."

Tia drew a long, unsteady breath. "Ain't but one thing left to do." She unpacked a poultice, laid her hand directly over the open wound and prayed, then placed the poultice on the broken skin.

Annie gulped. "Aren't you worried about infection?"

"We way past that point, child. Now I need you to help me. We goin' to draw that poison out of his body and into mine."

"But—we can't. What will the poison do to you? Your heart—"

Tia held up a hand, face stern. "My time on this here earth is almost up anyhows. We gots to try. Now. What I want you to do is find that gris-gris bag full of wormwood in my bag and sprinkle it all around us."

Annie hastily rummaged in the purse, pulled out a black satin drawstring pouch and held it to her nose. A pungent, bitter smell tickled her nostrils. "Is this the one?"

"That's it. Now you get to work and recite parts of Psalm 91. And don't interrupt me, no matter what. You hear me?"

Her upbringing left her no choice but to respond properly to the authority in that voice. "Yes, ma'am."

Tia's eyes softened, and the rigid set of her face melted. "You always been a good girl," she said. "My shining star with the gift. You hear music where the rest of us hear silence." She turned abruptly away. "Now get to work like I taught you."

It felt like a farewell.

Surely not. Grandma Tia was no voodoo hack. She was the real deal. Knew things, sensed things, felt things.

Annie circled around them, a few feet out, crumbling bits of wormwood petals and letting them fall onto her path. The words of the psalm were ingrained since childhood.

"Thou shalt not be afraid for the terror by night, nor for the arrow that flieth by day, nor for the pestilence that walketh in darkness, nor for the destruction that wasteth at noonday."

Heat singed upward from below where her grandmother knelt beside Tombi's body that was sprawled on the hard ground. The sweltering air battered Annie's temples with headache. The wormwood's bitter, camphoraceous scent deepened, and her fingers tingled with numbness—some toxic effect of the herb intensified by the spell. A golden light flowed between Tombi's chest and her grandma's hand.

Annie stopped her recitation, mesmerized by the etheric glow.

Tia cast her a sharp glance. "Don't stop."

She cleared her throat and continued circling. "No evil shall befall thee, neither shall any plague come nigh thy dwelling. For he shall give his angels care. They shalt tread upon the lion and adder."

The swelling and redness of his skin decreased. Tombi stirred and wet his lips. A low moan escaped.

"It's working," Annie exclaimed, wanting to tap-dance around the sacred circle. The golden, healing energy had wrought a remarkable change. There was still some swelling, but the angry red streaks of infection had disappeared. "You did it, Grandma—" She stopped abruptly.

Tia's olive skin had grayed and wrinkled even more, to

the point it resembled elephant skin. Her eyes held an un-healthy glaze, as if she were burning with a fever.

Annie sank on her knees and hugged her grandma. "Don't leave me," she begged. "Tell me how to help you."

A laugh so faint that even she couldn't hear it—it could only be felt from the rumbling of Tia's chest and throat. "It's all in the good Lord's hands now, child."

Annie burrowed her head in her grandma's gray hair with its witchy, herbal smell. The smell of home and safety and love. Her grounding force in this world.

"I'm going to get help," she promised, mind whirling with the action she needed to take: get up, run to the cottage, find her cell phone and car keys. Call the ambulance, drive through the field, manage to get these two in the car and drive them to the cottage for the ambulance to transport them to the hospital.

Once at the hospital, the doctors would demand to know what happened...

"Hey," Tombi asked with a note of hoarse puzzlement. "What's going on here?"

A frisson of resentment washed over Annie. This had been *his* fight. Not hers. And certainly not her grandma's. If she'd never met him, her grandma wouldn't be hovering at death's portal for the afterlife.

She'd sacrificed her own safety and, worse, her grandma's health. All for a promise. One that Tombi didn't seem in any hurry to fill.

"My grandma absorbed the poison meant for you," she said, hot tears scalding her cheeks. "I wish I'd never met you."

Chapter 4

Tia's deep olive flesh turned ashy. The glaze of her eyes and burn of her skin indicated a dangerously high fever, as if a volcano had exploded inside her body.

How much longer for that ambulance? Seemed as if it had taken hours to get her grandma back to the cottage and make the call for help. Annie held Tia's hand and stroked her hot forehead. "Isn't there some kind of special tea or gris-gris bag I can get for you?"

"Fetch my crystal from the altar and light a candle." Tia's voice was weak and hoarse. She swallowed hard. "And say a quick prayer while you're at it."

Annie scurried to do her bidding, glad to take action. Seeing someone in pain, especially the rock of her universe, was to suffer alongside them.

Don't die. Sure, she'd known Tia's heart was winding down, but Annie had expected weeks, if not months, to share with her grandmother. Time to soak in her care and wisdom. Time also to be trained in root working and to, hopefully, cajole a reverse spell to banish the musical auras that assaulted her mind.

At the altar, Annie grasped the large chunk of polished carnelian that, despite its vivid orange-red color, was cooling and soothing to the touch. With shaking hands, Annie struck a match. It hissed loudly in the quiet and emitted a whisper of sulfur. She applied the flame to the white columnar candle that smelled strongly of patchouli and cloves. Beside the candle was a framed print of a stern angel with spread wings.

Annie collected her panicked thoughts and prayed. "Dear God…universe…angels…help my grandma," she whispered in a rush. "She's done nothing but help people all her life, and now she needs you. The time isn't right. I'm not ready." Annie drew a deep breath, ashamed she'd wandered into selfish territory. A groan from the next room, and she drew the prayer to a quick close. "Please and amen."

She hurried to the den, where Tombi leaned over the sofa toward Tia, as if drawing closer to hear her speak. Or check her breath for life.

A jab of fear wrung her gut. "Is she…?"

"She's alive," he said with grim authority. "But her pulse grows faint."

A siren sounded from far away.

Tombi straightened. "I'll wait out front for the ambulance. Make sure they don't have trouble finding this place." He brushed past, and Annie lifted her chin, turning her body to the side to avoid accidental contact. It might be unfair to blame him for Tia's condition, but she couldn't help resenting him, nonetheless.

Tombi raised a brow but said nothing.

The door shut behind him, and Annie let out a deep

breath, resuming her place by Tia's side. She slipped the carnelian crystal into her grandma's weathered palm, and Tia curled her fingers over the rock.

"Does this help you?" Annie asked, hoping it eased the pain.

Tia nodded. "Helps me focus. To say what needs sayin'."

Her grandma took a long, raspy breath, and Annie winced at the rattle that sounded like oxygen was leaking and gurgling from her lungs. She eased down and sat beside Tia's sprawled body. "Take your time. I lit the candle and said a prayer like you asked."

"Ain't much time left."

"Don't say that," Annie scolded. "You're going to be fine."

"Listen." Tia struggled to rise on an elbow, but gave up and sank back into the cushions. "I know I been a disappointment to you this visit."

Annie started to deny it, but Tia cut her off.

"We ain't got time for nothin' but the truth between us. And the truth is, you need to help Tombi. He needs you. He needs your gift."

But what about me? It's not what I want.

Tia frowned, eyes sparking with reprimand.

No doubt she'd heard the selfish, unspoken thought. Guilt and shame washed over Annie in a heated flood of remorse.

"You listen here, Annie girl. You help that man. Now. Tonight."

Annie shook her head again. "No way. I'm staying with you."

"I'm goin' somewhere you cain't follow."

"You aren't going to die," Annie insisted.

"I mean it, missy. You go with Tombi. Promise me."

Her tone was fierce, insistent—one that Annie remembered as a child. A you-better-mind-me-this-is-your-last-warning kind of voice. The siren's wail grew distinct and piercing.

Annie crossed two fingers behind her back. "Okay."

Tia tugged Annie's right hand around to the front of her body. "You stop that childish nonsense, or I'll haunt you all yer living days."

"Yes, ma'am."

"Now, then. They fixin' to take me to that infernal hospital." Tia sniffed as if she'd smelled something unclean. She hated the hospital and always said they hurt more than helped. "Guess it's for the best in this case."

"They'll take good care of you. You'll be better in—"

"Hush. If you ever loved me, if you ever trusted my judgment…don't go to the hospital with me. Say you won't."

Annie's shoulders slumped. "Okay," she whispered in defeat, crushed at the mandate. "Is there at least some spell or working I can do while you're gone?"

"No. You be my good girl and help Tombi." Tia's eyes filled with tears that poured down her cheeks like trickles of rain.

Annie couldn't ever remember her grandma crying, except that one time when Annie's mama got in a huge argument with Tia and walked out, saying she would never come back to this backwater hell. That day, Tia's great shoulders had heaved in silent sobs.

Flashing red lights strobed through the window like a disco party from hell. Annie squeezed Tia's hand.

"You always were my special girl." Tia nodded. "But now it's time for my release. Tombi is your destiny now. Ya hear?"

The screen door burst open, and two men in dark blue

uniforms entered with a stretcher, Tombi close at their heels.

The men hurried to Tia's side and took her pulse, listened to her heart, assessed for damages. Tombi explained what had happened, and Annie sank to her knees, hands covering her mouth. How could her grandma expect her to stay here while she went to the hospital?

Tia was transferred to the stretcher, and the men labored to the door with their heavy burden. She still clutched the carnelian in one hand, taking a piece of home with her to a foreign place bustling with antiseptic, modern doctors who prodded you with needles and probed your flesh and innards with an impersonal, impatient air.

It was about as far from hoodoo healing as you could get.

"We're taking her to Bayou La Siryna General Hospital," one of the young men said.

She couldn't speak past the clogged boulder in her throat, but Tombi responded. "Thank you. Family and friends will follow shortly." He walked the EMR staff to the door and shut it behind them.

Annie curled into the sofa. The cushions were still warm from her grandma's fever and smelled like her special scent of cinnamon and sandalwood. She punched a throw pillow, aching with the need to follow her grandma.

But she'd promised.

She gave in to her grief and sobbed into the battered pillow.

A warm hand touched her shoulder. "Annie?"

She jumped. She'd completely forgotten Tombi was present.

"You," she spat.

A flinch danced across the hard planes of his face, so

fleeting that she wondered if she'd misread it. He withdrew his hand.

"I'm sorry about your grandmother." He stood erect and awkward, as if unsure what to do or say.

Annie swiped her eyes and edged away from his presence. She tucked her feet beneath her on the sofa and hugged her knees to her chest. "Why don't you go away and leave me alone?"

She didn't care if she looked or sounded childish. Grandma Tia was gone. And it was all his fault. If she'd never met him, never made the mistake of following the will-o'-the-wisps into the woods, her grandma would still be here.

I'm going where you can't follow. Was Tia talking about her death? Or something else?

"Is there someone I can call?" Tombi asked. "Family? A friend?"

Annie didn't want to call her mom. It would take her hours to drive down from the north Georgia mountains. That was, *if* she came. And she'd be impatient and cross that Annie hadn't gone to the hospital. No matter that she'd shirked her own daughterly duties. Best to wait a bit for some news on her grandma's condition before calling.

Annie nodded at the desk by the far wall. "Open up that middle drawer. There's a blue address book in it."

She watched as Tombi rummaged in the drawer. His green T-shirt was streaked with red clay dirt, as were his blue jeans. It reminded her that he'd been lying on the ground deathly ill less than an hour ago. She shouldn't care but…

"Hey, are you okay?" she asked reluctantly. "Maybe you should have gone to the ER, too."

He shut the desk drawer and came toward her. One side of his mouth twitched upward. "Nice to know you care."

He handed over the battered book, which was crammed with names and addresses scribbled in Tia's large, dramatic script. Grandma wasn't one to trust computers for storing information.

Annie found Verbena Holley's name and picked up her cell phone. Verbena was a longtime family friend who would drop everything and stay with Tia at the hospital. She also wouldn't question Annie about Tia's demand that she remain at home. Verbena was almost as eccentric as Tia and possessed absolute faith in Tia's wisdom.

That done, Annie hung up and let out a deep breath. She felt a fraction better that her grandma would have a familiar face by her side this evening. Outside, shadows lengthened, and twilight wouldn't be far behind.

Tombi paced their small den looking large and out of place. He belonged to the night and to the swampland, not here in this mystical room with its herbal sachets, saint statues and candles. His stride was cramped, his posture rigid. He kept his eyes to the ground, hands tightly interlaced behind his back.

"You don't have to stay," Annie said. "You should go back to your friends." After all, Grandma Tia hadn't said she had to help him immediately. It would be best if he left, and she could gather her wits and form a plan. "They probably wonder what's taking you so long to return." And no doubt would blame her for his injury.

He stopped pacing and gave her a ferocious stare. "I'm not going back without you."

Beneath the glare of his eyes, exhaustion and pain had left a faint trace. Annie wanted nothing more than to demand he leave, but she couldn't send out a man who had been so near death.

My destiny. Was her grandma just being fanciful?

Annie stood and pointed to the sofa. "Why don't you

sit, and I'll fix some tea. Something to make sure the fever lessens."

He narrowed his eyes. "What kind of tea?"

"A little this, a little that." Realization struck. "What did you think I'd put in your drink?"

"Poison, perhaps." He arched a brow. "What do witches brew? Toadstool soup with dragon blood and gator claws?"

That was rich. The guy practically killed her grandma and then suggested *he* didn't trust *her*? "Don't forget magic mushrooms and bat whiskers," she drawled.

Too bad she didn't have access to something like truth serum to find out more about his background and intentions. Still, her healing nature couldn't ignore Tombi's underlying suffering. And keeping busy was her preferred method for dealing with sorrow and worry.

In the kitchen, her safe haven, Annie set the iron teakettle on the stove and mixed together a pinch of elderberry, angelica and feverfew for taking out any underlying fever, plus a dash of chamomile for relaxing. Not truth serum, but maybe if Tombi relaxed he would open up more. Couldn't hurt.

She reached up on tiptoes for the container of stevia.

"Interesting place."

Annie spun around like a ballerina *en pointe*. "I didn't hear you come in," she sputtered. "Sneaking up on me?"

"No. It's just my way. The way of most hunters. I came to see if I could help."

Annie leaned against the counter and folded her arms. "I think you wanted to keep an eye on me." She waved a hand around the kitchen. "Go on and look. We're fresh out of arsenic and eye of newt."

Tombi squinted at the jars of dried spices and roots lining the countertops, the basket of pink mojo bags she'd assembled earlier that morning and the bunches of dried herbs hanging above on the ceiling. "Unusual, but nothing overtly suspicious, like a box of rat poison."

Was he serious? Annie frowned. "Now, look here, you can't just—"

Tombi opened the pantry door, and she drew away from the counter, spine stiffening. "Who said you could go poking about everywhere?" she demanded.

"You said I could look around." He stepped in the pantry and ran a finger over the shelves. "Ah, now it's getting interesting. Graveyard dirt, coffin nails and—" he picked up a sealed jar and turned "—swamp juice?" His nose crinkled at the puke-green cloudiness. "Looks like it could kill someone. Bacterial infection would be a gruesome death."

"Put it back, and mind your own business."

He returned it to the shelf, and Annie poured steaming tea into two mugs. She lifted the silver ball that held the loose ingredients in the teapot and waggled it. "We're drinking from the same pot. Just so you know."

Tombi sank into one of the cane-backed kitchen chairs, and Annie sat across from him at the table. He filled the room with his strong presence, overpowered what was once her peaceful sanctuary. Made it disturbing.

Exciting.

Even the air she breathed reeked of masculinity and testosterone—forceful and heady.

Annie slid the ceramic bowl filled with packets of sugar to the middle of the table. "You'll want to sweeten up that brew. It's a bit bitter. If you'd rather use honey, we have some."

"This will do."

She couldn't meet his eyes, instead staring at his lean, muscled forearms and large hands as he ripped open a sugar packet and stirred his tea. What would it be like to have his hands touching her all over? A warm flush blossomed on her cheeks, and she gripped her mug with both hands to steady the turmoil Tombi awoke in her body.

Stop it. He can't be trusted. So far, he had brought nothing but empty promises and disaster.

Tombi swallowed a mouthful of the astringent tea and struggled to conceal his revulsion. But if it would help strengthen his aching limbs and exhaustion, he'd drink every drop.

Annie regarded him, lips curled sardonically. "That's right, my dearie," she crooned in a crackly, crone voice. "Drink every last drop or the poison is no good."

He set the mug down with a bang. "You wouldn't." A heartbeat. "Would you?"

She folded her arms. "What do you think?"

"You wouldn't."

Her eyes narrowed. "Don't be so sure about me. After all, you might have got my grandma killed today. Things like that tend to piss people off, you know."

"It's highly unusual for Nalusa to attack before nightfall. It's as if he were lying in wait for me. As if someone had tipped him off."

"What the hell is that supposed to mean?" She jumped up, hands gripping the table with white-knuckled anger. "You think I contacted a…a…snake? I never even heard of Nalusa until yesterday."

"So you say."

Tombi couldn't let it go. He'd become a jaded man, not by birth disposition, but because of the deaths and trapped spirits he'd witnessed over the past ten years. He and his tribe tried to release all the ensnared souls, but they kept growing in number. Secretly, he despaired there was no stopping Nalusa's increasing spread of misery. How was he supposed to trust this girl—this witch who mysteriously appeared in the dead of night in the swamp and claimed to speak to Bo?

Annie made a disgusted clucking noise and noisily set about tidying the kitchen. "Don't drink the tea, then. Suffer. Means nothing to me."

She dried some silverware and threw it in a drawer, where it clanged. "If anyone's scared, it should be me."

"Scared? I'm not scared." For spirit's sake, he faced creatures of the dark on a daily basis.

She stared pointedly at his half-filled mug and raised an eyebrow. "Really?"

Tombi lifted it to his lips and took another experimental sip. The liquid had cooled considerably. He raised the mug in a salutatory gesture. "To good health." He downed the whole mess in four gulps.

Great Spirits almighty, that was nasty stuff.

Annie threw the dish towel in the sink and stared at him. "Your skin is starting to get a little pale and clammy," she noted. "Perspiration's beading on your forehead. You sure you're okay? Maybe I poisoned you after all."

Tombi lifted his right arm a few inches, then dropped it by his side. He'd almost given her the satisfaction of touching his forehead to check.

"Your jaw is twitching, too."

"It tends to do that when I'm annoyed."

"Better annoyed than worried sick like I am." Annie glanced out the kitchen window, and her body slumped, as if the fight and anger had melted from her spine and left her in a pool of misery.

Damn. He fought the guilt that pestered his gut. He didn't ask that old lady to save him. "Look, Annie, I'm sorry about your grandma."

She waved a hand dismissively, back still toward him. "Maybe you should go to the hospital," he drawled, reluctant to encourage her but compelled to show compassion. Tia Henrietta had saved his life; he owed her.

"She'd kill me. She specifically begged me not to."

"Did she say why?"

Annie sighed. "She seems to think you are some kind of hero or something."

"I wish she hadn't taken the poison," Tombi offered.

She faced him and tilted her head to one side. "Did she say something to you right before the ambulance came? I saw you lean over the couch where she lay."

He shuffled in his seat and shrugged his shoulders. "She moaned, and I got closer to see if she was trying to talk. But she was mostly incoherent."

Mostly.

The word and its meaning seemed to slip by Annie. Thank the spirits.

"She has a weak heart. I don't see how she can recover from this." Her eyes were a reproach.

Tombi frowned, hardening his heart. He couldn't let his resolve to mistrust all strangers end. He had a mission. His people depended on him. Should he fail… No, he couldn't go down that dark corridor of possibility in his mind. Bad enough the worry haunted his dreams.

Her voice rose an octave. "And to top it off, you seem to believe I brought all this on myself and my grandma."

Tombi pursed his lips. "You could have set a trap, not knowing your grandmother would come swooping in to save me at the last possible second."

"Of all the ungrateful…" she sputtered. "If not for us, you'd be dead or ate up with fever."

He paused, struck by the fact that he was ready to return to the hunt, full of vigor. "That tea actually helped," he let slip in surprise.

"Of course it did. You…you…" Again, she was so angry

that words failed. She planted her hands on her hip and glared.

He smiled, and she stepped close to him.

"Stop smirking." Annie pushed against his chest. She was so small, so petite, the top of her head hit him only chest-high.

Instinctively, he grabbed her arms and pulled her closer into him. She smelled mysterious—like herbs and musk and a touch of some flowery scent that was deliciously, dangerously feminine.

He remembered their kiss. Would she ever want to kiss him again—now that she held him responsible for Tia's illness? Loss and regret swept through him like an errant breeze.

If circumstances were different. If there wasn't so much at stake. If only… But it did no good to wallow in "ifs." It wasn't as if he'd had any choice in the matter of his destiny and duty. His hands still held her forearms, but they loosened—and she didn't pull away. He hardly dared move for fear of shattering the magic.

The only sound in the room was their joined breathing, hers lighter and more rapid than his. Her chest gently expanded and contracted. And then, oh-so-slowly, they eased their bodies together, and her cheek lay on his chest. Tombi leaned down and rested his chin on the cinnamon warmth of her dark hair.

Outside, the sky darkened. Leaves and moss would begin to rustle in the ancient oaks. Soon, birds of the night would swoop from branch to branch, screeching and spying and reporting back to Nalusa on the hunters' movements. *Ishkitini*, the horned owl, was the most ominous bird of prey, because his screech foretold a sudden death or murder. Will-o'-the-wisps would glow and skitter about with the energy of the trapped deceased.

The windowpane's reflection captured their joined silhouette like a flickering trick of the eye. Nebulous and passing, a fragile thing of impermanence. Tombi closed his eyes and stroked her arms. They were as soft and slender as a robin's wing.

The phone rang, and she jerked and wiggled out of his embrace, returning to the table to pick up her cell phone.

"How is she?" Annie asked, face set in tense worry. "Uh-huh. That's good…right?"

Reassured the call wasn't death news, Tombi let himself out the front door and stood on the porch. She'd appreciate her privacy. The heat and the night pressed down on him, cloying and heavy.

He had to return to the others. His duty was clear. Somehow, he must convince Annie to come with him. This cottage wasn't safe for a young woman alone. She'd been lured once by a will-o'-the-wisp. It could happen again. Their call was almost impossible to ignore.

And then there were Tia Henrietta's words. *Annie is your destiny. Without her, you fail.* And as he'd started to straighten, the old woman's hand had gripped his with surprising strength. *Take care of my granddaughter.*

Destiny? Destiny be damned. It was enough that the gods had placed this duty on him, this infernal battle with Nalusa and his shadows. No doubt Annie could prove useful with her extraordinary hearing. But that tiny woman wasn't a key to battling evil. She didn't stand a chance against dark forces she'd never before encountered. *If* she was an innocent, he reminded himself grimly. And as far as taking care of Annie…wasn't it enough that his fellow hunters depended on him as their leader? He didn't need another burden.

The door creaked open, and she stood beside him.

"How's your grandmother?"

"Miss Verbena says her vital signs are stabilized, but she's in a coma."

He tried to find comforting words. "Her brain just needs a rest while she battles the poison."

"I don't like it." Her voice was small, weak.

He should say something sweet, something comforting. But he didn't know how. Even his twin, Tallulah, wasn't much good at sweet-talking. If Hanan were here, he would know. His friend was always quick with the comebacks and the right, appropriate thing to say. A real asset in his job as the county sheriff. Tombi stiffened, feeling awkward. "Come with me. Stay with my people."

She shot him a sideways glance. "Why?"

"So you can help us."

She sniffed and turned for the door.

He'd said the wrong thing.

"And because we could use your gift. We…apparently, need you."

"Well, I don't need you. Grandma made me promise not to go to the hospital, but she can't make me leave this house. I'm staying here in case Miss Verbena calls with more news."

"You can take your phone with you."

"Coverage is spotty in the woods. I can't chance it."

"But even if there's news, good or bad, there's nothing you can do," he pointed out.

She gave him a look that would surely curdle even Nalusa's milky venom. "I want to know everything the moment it happens." Her words were slow and deliberate, as if she were talking to a not-so-bright child.

An unexpected warmth flushed Tombi's cheeks at her condescending tone. He scowled to cover his embarrassment. Time to show his ace in the hole. "Your grandmother asked me to take care of you."

"When?" Her eyes narrowed to suspicious slits.

"That time you saw me bending over her before the ambulance came."

"You said she was incoherent."

"I was trying to save your pride."

They glared at one another. In the distance, an owl screeched. A bad sign.

Very bad.

Chapter 5

Annie shivered, breaking the tension. "That owl sounds creepy."

"Ishkitini," Tombi grumbled. No good ever came of the horned owl's cry. It often foretold death. But no sense troubling Annie with that information. She'd assume it was an omen about her grandmother, and then she'd never agree to go with him. Plus, he had to admit, he didn't want to upset Annie.

"A dangerous night to be alone. You'd be safer on the hunt with me," he said.

Her eyes shifted to the woods and back to him.

She was weakening.

"Besides, you shouldn't be here alone tonight worrying about your grandmother. Go on the hunt with us. It will take your mind off your problems."

"Why should I go? It's obvious your friends don't want me around. At least at home, I won't be insulted."

Damn Tallulah and the others for their hostility. It had been a mistake to tell them he'd brought Annie to possibly find a traitor. Nobody appreciated a messenger with bad news. "You'll be by my side during the hunt," Tombi promised. "The others follow their own path in the night darkness."

She glanced over to the woods again. "I have to admit I'm curious about your hunt." Her eyes met his. "Does what you do involve anything gruesome? You know, like, bloody stuff?"

"Not usually."

"Good." She pinned him with a hard look. "And in return for going tonight, you'll teach me how to control my hearing?"

"For one night's work?" The words tumbled out, unfiltered. Oh, hell. By the look on her face, he'd lost any chance of getting her cooperation.

Annie marched back into the cottage, slamming the door shut.

He opened it and followed her inside. At least she hadn't locked him out. "How about this? Spend time with us, and let me know if you have suspicions about anyone. In return, I'll teach you what I can."

Anger twisted her delicate features. "Teach me? I didn't think I'd need lessons."

"How else did you expect to learn to control your gift?"

"I thought… I thought…" She sputtered to a stop.

"I never said it would be easy."

"You never said it would be hard, either." She rubbed her temples. "Just how long will these lessons take?"

"Hard to say." He folded his arms and considered. "Could take weeks, could take months. That is, if you can follow my teachings. Not everyone can control their energy."

Annie sat on the sofa and took a deep breath. "Okay, there are a couple of things troubling me about what you just said." She held up an index finger. "One, your people can guard against leaking their energy, making it difficult for me to hear their auras. So I can't guarantee I'll be able to pinpoint this person."

She held up a second finger, but Tombi interrupted, "Let me take your objections one at a time." He sat across from Annie, their knees almost touching. Warmth radiated from her slight body, and he clamped down the passion she aroused as he cleared his throat. "After a night chasing shadows, we gather back at the campsite and fill each other in on the night's events. We'll eat a light meal and then go to our tents and sleep until the heat of the day drives us out. Usually about noon."

"I don't see what this has to do with—"

"I'm getting to that," Tombi promised. "Stay alert while they sleep and walk around the camp. See if you hear anything suspicious then."

Her brow creased and then cleared. She nodded. "They must let down their guard during sleep."

"Exactly. Now what's your next objection?"

"You said you would teach me *what you could*. What the hell does that mean exactly? First you claimed you could cure me of this gift. Now it sounds like you're waffling."

"No waffling."

"Then are you saying I'm unteachable? I can assure you, that's not true. Not at all. There's nothing wrong with my intelligence."

Tombi raised a brow and regarded her silently.

She had the grace to look sheepish. "Sorry. Touchy point with me. I was teased unmercifully in grade school because I had to be taught in a separate room one-on-one with a teacher's aide. The music from all the other students made it impossible for me to concentrate in a regular classroom." She took a shuddering breath. "They used to call me Crazy Annie."

That must have been tough for a sensitive girl. "Kids can be cruel. I promise I wasn't making a comment on your intelligence. What I meant was that I'll show you how I block my energy. It's a skill my parents taught me, so it stands to reason that, with the right training, you can do the same."

A wistful sadness shadowed her eyes.

"You don't think you can do it?" he asked gently.

She bit her lip. "Oh, it's silly. But what I was really hoping is that you'd arrange for a shaman to remove it. You know, something quick and easy."

He fixed her with a hard stare.

Annie flushed. "I know. That's awful of me. I just want to get on with my life."

"Meaning what? What would you do without your special hearing ability that you can't do now?" Annie was hard to understand. He could control his senses to some degree, yet it didn't change who he was, or his purpose in life.

She threw up her hands. "You can't laugh."

At his steady wait, Annie admitted, "I want to be a librarian."

"Then do it." He shrugged. "Now. No one's stopping you."

"Even in a library, the noise gets to be too much after a while. There's more peace and quiet there than any other public place, but it still grates. I can't see me working as a librarian forty hours a week."

Annie stood and walked around the small den, picking up stray items and straightening stacks of books and magazines. "And it's more than wanting to work a full-time job. I'd like to have friends, a family, a social life."

"The music is that disruptive for you?" It might be hell

for Annie, but this extraordinary ability could only be good for his hunters. And he would try to help her control her gift.

Eventually.

Once he'd gotten all he could from her. Duty first, always.

For the first time in days, a surge of hope fueled a fire within him. "Then what do you have to lose by helping me?" he asked. "I'll make sure no harm comes to you."

She carefully placed a book back down on a coffee table. "I really, really, really hate snakes," she said, dead serious. "So you'd better protect me like you promised."

"I will," he vowed. "With my life." This he could say with no guilt or deception.

Annie picked up a picture of her grandma and bent her head over it. Her long, wavy hair covered her face, but her shoulders shook, and he knew she wept. Surprisingly, it made him long to put his arms around her and kiss away her tears. He hardened his heart—this wouldn't do at all.

"It's what your grandma wanted, too," he reminded her, pushing Annie to make a commitment.

She nodded, slowly putting down the picture. "I'm ready."

He tamped down a satisfied smile. What the hell was wrong with him? Her grandmother was probably dying. A familiar fear flickered along his nerves. He was turning into the shadows he hunted, losing his humanity and compassion.

"Should I bring anything?" she asked.

"No, I have all the provisions we'll need."

She set about blowing out the scattered candles flickering in the room, grief making each act seem like a small goodbye.

"You'll be back tomorrow afternoon," he said.

"I wonder when—or if—Grandma Tia will ever come back. This place may not be much, but she loved it."

He considered his surroundings more carefully. The worn furniture, the framed pictures, saint paintings and jars full of wildflowers strewn everywhere. It was an unexpected blow to his heart, reminding him of a similar modest place filled with colorful wool rugs and books and carved statues his father had whittled. A home that always smelled faintly of corn bread and wood shavings. A place swept away by Hurricane Katrina, along with a peace he never expected to find again.

"It's her home. Your home," he said simply.

"Yes. I only lived here during the summers, but it felt like my true home. The one place where I was wanted." Annie cleared her throat and set her shoulders back. "Let's go."

She didn't need to tell him a third time. "Okay. I'll wait for you outside."

He left, sensing she needed to collect her emotions before leaving. Night had come once again, bringing with it danger and whispers in the wind. But it was also beautiful in its own dark, mysterious way. The full moon shone bloodred, and the tall trees stood like sinister sentinels of doom.

Annie popped her head out the door. "Do we need flashlights?"

"Not necessary."

She gave him a quizzical look as she shut the door and locked up. "How about you explain a few things to me before we get to the campsite?" She pocketed her keys in a small, crocheted purse and joined him.

"What questions do you have?" he asked reluctantly. Tombi set off in long strides toward the trail. Normally, he evaded questions from outsiders, but Annie would be part of the hunt tonight, and she had a right to ask.

"For starters, how do you see so well in the dark? And slow down before I trip on a tree root or run into a tree."

He slowed. "Sorry. I'm not used to being with an outsider."

"I'm always an outsider," she mumbled.

"No offense. It's just a word we use for those not of our nation." He took hold of her hand. "It will be safer this way."

To hell with that. It was electric. He guessed from Annie's sharp inhale that she felt the same current buzzing through her body. He forced himself to focus on the path. This was no time to indulge in lustful distractions. Mistakes out here got a man killed.

"Lesson one. I have unnatural night vision, as do the rest of the hunters. It's how we were first identified by our ancestors. And since all natural gifts have a purpose—" he squeezed her hand "—they soon found why. It was one of the gifts from the spirits for us to fight and protect ourselves from the evil ones."

Annie snorted. "I don't believe all so-called gifts are for a reason. Sometimes things just are. Like genetic mutations. And why does evil exist in the first place? The spirits didn't have to allow Nalusa power."

"Why does your God allow the devil to live?" he countered. "It's impossible to question such things. We have to deal with what is instead of trying to pry into the intelligence of our creators."

"You have a point," she admitted grudgingly. "But go on—what other abilities do you have as a shadow hunter?"

He continued, glad Annie's questions seemed to keep her distracted from her anger against him. "As you guessed, we can control our energies. Which usually means creatures don't sense us until we are very close."

She stumbled slightly, and he steadied her. "I can see how that's useful. What powers do your enemies have?"

His enemies. Tombi searched the gathering twilight. "They can't sense energy as well as we can, but they have their own elements of surprise. Nalusa can shape-shift to other forms. You saw him as a snake."

Her tiny hand trembled in his own.

"Sometimes he appears as a tall, dark being with small eyes and pointed ears. And there are the will-o'-the-wisps he controls. They can take you alive or steal a soul that's not yet crossed over to the land of the dead."

"But why? What does he gain?"

"Evil doesn't always need a reason to exist. It's the nature of the universe, the duality of our world. But in Nalusa's case, any kind of death or destruction, any human suffering, contributes to his power. He feeds off our misery."

"He sounds like the very devil," she whispered. "Sorry, but I hope we don't run into him tonight." Annie shivered but continued to pick her way through the woods with his guidance, carefully stepping forward and trying to avoid the large, gnarly tree roots that erupted from the soil.

Even with his heightened senses, Tombi's night vision was limited. He could see enough to break the dark into lighter and darker shadows and to be sensitive, like a cat, to any kind of movement, even from a considerable distance.

They would arrive at camp in minutes. Would she find any of his people were really betrayers, working against them and for the dark side? That was the worst part of the shadow world; they could insidiously invade your mind and heart. You had to be constantly on guard against their influence.

"What, exactly, do you do when you find Nalusa or a wisp?" Annie asked, breaking his melancholy thoughts.

"I'll tell you when we get to camp. It's not wise to speak of such things out here in the woods."

Her eyes darted around the path, as if expecting Nalusa to grab her any second, but she kept moving forward.

He silently kept watch over her as she stumbled along, wondering at her story. He couldn't afford to discount Annie's claim of speaking with Bo. His friend—so powerful and so close to the tribe—might have found a way to do what no other trapped soul had done before: break through a wisp's barrier and speak a warning.

That was, if Annie wasn't lying, if she wasn't under any shadow influence. There was no way to judge. He'd observe her closely for any inconsistencies or suspicious moves.

Because that was the worst power his enemy possessed, the most dangerous. He could rot your soul on the inside, could find purchase in the flimsiest of your sins and make them into something larger, until they became a wicked cancer that contaminated your mind. All the while, on the outside, your friends and family couldn't tell the invisible transformation beneath skin and bones.

The worst evil was the one that lived in your own heart, waiting to be fed and exploited by the shadows.

As always, Annie heard before she saw: a low murmur of voices, a rustling of feet against earth and a thrum of excitement like the muted power and hum of an ocean undertow.

And she was about to be dragged down into the strong current.

The closer to camp, the stronger the pull. At last the other hunters came into view, dark shadows with eyes that occasionally glowed like a cat's with refracted moonbeams. Those pinpricks of light focused on her and Tombi, but mostly her.

"How come your eyes don't glow like that?" she whispered.

"Those of us who are masters at containing our energy are able to suppress any sign that gives away our location."

"There's more people tonight than the group I met earlier."

"You only met my inner circle this morning."

One of the shadows moved closer. "We wondered where you were," said a low voice.

Annie recognized that voice. Hanan. Some people never forgot a face; but she never forgot a voice.

"So you brought her again." His voice was flat, neutral as Switzerland, but Annie registered the dig.

Tombi's hand rested on her shoulder. Possessive, comforting. Her insides warmed from the contact.

"Annie might help us turn the tide against Nalusa."

She silently berated herself. She was only important to him if she suited his purposes. Best to remember that.

Hanan nodded. "Barrett needs to speak with you before he sets out."

Tombi released her shoulder. "Be back in a minute."

The two men walked off together beyond her sight and sound. Annie marveled at their self-containment. She was in a group of over twenty people, yet the music was subdued and manageable.

A sharp pinch at her elbow caught Annie completely by surprise.

"You may have my brother fooled, but not me," Tallulah said in a fierce whisper. Her eyes glinted with suspicion. A jangle of minor keys plunked the air surrounding her tall, lithe figure. "You never talked to my Bo. If he could talk, his spirit would have come to *me*, not you, witch."

Her Bo. So that was how it had been between them. Tombi should have mentioned that the two of them were lovers. Still, it was hard to find sympathy for the malicious Tallulah.

"I didn't seek him out," Annie protested. "I can't help it."

"I can't help it," Tallulah mocked in a high-pitched trembly voice. "What's your real game? Who sent you here?"

Where was Tombi? Annie scanned the campground, where hunters' shadows moved into the woods and disappeared into darkness. They moved alone or sometimes in groups of two. Loners. Instead of talking, they used a series of hand signals to communicate. A few she could understand—wait, this way, goodbye—but most she couldn't decipher.

Tombi appeared suddenly from behind. "Go," he told Tallulah in a low, harsh voice.

Chulah materialized by Tallulah's side and motioned for her to join him.

But Tallulah wasn't finished. She edged closer, and her harsh breath was in Annie's ear. "I'll be watching you." With that, Tallulah spun around and sauntered into the woods, Chulah close at hand.

"She's had a hard time since Bo's death," said Tombi.

Of course he'd defend his sister. But Annie found it hard to muster understanding for that Amazon. Tombi's twin possessed a black panther's stealthiness, a feline wildness marked by sharp claws and growls and hisses.

Annie would come out on the losing end of that catfight.

"We need to talk." Tombi motioned, and she followed him into his tent. The darkness was utter under the canopy. She sat down on a pallet made of blankets. A low, throbbing drumbeat suffused the tight space between their bodies.

She wanted to sink into that sound, to lie down and fold into the steady, pulsating notes. Feel its vibration stroke her naked skin.

"The tent will muffle our voices a bit. I'm laying down a few rules before we start."

The baritone filled the cramped space with its power. Too bad his words tempered the sexy effect of his music.

"I won't cause trouble," she whispered, curtailing the teenaged desire to roll her eyes. "I'll stick close and keep quiet."

"Good." He leaned over, and she felt the hot skin of an arm and the side of his waist brush against her chest and face. Her breath quickened. His scent, his aura, drew her to him, and she was helpless to fight the pull. Being near him was sexually hypnotic. How easy it would be to reach out and pull him closer. Feel the weight of his body on top of her own. Despite the sadness of the evening and her chaotic thoughts, she was drawn to his music, as if her were the Pied Piper of the bayou.

The tent was intimate. She didn't want to hunt, she wanted to stay here, with Tombi. Safe and protected and exploring the pleasure of his body.

Crazy.

Wrong time, and possibly the wrong man.

But as if her arms weren't controlled by her brain, Annie reached around his back and drew him to her.

His back muscles tightened beneath her touch, and he drew in a ragged breath. Tombi stilled, as if warring with his sexual desire and his duty in the world outside the tent.

Annie wanted him desperately, just for a few minutes, a little slice of time. She saw how much he gave to the others, how they looked up to him. She saw how he defended his sister. In spite of Tallulah's nastiness, he made allowances for her grief. Didn't he deserve a few minutes of happiness for himself?

Didn't she?

Who knew what dangers the night and the hunt might bring?

In the hushed darkness, their breathing forged wisps of desire that swirled in the confined area.

Tombi groaned, as if admitting defeat, and his weight slammed into her, sending them both down, bodies pressed hard against the earth. His lips and tongue were on her, in her, warm and electric.

He moaned again—no, wait, that was *her* this time. Her body was in a fever of longing. Annie couldn't remember the last time—if ever—she had been so desperate with desire. Need curled and twisted her gut.

"You're so damn sexy," Tombi ground out.

Passion flamed hotter in her veins, along with triumph and humble gratitude that she, misfit Annie Mathews, could affect him so much. She arched against him, and his mouth tracked kisses down her neck and past the hollow at the base of her throat. He pushed up her T-shirt and unhooked her bra. One of his hands glided to her breasts and palmed her rounded flesh. His mouth lowered and covered a nipple, his tongue flicking the bud, sending unbearable need to her core. Tombi's full manhood ground against her, hard and insistent.

"Tombi? Tombi? You there?"

The insistent whisper outside the tent flap exploded on their private ecstasy.

"Damn it," Tombi muttered. In a heartbeat, he pulled away and ran a hand through his long hair.

Annie watched him scramble out the tent and hugged her arms to her waist, missing his heat and touch. Quickly, she hooked her bra and pulled down her shirt. She felt disoriented. Seconds ago her mind and body had been united and focused on physical release. Now her thoughts were chaos.

Low murmurs sounded nearby. Was there some kind of trouble? Annie silently crawled to the tent's front and poked her head out the slotted opening. Tombi and Hanan were several feet away, and they immediately turned as one to stare at her.

Not much, if anything, would get past these men. They could probably pick up a frog's croak from a hundred yards out. She ducked her head back inside, as if she'd been caught eavesdropping.

Tombi crawled into the tent and sat as far from her as he could in the small space.

The passion party was definitely over.

"So here are the simple rules," he said, as if nothing had happened between them. "Stay within arm's reach of me and avoid talking unless it's an emergency. I'll be searching for will-o'-the-wisps, and when I come within range, I'll shoot it with a slingshot. We aim for the glowing heart in the middle. If we hit it dead-on, the wisp will release the spirit and lose its power."

"And the trapped spirit will be freed?"

"Exactly." He hesitated. "I've been searching for one wisp in particular."

"Bo," she guessed. "You want to help your friend."

He nodded. "If you hear Bo again or sense he's near, point me in the right direction. Other sounds to beware of are snake rattles or music from the wisps. You might hear them before me. If you do, tap my arm."

She cringed at the thought of snakes. "Seems like the wisps would be easy targets with the way they glow and the music they make."

"But nature's provided them with speed and the ability to momentarily lose their light. Makes it hard to zero in on them."

"And what has nature granted you? What does it mean when you say you can control your energy?"

His eyes shifted to the opening, as if impatient to be on the move. "The quick and dirty version is this—we can create a field around our bodies that makes it hard for Nalusa and his wisps to see, smell or hear us in the dark."

He reached behind her, pulled out a camouflage duffel bag and slung it over his right shoulder.

So that was what he'd been looking for earlier when he'd leaned across her body. And she'd grabbed at him like an out-of-control hormonal teenager. Annie winced inwardly. But she consoled herself, knowing that he had obviously enjoyed their kiss.

"Let's go."

His command cut through her musings. She followed him out, and they walked across the open field. Annie took care to stay close and stay silent.

It was like another world at night. Although it was still hot, the humidity was at a bearable level, and she became even more hyperaware of sound and smell—the gentle lap of the Gulf water, the crickets, the unnerving screech of an owl. The breeze smelled of pine and moss and sea salt that invigorated. It was the smell of childhood summers and freedom.

Tombi kept a slow pace, most likely for her ease, and managed to avoid most twigs and dry leaves. Annie winced at the first few crunches her footfalls produced. Somehow, though he weighed twice as much and his foot size was a great deal larger, Tombi walked almost soundlessly.

To his credit, he didn't utter a word or give a disapproving warning look. *Because you are doing just what he wants you to do. He needs you to find Bo again.* Tombi didn't care so much about stalking prey as he did about finding his friend. And she was his key.

Her legs tired, and her arms burned from scratches and brushes with foliage and bark. On and on and on they walked until she'd lost all sense of time. Her jeans were hot, but at least her legs weren't getting sliced and battered like her arms. How long would this go on? She'd assumed it would only be a couple of hours, but now she feared he would keep hunting until dawn.

Every few minutes he would turn and look at her, an eyebrow raised in question. *Have you heard anything?*

And each time she'd had to shake her head "no."

Annie kept her senses fully opened, a rare event. She heard more intricate, softer sounds now, rustling leaves, a lone car passing by from a great distance. The other noises she'd heard earlier deepened, and she awakened to the more subtle tones like tree roots pulsing and pushing the earth, inch by inch, mining for nutrients. The ocean lapped the shore with a splash, announcing the end of its journey until the undertow pulled it back to start a new one. Insects droned and squeaked in their thirst for survival. Small critters like squirrels or rabbits or foxes skittered amongst dense underbrush.

Eat or be eaten. Perish or thrive. The cadence of survival was a constant dance of retreat and attack, a crescendo and decrescendo of noise.

Tombi unexpectedly pulled her close to his side. His mouth covered one of her ears. "Do you need to rest?" he breathed. Her skin and insides vibrated with arousal.

She nodded, and he led her to a fallen limb where they could sit. Annie sank on to the rough bark and fought the urge to break into a loud sigh of relief. Tombi removed the camo bag from his back and produced a water bottle. Wordlessly, he handed it to her.

Annie gulped the cold water. She lifted it to her lips for another draught, pausing at the faint, floating notes wafting in the breeze. Bewitching, evocative notes that pulled her inside, urging her to come forward, to more clearly enjoy the exquisite melody. She dropped the water bottle and rose to her feet, circling to catch the direction of the music.

The music grew more distinct. And even though she knew its charm held an ugly underside, the need to follow the sound twisted her gut with longing to be closer, to bask in its loveliness.

Tombi's touch on the middle of her back steadied her. Again, he whispered in her ear. "Is it Bo?"

She considered. "I don't think so," she said, keeping her voice barely above a breath.

Disappointment tightened his face.

"But there's more than one," she added. "It's a blended sound. I'd guess at least five or six separate voices."

"Damn. How far away?"

"About fifty yards." She pointed toward the east. "In that direction."

Tombi pulled out his slingshot and palmed several rocks. "Can't wait here and let them circle us in an ambush."

"What would happen if they did?"

"Your soul would be in jeopardy. They invade your mind like a cold smoke. A vapor that seeps in by any crack in your mental armor."

"I'll go with you," she said hurriedly. "I can help throw stones."

"No," he said, cutting her off at once. "You'll be safer here. Stay put and don't go anywhere."

He placed a couple of stones in her hand and left, disappearing in sudden, silent movements.

Jerk. He'd promised to stay close by her side, yet at the

first whiff of a fight, he'd abandoned her. Annie sat back down on the log, put the stones in her lap and pressed her fingers to her ears, trying to at least partially block the will-o'-the-wisps' alluring call. It helped, but it wasn't perfect. Annie resorted to her second round of defense; she sang silently inside, blocking outside sound from overpowering her emotions.

Much better. Not perfect, but better. It was tolerable. Good thing, because her last defense was running away, and right now that wasn't an option.

The relief was short-lived.

A stealthy note of caution and cunning crept over her flesh like sticky syrup. Something or someone was at the edge of her awareness. Annie dropped her hands in her lap and stared into the inky void.

A rumble vibrated in her mind, like she'd imagine an earthquake would produce. But the ground wasn't trembling. Where the hell did it come from? Even the wisps had fallen silent. Did this mean Tombi had been hurt or captured? Dread prickled her scalp.

A harsh noise like grating metal erupted. Annie jumped up, nerves jangling with adrenaline.

The rumbling and grating ceased, and a small childlike voice whispered in the night.

"Help me. Please."

Annie's breath was so loud and ragged she might as well have had a beacon of light shining on her, telegraphing her location.

"I'm trapped," the voice said plaintively, louder this time.

It called to the healer in her even more than the wisp's enchanting songs.

She had to help.

Chapter 6

"Over here."

Annie squeezed the rocks fisted in both her palms and took a couple of steps forward. She held her hands out in front of her to avoid slamming into anything and carefully followed the voice.

The exquisite music returned, and she realized the voice was a soul trapped in a wisp. Thankfully, it appeared to be solitary in its flittering about the swamp. If only Tombi were here, he could help this poor soul. As for herself, she was always the last one picked for any kind of sport at school, including softball. So her strength and her aim were highly suspect. She'd be lucky to hit a large target even at the mere distance of ten feet.

Forward progress was painfully slow, but the volume of the music increased, and Annie knew she was close. She leaned against a tree and took a deep breath. Might as well speak up; the wisp already knew she was present. "If you want my help, come to me."

A swirl of pink and purple shone through a patch of brambles a few yards ahead.

"That was quick," she muttered.

Symphonic music emanated from the wisp, soothing her fear.

Be careful. Annie focused on the rocks balled in her hand, their sharp edges scratching into her flesh. *Focus on the soul who wants freedom.*

In the span of time it took for a struck match to catch flame, the wisp floated to within six feet of where she stood with her back pressed into the jagged bark. Its brightness lit the woods stronger than any lantern. At its center, a heart shone violet blue like the color at the base of a candle flame. That was her target. Her mouth grew dry. Could she really do it? Tombi never said what would happen once the spirit left a will-o'-the-wisp.

"Whoever, whatever you are inside there, you better help me if I free you." Annie stepped away from the tree, raised her arm and threw the stone in her right hand.

It landed several inches above the heart, harmlessly passing through the wisp's pink-and-purple vapor. The beautiful music stopped, and a growl rumbled in warning. Quickly, she transferred the rock from her left hand to her right and whirled it again at the glowing heart.

Dead-on.

A high-pitched screech wailed, and gray smoke shot out of the wisp's center. The rest of its glowing form collapsed upon itself, as if it had lost its skeletal base. Its shine dimmed and grew smaller, until it was about the size of a basketball. Would it retaliate? The need to run fueled her body, and her veins pulsed with adrenaline, but how could she run in this darkness?

"Follow me," said a tiny voice from below.

Annie looked down, and floating only a few inches from the ground was a swirling ball of gray-yellow smoke.

"You have only a few minutes before either the wisp regenerates or other wisps hunt you down."

Chills chased up and down her spine. "But how—"

The light wobbled in the air. "There's enough light that you can see a few feet ahead of you at a time. I'll take you down a path that leads to a paved road. Hurry!"

A faint rumble near the wounded wisp was all the encouragement she needed. Annie picked her way along the dirt path, frustrated with her slow pace.

"Hurry," the light urged again.

"I can't go any faster."

"Try."

The light streaked ahead, and she quickened her step to keep up. "Don't leave me, you ungrateful little…" Annie bit her lip to stop the insulting words. It would be foolish to anger the tiny soul helping as best it could. Tombi was nowhere around, for damn sure. Some protection he turned out to be.

She plunged on, her focus on the small soul she'd rescued and the lucent beam it cast. Red clay, pine needles and twisted tree roots had never appeared so beautiful. Nothing mattered except continuing, one foot, then another, doing what was necessary for survival. Her breathing was labored and unnaturally loud, a roar in her ears.

"You're almost to the road," the soul squeaked in its small voice. "You're on your own from there."

"Where are you going?"

"I'm crossing over."

"You're entering the afterlife? Is that a good thing?"

"The best."

At least one lovely incident occurred this evening. A

soul's passage from Earth was a solemn, miraculous rite. "What's your name?" Annie asked.

"Not important. All that matters is that you make it home."

The soul surged to Annie's eye level, the swirling ball of color changing from its original grayish yellow to a blazing orange.

Her feet hit pavement, and she wanted to weep with relief at the sight of the open road.

"Keep going," the soul warned.

Panic returned. Annie looked up and down the road, but nothing appeared familiar. "At least tell me where I am."

The light whooshed away at a dazzling speed, pitching her into sudden darkness. It was leaving her, after all she'd done, all she'd...

The soul returned. "Another mile ahead is the intersection of County Roads 82 and 40."

Not far from home after all. "Thank you," she said, exhaling deeply with relief.

"Go." The soul slowly floated upward.

"Wait! I still can't see much without you."

It kept floating until it became one with the night. "You could have at least said thank-you," Annie complained, her face tilted skyward.

The grating metal noise sounded again from the edge of the woods. Annie took off on a brisk walk. There was a sliver of light from the moon now, but not much. It would be a miracle if she didn't trip and bash her head a dozen times on the blacktop surface before she even came to the four-way stop.

Damn Tombi. He should never have left her alone.

A captivating song unexpectedly entered her mind. One she'd never heard before. But how? This never happened unless she was near someone. And right now she was utterly alone. The song continued, like a balm easing soreness, a lullaby for frayed nerves. It wasn't the enchanting music of the wisps; this was more…relaxing and peaceful.

Annie's breath slowed while her feet continued their ceaseless march forward. If she had to run at some point, she would. She'd faced and defeated one wisp; she could do it again if needed.

"Thank you." The words were a brushed whisper in her mind. The rescued soul hadn't abandoned her at all. It had come back and provided comfort for the long journey home.

It was one of the sweetest acts of kindness she'd ever experienced. Annie's throat tightened. "You're welcome," she said aloud, past the aching lump.

The music played on. The sweet notes kept her steady, kept her from stumbling on legs burning with exhaustion. A side stitch smarted, like a surgeon's knife had sliced through half of her torso, and dehydration left her parched and with a headache. But the music kept playing until she'd arrived at her grandma's cottage. A long, cool glass of water, and she was falling into bed. A shower could wait.

Where the hell was Annie?

Tombi paced back and forth by the log where he'd last seen her.

"We've searched everywhere." Chulah arrived with two others. "I checked in with all the hunters. No one has seen or heard her."

"Keep looking," he snapped. Worry racked his mind until he thought he would go mad. He'd said he'd protect Annie. And now she had vanished.

His fault.

He should never have left her alone. Not even for a shot at capturing Nalusa.

His brain froze in horror. Did Nalusa get to Annie?

For the hundredth time, Tombi walked around the log, hoping to track a smell or visual sign for a clue. He slowly tracked in ever-widening circles. This time, a faint sulfur odor, mixed with balsam fir, drifted up from the ground. Tombi knelt down and found a sprinkling of ash dusted on pine needles.

"Hey," he said, looking over his shoulder. "We have burnout."

Chulah knelt beside him, picked up a powdered needle and held it beneath his nose. "Happened well over an hour ago."

"Has anyone else hunted in this area tonight?"

"I already told you—no. The girl must have done it."

Tombi kept searching until he found two small, round rocks several feet nearby. The ones he'd given her for protection. "I shouldn't have left her side."

"How were you supposed to know it was a trap?" Chulah asked. "You thought a band of wisps might encircle the two of you."

"Better that than to leave her defenseless."

"You left her the rocks, and she defended herself," Chulah said, standing. "There's enough light now that it's possible she walked home. She's probably in bed asleep."

His friend lied to reassure him. Tombi stood as well, dread slowing his movements. He'd promised to protect her. What if another wisp had heard the burnout when the soul was released and made its way to Annie, bent on retaliation? His gut clenched.

"Why are you so worried about that girl?" Chulah frowned. "One explanation is that she defended herself and got either bored or tired of waiting on you to return and went home."

"*That* girl?" Tombi said, crossing his arms. "She's a

woman, not a girl, and you know damn well she must be in trouble." He remembered the press of her body against his, the warm feel of her skin against his own. Annie Matthews was a woman. A passionate woman.

Twigs snapped, and leaves crackled beneath a careless foot. Tallulah burst through the underbrush to his side. Her eyes were fierce and focused as she strode to where he and Chulah stood.

"We've wasted enough time searching for that foolish woman," she snapped. "Let's get back to camp."

"She's not foolish. Why the hostility? She's offered to help us."

Tallulah tossed back her long hair and lifted her chin. "Because she's under Nalusa's influence. He sent her here to spy on us and make us mistrustful of each other. There's no traitor."

His sister voiced his own misgivings, yet he found it increasingly difficult to believe the worst of Annie.

"Her grandmother is critically ill, maybe even dead, because she absorbed the poison Nalusa meant for me," Tombi reminded them.

"And Annie could have set you up to be bitten," Tallulah said. "Her grandmother might not have known what was going on. Why are you so blind?"

If she wasn't his sister, if he didn't know how grief-stricken she'd been after Bo's death, he wouldn't be able to control the temper heating his veins. "I've been leading this group for ten years. You've never questioned my judgment before."

The fierceness in her eyes faded, and her shoulders slumped. "I don't want you to get hurt, Tom-Tom."

She hadn't called him by that childhood name in years. His heart softened, remembering everything they'd been through together—the death of their parents and a new lifestyle with a host of duties thrust upon them at a young age. For spirit's sake, they'd only been nineteen when Hurricane Katrina had washed away the solid foundation of their world.

"Don't worry about me," he said softly.

Chulah stepped in and placed an arm over Tallulah's shoulder. "Let's get back to camp and eat breakfast. We're all tired and hungry. You, too, Tombi."

"Not until I find out what's happened to Annie. Go if you want, but I'm going to keep tracking." He had to see her, had to know she was safe. The need to touch Annie, to hold her and apologize for leaving, was an ache deep in his soul.

Sleep was impossible.

Annie drank the tall glass of water she'd craved and collapsed on her bed, but an unease settled over her, a conviction that something bad had happened. She got up and went to the altar in the den, intent on lighting a candle to pray for Grandma Tia. A note from Miss Verbena had been propped on the mortar-and-pestle bowl, informing Annie that her grandmother had suffered a stroke.

A punch in the gut.

Sooner or later lack of sleep would catch up to her, but for now Annie was fueled with adrenaline and the need to check on her grandma. She showered, put on a clean pair of jeans and a T-shirt, and drove to the Bayou La Siryna hospital.

To hell with that coerced promise to stay away.

Annie's resolution stayed strong until she walked down the long hallway of the critical-care unit. From every door she passed, she heard a funereal fugue with its long, melancholy strains, as gloomy as Baroque organ music. Worse were the open doors to rooms housing patients in intense pain. Their aural music was sharp as glass shards, slicing through her consciousness. *Deep breaths. One step at a time.* Only her love for Tia was worth suffering these symphonies of agony.

Room 3182. She'd made it.

Annie pushed the cool metal door open and entered. All was quiet. The sweet scent of violets triumphed over antiseptic's odor. Which meant Miss Verbena had recently been here, had been in vigil by the bed when *she* should have been the one doing so.

Tia's eyes were closed and her breathing steady, as if in peaceful slumber. As if her physical agonies were in a state of suspension.

Annie took her grandma's right hand in her own. Tia's fingers were cold and rough. Her grandma would hate that. She always said that if she were meant to tolerate the cold, she'd have been born a Yankee.

She found some lotion in the hospital toiletry bin and rubbed the balm into her grandma's cold flesh, pressing and kneading the rough skin, massaging in healing warmth. All Tia's flashy rings were gone. She looked bare without them, oddly lonely and vulnerable.

Tia's hands should be active—mixing potions, dealing tarot cards, lighting candles. Even saddled with a bad heart, her grandma would sit on the sofa in the evenings and read through old magic books, an index finger gliding down the page like a third eye, absorbing words. Or she would shuffle the cards and lay out spreads, searching for messages from the beyond.

Inside a metal locker was a blanket, and Annie tucked it over Tia's unmoving body, remembering all the times her grandma had tucked her in bed as a child. She'd never felt so loved nor as safe as when Grandma Tia chanted and hummed, asking for the saints' protection over "the

young'un" while she slept. Tia would slide the sheets up
to Annie's neck and pat her large, warm hands on Annie's
slender shoulders, as if to seal in a prayer.

"Rest well, Grandma. I'll watch over you now." Annie
pressed her palms into Tia's broad shoulders. "Saints be
with us."

The air pressed down, and a humming rang in her ears,
as if she'd been submerged in a cave. What was happening? The contact with Grandma Tia had set something in
motion. Every sound magnified: the grind of tires on the
distant highway, a clock ticking. Down the hall, a voice
called for a nurse. The sounds were distinct yet muted and
slowed down. Annie sank into the chair by the side of the
bed and squeezed Tia's hand.

"Are you there, Grandma? It's me, Annie."

Tia's chilled, lifeless hand suddenly warmed, then
burned into Annie's palm and fingers. Instinctively, Annie
started to pull back but stopped, afraid she'd lose this connection. Possibly the last she'd ever have with her grandma.
She closed her eyes and concentrated. *I'm here. Don't be
mad. I had to see you.*

A pinprick of light danced behind Annie's closed eyelids. With each flicker, a tiny note pinged…sounding like
the metal triangles of elementary school. No, wait, that
wasn't right. The notes were more like the Native American flute Tombi had played in the woods.

She didn't want to think about him. Yet, she couldn't
escape the feeling that he was calling her somehow, that
he needed her. Why was Grandma Tia always pushing
him toward her, even while unconscious? An image of
a flute pressed into her thoughts. It was more decorated
than the one Tombi had played, as if it were used in ceremonies and rituals.

She'd never seen it before. But Tia had.

"What are you trying to tell me?" Annie asked.

The image, and the music, faded to a black void. Tia's hand cooled to a normal temperature.

The moment had passed.

Annie's eyes flew open, but Tia's calm mask of sleep was undisturbed. Profound relief washed over her body, and with it came a great weariness. She sank into the chair and slept.

Violets…the scent tickled her nose. Miss Verbena's lined face came into view.

"Annie, are you okay, dear?"

She jerked to an upright position and looked out the window. How long had she been asleep? The late-afternoon sun washed the air with bright power.

My name means ray of light in Choctaw, Tombi had told her. *We once revered the sun's power.* At the time, she'd laughed over his not-so-sunny personality, but his name fit. He was powerful and strong and important to his people, a central figure in a fight against shadow beings who wanted to block the light.

Her anger melted like butter in the heat. If Tombi hadn't ever returned to find her, he'd had a good reason. A chill settled in the pit of her stomach. What if he'd been injured last night?

She had to find him at once.

"You're so pale," Miss Verbena said. "I'll fetch you a glass of water. Have you eaten today?"

Her mouth tingled at the mention of food. "No. I guess I forgot."

"Lord a-mercy, I wish I'd forget to eat a meal." Miss Verbena patted her ample belly and dug a pack of peanut-butter crackers out of her straw bag. "This should tide you over until dinner."

Annie scarfed them down greedily as she gathered her pocketbook and car keys. "I have to run," she apologized. She hugged her grandma's dear friend. "Thank you for staying with Grandma Tia. I'll be back as soon as I can."

"'Course you will. You've always been a good girl, unlike your…" She clamped her mouth shut in a tight line.

"Unlike my mom," Annie said. "Have you called her? I know I should but…"

Miss Verbena shook her head. "That's your business. Doubt she'd come, though. Always swore she never wanted to come back here again after they had that big blowout years ago." The scowl on her face softened. "Don't you worry, honey. I have a feeling ole Tia's gonna pull through this just fine. You go on and do what you got to do."

She carefully hugged the old woman, throat constricted with tears. "Thanks for understanding."

Annie hurried out, knowing that she had to find Tombi.

Chapter 7

Tombi kicked at the campfire ashes, placed his elbows on his knees and rested his head in his hands. He should be sleeping like the others in preparation for the last night of the hunt. Instead, his mind kept asking the same question over and over. *Where is Annie?* He'd checked her cottage, of course, but she wasn't home. Neither was her car, which meant she could be anywhere. He'd called and left messages on her cell phone, but she couldn't, or wouldn't, answer.

The air's vibration shifted, and the soles of his bare feet prickled from a subtle tremor. Someone was approaching. Tombi raised his head, and his eyes went immediately across the clearing to where a woman entered from a wooded path.

Annie.

Others might have mistaken her for a girl, but he knew better, had explored the rounded curves of her breasts and the slight swell of her hips. He rose slowly to his feet, his mind churning with passion, anger and relief. Mostly relief.

Graceful as a woodland sprite, she walked across the field, her brown wavy hair tossing in the breeze. She seemed to draw energy to her, as if the natural world became more animated in her presence. A dark angel, a whimsical witch who heard music where others experienced only silence.

Tombi went quickly toward her, away from the tents of sleeping hunters. A few were already stirring, preparing for various camp duties before the night's hunt.

"Where have you—" he started.

"You're okay. I thought maybe—"

They both stopped. Tombi reached for her, and she willingly walked into his arms. All the worry and anxiety of the past few hours vanished under the solid feel of her body pressed against his. He kissed the top of her head, inhaling the scent of flowers and musk. But he was conscious that the others would soon be stirring from their tents. Now wasn't the time to kiss again—they would be certain she'd bewitched him. He stepped back and scanned her body, checking for injuries.

"The wisp didn't hurt you?"

Annie blinked. "How did you know I was attacked?"

"We found the stones you threw and ashes from a released spirit." He had to know, dared to hope. "Was it Bo?"

"No, sorry. I had the impression the soul was a girl. And she never told me her name."

Tombi shook off the disappointment. It had been a longshot chance at best. "I tried to find you. Even went to your grandma's cottage, but your car was gone. I've been worried."

She shrank into herself. "I went to the hospital to see my grandma," she said shortly.

Did she still blame him for her grandmother's illness?

Hell, it wouldn't be any worse than the guilt that nagged at him over what had happened. "How is she?"

"She's still in a coma. The doctors said she had a stroke but they never mentioned poison, which I find strange."

"There never is. Nalusa's venom won't register on medical tests. People he's bitten were diagnosed with other conditions like heart attacks or allergic reactions."

"Has anyone been bitten and lived?"

Her eyes were so sad, so anxious, he couldn't tell her the truth. "Maybe," he hedged. "I can't be aware of every instance he's attacked or bitten."

"What happened out there in the woods? You never came back to me."

"I was drawn away. I'll explain later. But first, I need your help. Quick." He looked back over his shoulder at the campsite. "While everyone is still asleep."

She nodded. "That's why I'm here. I did promise."

Annie brushed past him and strode purposefully toward the tents. He followed a few yards after, hands clasped behind his back. None of his people would betray him; he was almost 100 percent certain of their loyalty.

Almost.

If Annie heard nothing incriminating, he'd report her finding to the others, and they could continue on as before, without the worm of mistrust wiggling in some dark recess of their minds.

She walked carefully among the tents and paused at one. A large moan erupted from inside, and she blushed. Even he recognized the music of passion. Annie scurried away, and he laughed.

She circled around a tent on the outside of the ring, her head cocked to the side. He raised an eyebrow at her, but she shook her head and moved on, tapping her lips and chin as she concentrated.

Only one more round of tents, and she would be finished. He silently willed her to hurry and be done with it. Before the last tent, the one closest to his own, she stopped. Her brows creased as she listened.

Tombi couldn't move, couldn't breathe. *No.* Not this tent. *Move on*, he wanted to scream.

But she didn't. She faced him and extended her right arm at the tent, pointing her finger. Quickly, he walked to her side and guided Annie away by an elbow.

"There's your man," she said.

"Not possible. You're mistaken."

Her eyes widened. "What's wrong with you? You've begged me for two days, and now you act like *this*? Sounds like you're making excuses for somebody." Her voice rose. "Who are you protecting?"

"No one," he denied, his own voice rising in anger. "Forget about it."

Annie put her hands on her hip. "Bo spoke to me. He said to warn you about a betrayer. Well, I've done my duty. If you don't want to listen to me, that's your problem."

Bo. Even now, hearing the name of his best friend pinched his heart.

Annie turned her back on him and stalked away from the center of the campsite. Already, hunters were stepping out of their tents to see the commotion. He hated public displays. He was a tracker, damn it. Controlled, in charge and rational.

Tombi caught up to her. "Where are you going?" he whispered harshly, not wanting everyone to hear their conversation.

"Home."

He grabbed her hand. "Wait. I want—"

She jerked out of his grasp and kept walking. "I don't care what you want anymore."

Annie couldn't leave. Not like this. He could still use her help. And she was his last living link to Bo. "I'm your only hope of learning to control your gift," he reminded her.

She stopped, and Tombi scrambled in front of her.

"When do the lessons start?" she asked through tight lips.

"Tomorrow morning."

"What kind of lessons are you giving her?" Hanan asked, arms crossed. He stood in front of his tent.

The tent that Annie had fingered.

Annie looked from Tombi to Hanan, eyebrows raised.

"He's my right-hand man, my closest friend since Bo died," Tombi explained in a low voice. "I trust him."

"Believe what you want." Her posture was stiff and her words clipped.

He'd hurt her feelings. Tombi tried to consider their argument from her perspective. She found his rejection of her findings as a rejection of *her*. Which wasn't the same thing at all.

Hanan ambled over and nodded pleasantly at Annie before speaking to Tombi. "Is it something I can help you with? I know you're pressed for time finishing the Anderson project."

"Maybe. I'll let you know." It was true he was behind on his carpentry jobs, but Tombi doubted Annie would want Hanan as a teacher. Not now.

"Sure, if you can help teach me to guard my energy like the rest of the hunters." Annie smiled sweetly and held out her hand.

All the frosty stiffness had melted. What was her game?

Hanan accepted the outstretched hand, covering Annie's small hand with both of his own.

Tombi frowned at the sight. The touch was held a moment longer than necessary. Hanan broke contact first.

"Chulah and I need to talk with you when you get a minute."

"Be with y'all shortly."

Hanan sauntered off, joining the other men in preparing a meal.

"You would really take lessons from Hanan?" Tombi asked.

"Someone needs to keep an eye on him." The lemontart tone returned. "What time should I come back tomorrow for a lesson?"

"Tomorrow?" he sputtered. "I thought you would stay the night."

"And go on another hunt? No, thank you."

Incredulity and frustration battled in his gut. He was used to directing everyone's moves. But Annie? She had her own life, separate from his people, and she had her own secret agendas.

Annie bit her lip to keep from smiling at Tombi's discomfort. He liked to wield power and expected others to fall in line with his wishes. But she was afraid if she allowed him to exert that same power over her, he'd stretch out the lessons and string her along until he got what he needed.

He took a deep breath. "Please, stay."

"Why do you want me to?" she asked, confused at his insistence. "I mean, it's not like you listen when I tell you what I hear."

"I do listen," he argued. "It's just, in this case, you're wrong. You heard thoughts about a dream he was having. Hanan isn't conspiring with Nalusa."

Self-doubt, her constant companion, crept in. It was possible he was right. Although, usually when she picked up dream music, it had an otherworldly, faint kind of vibe.

Not the distinct, ominous tone that had emanated from Hanan's tent. The only way to know for sure if Hanan was a traitor was to spend more time with him, to catch him unawares.

No one could keep their energy contained all day, every day. Even Tombi couldn't. At unguarded moments, or at times of high emotion like when he kissed her, she heard the pounding of his heart like a snare drum vibrating in her gut. Still, other times, when he was wrapped up in his thoughts, she'd hear the notes of the Native American flute he was so adept at playing.

"Look, Tombi, I didn't get much rest last night. Let me sleep in my own bed tonight, and I'll stay for the hunt tomorrow night."

He shook his head. "That's no good. The week of the full moon ends tonight."

"Meaning what?"

"We all return to our real lives. The hunt won't resume again until the next full moon."

"You don't need me for hunting. You've done it for years on your own." She studied him closely. "I think what you really want is to see if I can speak with Bo again."

Tombi looked over her head, across the field to the woods. His face was hard and set. "He's out there, trapped. I'll do anything to release his spirit. I owe him at least that much."

Annie felt his pain like a lump in her own chest. "And he would do the same for you if the situation were reversed," she said gently.

"Tombi." Hanan waved him over to his group of four hunters.

"I have to go." He faced her at last. "I can't make you stay. As you've said, this isn't your fight."

How could she rest tonight leaving Tombi with such

sadness? And Grandma Tia had fought hard to communicate with her at the hospital—to tell her that Tombi needed her. "Since you put it that way…I'll hang around."

His shoulders relaxed, as if a weight had rolled off. "Thank you. I guarantee to not leave your side this time."

"Go ahead and see your friends," she said.

"My tent is yours. Go take a nap until night falls."

"More orders?"

A smile broke across the grave landscape of his face. "Just a suggestion. Up to you."

Annie watched as he left her side, her heart lightened that she'd made the right decision in staying. And he was right. A nap would help keep her strengthened for the night ahead. She turned to walk to his tent and then froze.

Tallulah slipped out of Hanan's tent flap, as silent and fluid as a cat with her long, thin body. She stood and ran a hand through her tangled, mussed hair.

Her face was relaxed and peaceful in a way Annie had never seen. It transformed her stark, aggressive features into something lovely. Tallulah's gaze swept the area, then zeroed in on Annie. Her dark eyes tightened to suspicious slits.

She wasn't up for this. Not after seeing her grandma in a coma, not after the fight with Tombi. And not in a sleep-deprived fog. Annie went to Tombi's tent.

"Hey. Where are you going?"

Annie ignored Tallulah's strident demand. Everyone stopped what they were doing and stared; their eyes burned into her skin. She walked quickly, but lifted her chin and didn't glance right or left. Straight ahead lay safety. A few more feet and she could enter Tombi's tent and zip out the rest of the world a few hours.

Hot breath brushed the fine hairs at the nape of her neck. "Nobody wants you here. You don't belong."

Annie's skin prickled at the hostility, and her lips trembled. Stupid to let Tallulah's anger cut her to the quick. She pressed her mouth into a thin line. She wouldn't cry in front of everyone watching. Three more steps and she would be rid of the woman. Quickly, she reached the tent flap and knelt to enter.

Tallulah dropped to her knees alongside her. "What does my brother see in you?" she continued in that same dark whisper. "You're a coward. A lying coward."

Annie's hands fumbled at the zipper, and she tugged at it, eyes burning with tears.

I will not cry in front of them. Yes, it was true. She'd rather curl up in a little ball all alone than face Tombi's pit viper of a twin. Metal grated on metal, and nirvana opened. Annie ducked inside and battened down the hatch, allowing the salty tears to spill from her eyes.

Low-pitched laughter rang out inches away from the thin canvas lining. "Coward," Tallulah seethed again.

"Tallulah!" Tombi's commanding voice cut through the air.

How much had he heard? Despite the smothering heat, Annie curled up in the corner and pulled a sheet over herself, a turtle retreating into its shell. Shame smothered her as thick as the Alabama humidity. *You don't belong.* The words ricocheted in her brain, fast and deadly. She never belonged, and she never would. Even with a band of supernatural shadow hunters, she was branded as a misfit.

Hysterical laughter bubbled up, and she covered her mouth with the sheet to keep anyone from overhearing.

The sound of a zipper unfastening had her hastily rolling onto her side, back to the entrance. She didn't want Tombi to see her like this. Couldn't bear to see either pity or disgust on his stoic face.

"Annie?" he called out softly. "You okay?"

She feigned sleep, keeping her breathing deep and rhythmic. The air crackled with his scent, with his strong, commanding aura. Her heart pounded in time to the drumming that was his unique music.

A heavy warmth brushed against the back of her scalp as Tombi's fingers stroked her hair. The tenderness almost undid her. She'd experienced passion before, but gentle gestures like this were foreign territory. Annie relaxed and stilled under his touch.

Tombi left in his quick, silent way, and she rolled onto her back. The smell of bacon and biscuits permeated the air. People shuffled around the campfire, speaking in low murmurs.

She longed to be a part of community like this. Mom and her string of stepfathers and stepsiblings merely tolerated her, and no one wanted to be friends with Crazy Annie.

Enough of the self-pity. Tallulah had hit a soft spot, and she'd overreacted. With any luck, no one had seen her tears. Her cheeks burned that everyone had witnessed her hasty scamper to Tombi's tent. Bet none of them had ever disgraced themselves by running away. The warrior spirit in them probably never backed away from a confrontation. Annie sighed and closed her eyes, imagining herself as one of them, eating and laughing together instead of lying in the hot, stifling tent alone.

She indulged in a familiar fantasy. She'd find a way to get rid of her supernatural hearing and go about her life doing all the ordinary things others took for granted. A job, a family, or even simple things like shopping at the mall or going to a concert. Maybe she'd even go back to school and get a college degree.

A smile tugged her lips, and she curled up, sleepy at last.

* * *

"Annie? Wake up. Time to eat."

She bolted to a seated position and inhaled sharply at the intimacy of Tombi's nearness. Memories of their previous kiss in the tent made her skin heat and her body yearn for more of the same.

Tombi retreated, even as his breath grew raspy and his eyes darkened. "A quick bite and we need to get a move on."

He was in full warrior mode, ready to hunt once more. Damn her traitorous body. She needed to remind herself that his focus was on defeating the shadows, and she was merely a tool in helping him win the battle.

Annie clambered out of the tent and followed him to the center of the campsite. The fire was long gone, but white-hot firewood gave off heat. Tombi piled an aluminum pie plate with several bacon slices and a couple of biscuits and handed it to her.

The smell set her mouth salivating, and she dug in. She hadn't eaten since the crackers at the hospital. Tombi silently poured her a glass of sweet tea, and she washed down the food with the sugared brew. Perfect. Food always tasted better when eaten outdoors. Either that, or she was really hungry.

Tombi sat across from her and leaned forward; his skin shone like bronze in the night. "Let's do something different tonight. Something a little safer."

Safer sounded great. "What?" she asked, setting aside her plate.

"We're going back to the spot where I first met you. Where Bo appeared and spoke."

She sighed.

"Thought you would like that."

"I feel like I'm damned no matter what happens tonight.

Either you'll be disappointed he doesn't appear, or he'll talk and you might not like what he has to say." She couldn't help the bitterness that crept in her voice. "Like today."

"I don't discount what you heard. You just caught me by surprise. I didn't consider the possibility of you picking up on dreams." He stood, signaling the discussion was over.

She stood as well, determined to hold her ground. "I know Hanan's your friend. But you never know what's hidden in others' hearts." *Like your sister.* But she would keep her lips locked on that possible deception. If Tombi couldn't entertain the idea of a friend as betrayer, how would he react over a sister? A twin at that. Two hearts that once beat within the same mother.

From this point on, she would filter whatever messages the music or spirits revealed. Tombi and his people might have supernatural gifts, but they were no more accepting than anyone else in the non-gifted world.

Tombi held out his hand. "Whatever happens tonight, I won't be disappointed in *you*. Always tell me the truth, and we're good."

His words soothed Annie's hurt pride, and she placed her hand in his. The electrical charge that flowed between them gave her courage to face the long, uncertain hours ahead. Under coral beams shining from the Thunder Moon, she followed Tombi across the field and into the swampy woods. The constant chirp of cicadas and the eternal echo of the Gulf waters was a comfortable white noise in the background of her mind.

The stagnant smell of the bayou was more tolerable in the cooler nighttime temperature, and the occasional whiff of pine and brine was refreshing. Excitement unexpectedly rose within her. Whenever she was with Tombi, something exhilarating was bound to happen. Just being near him, touching him, made her feel alive. So different from the nights she had spent quietly at her grandma's cottage, grinding herbs and withdrawing from any human contact.

All this prowling about the bayou must have opened her senses in new ways, because Annie was able to recognize a few landmarks in the shadows. A familiar bend in the path here, a certain clump of saw palmetto there, a particular pattern of trees and moss…and they had returned to the place where Bo had spoken.

"This is it," she said softly.

Tombi led her to the fallen tree where she'd once heard him playing the flute. They settled down together, thigh touching thigh. Her skin tingled, and she was unsure if it was from the proximity of Tombi or the expectation of Bo reappearing inside a wisp.

Tombi's breath whispered against her ear. "Can't you conjure him? Use some of your hoodoo stuff?"

She started to roll her eyes, then paused. Not a bad idea. She didn't practice hoodoo spells much. Grandma Tia was so gifted and took care of everything, so she seldom needed to do a root work on her own. She'd have to rifle through her grandma's old grimoires and see what she could dig up.

"I'll do some research tomorrow. There must be—"

He placed a finger on her lip, and she realized her voice had grown too loud in the dark stillness of night. She stopped talking, and yet Tombi didn't move his finger. The pressure lightened, and his hand palmed her chin. Annie leaned into the caress and kissed his fingers, at last drawing one of them into her mouth and sucking the end of it.

In a swift move, Tombi had whisked her onto his lap. She straddled him and eagerly returned his deep kisses. Hot, wet, blistering kisses that she never wanted to end. The raw, honest need between them was unlike anything she'd ever experienced, not that she had that much experience. Just a couple of boyfriends who had found her convenient as an in-between kind of girlfriend until something better than Crazy Annie came along. She'd learned not to expect anything more. How could she, when she could barely tolerate their unceasing jumble of music every day and night? But Tombi kept his energy in check, and when it did pierce his aura, it was a drumbeat that matched her own heart.

He could be trouble for her heart. Big trouble.

But for now, she didn't care. The night was magical, and his kisses shattered her normal reserve. The barriers guarding her mind and spirit slipped away, and she immersed herself in the feel of his naked skin against her own, the silk of his hair, the calluses of his hands as he stroked her face, her neck, her arms, her back.

Ethereal music penetrated Annie's passion-fogged brain. She pulled back from Tombi and strained to hear better. Oh yes, she'd heard this tune before. Somewhere in the dark shadows, Bo had returned.

"What is it?" Tombi asked, his breath sharp with anticipation. "Is it Bo? Tell him I need to talk to him."

Don't tell Tombi I am near, Bo warned. *If I draw his attention, other wisps or Nalusa himself will pick up on it.*

Annie nodded. What did he want?

Find the music contained in the wind. Find it before Nalusa does, or all is lost.

She frowned. What was he talking about?

Tombi set her aside on the fallen tree and stood, peering into the shadows. "Bo? I'm still your friend. Talk to me." He turned to Annie. "What did he say?"

"To find the music contained in the wind. Or all is lost. Do you have any idea what he meant?"

He shook his head and gazed at the shadows. But the music had faded. Bo had vanished.

Chapter 8

Pink-and-purple light washed the sky. Annie yawned and stretched her arms. Her legs were stiff from sitting so long on the fallen tree, and her ankles were numb. Tombi was only a few yards away, pacing soundlessly, one hand to his chin as if deep in thought.

She walked to him, the crunch of twigs detonating like mini-explosions.

"We're done for the night, aren't we?" She pointed at the rising sunbeams. "And today you promised to start teaching me."

"I haven't forgotten."

Curiosity tripped along her nerves. "What's your secret? Why can't I hear your aura?"

"The spirit world assists us in blocking the energy we project. Let's go back to camp and have some coffee. I'll explain more."

She buried the scowl that wanted to break. More hostility from Tallulah and company? No, thanks. Besides, she was in dire need of using modern plumbing. "We're close to my cottage. We can have coffee there."

He nodded, and they made quick time, arriving at the cottage just as the sun rose over the horizon. To hell with dignity. Annie practically sprinted up the driveway and rushed to open the door. When she exited the bathroom, she found Tombi leaning in the doorway, lips twitching in amusement. Her bladder was too relieved to take offense.

"Go ahead and have a seat while I make coffee."

He dropped into a chair and crossed his legs at the ankle. Annie cast surreptitious glances his way as she went about brewing coffee. She cut two slices of coconut pound cake and set them on their best china.

"Dig in," she said, sitting across from him at the kitchen table.

He took a bite, and she waited expectantly.

Tombi didn't disappoint. "Wow."

"Grandma Tia grates real coconut and uses, like, a pound of butter in that cake. It's always a big hit." Annie sipped and set her cup down. "Now explain how the spirits help you."

Tombi took a long swallow. "Those of us who show paranormal ability during our teen years are given lessons by tribal elders on how to connect with spirits and seek their guidance. It takes concentration and a certain amount of dedication. For some, it's easier than for others."

"Bet you took right to it."

"Tallulah and I both did. Our father was very gifted himself—it seems to be passed down."

He made short work of the cake. Annie felt almost lightheaded with hope and excitement. The life she'd always wanted was getting a step closer. She interlaced her hands and squeezed her fingers. "Keep going. I want details. Who are these spirits?"

"It's different for everyone. The spirits can be in animal form, or it can be your ancestors."

She nodded. "In hoodoo, we petition our ancestors for help."

"Do you have a particular ancestor who serves as a guardian spirit?"

"No." Some of her hope wilted. "I've tried to connect with my ancestors, but I don't have the skill of my grandma. I've asked them to remove my gift, but they don't respond."

"Could be you're asking the wrong questions."

"Now you're sounding like Grandma Tia. Next, you'll tell me to thank my ancestors for this gift that's brought me so much pain."

"Not necessary. But you can ask them why you've been granted your ability and how to manage it."

The coffee soured in her stomach. "Is that the best I can do? Learn to control it? I want to be rid of it completely."

"I don't know if that's possible. Could be that you've been granted this hearing for a special purpose, and once your mission is done, the gift will disappear."

"You mean, help you fight Nalusa."

"You said yourself that Tia felt we were somehow linked together. Maybe she never helped you not because she didn't want to or didn't have the necessary skill, but because she realized it would help you or others one day."

She pondered his words. "Maybe. But you aren't getting off the hook that easy. I want my lesson, not a philosophical discussion."

His jaw tightened. "We're getting there. First, you need to know how energy control works."

"Okay," she conceded. "You mentioned animal spirits. Do I have one?"

"Everybody does. We all have animal guides that come and go in our lives—depending on what we need. But a totem is an animal spirit that stays with you your entire life."

The idea rekindled hope. "Great. What's mine?"

"You'll have to figure that out on your own." He held up a hand to forestall her next question. "You invite them to introduce themselves, much like you pray to your ancestors for their assistance. Ask them to appear in your dreams. Pay attention to animals that you're drawn to or that show up over and over in your life."

"I like cats," she said hesitantly. "Maybe a cat is my totem?"

Tombi shrugged.

Some help he turned out to be. Figured he'd give her homework to do on her own. "Okay, once I discover my totem or find an ancestor willing to work with me, what comes next?"

"The way it works for me is that I connect with my great-grandfather. I quiet my mind and ask for his help. He comes to me, and I'm able to see the world through his other-realm eyes."

"A veil between the realms. Hoodoo has similar beliefs." Grandma Tia often spoke of it. "So that's how you and the others see at night. It explains a supernatural ability you have, but it doesn't explain how you block others from sensing you."

"While we're in a semi-present state between shadows and earth, our guides cloak our energy—others' perceptions of us are dimmed. It allows for total focus on the hunt."

"So I need a guide that will cloak my supernatural hearing, not so that I can be invisible to others, but to prevent my picking up their auras." She smiled. "I'm ready to meet mine." Problem solved.

Tombi snorted. "Not many are able to connect on their first attempt."

"Then I'll keep trying until I meet him or her…or it, if my guide turns out to be an animal instead of an ancestor. Can we do it now?"

"Try it tonight at dusk. It is said that's the most opportune time, when the sun descends from the sky and gives way to the mysterious moon. When all around supernatural forces awaken and lengthen the shadows of men."

Which meant a wait time of several hours. "Will you be with me when I try?"

He shook his head. "It's something you need to do alone, in your own way. I'm sure you and your grandmother already have rituals for this."

"Hmm." Annie tapped a finger to her lips. She'd pore over her grandma's grimoire today and find a root working.

"For novices, most guides will appear in dreams. As you lie in bed tonight, concentrate on your intent to meet your guide in dreamland." He cocked his head to one side. "I'll sort of be with you, after all."

"Come again?"

"I want you to spend the night with me."

Annie's face flamed with heat.

"Not in the same bed," he hastened to explain. A slow, sexy smile carved his face. "Unless you want to."

Oh, she wanted. She spoke quickly, hoping he wouldn't sense her flustered nerves. "I'm sleeping here tonight, in my own bed, with only fifteen steps to a working toilet—thank you very much."

"We wouldn't be sharing a tent in the woods. The hunt

is over for this month, remember? You could stay with me at my cabin."

"I think I'll do better here at my own home, working at my own altar." Here, she felt closer to her grandma's presence, could perhaps draw on Tia's energy for help. "Besides, I've got a ton of stuff I need to get caught up on—groceries, bills, the usual."

"And I'm sure you want to visit your grandmother again. How is she doing?"

"Still in a coma."

He swore under his breath. "I'm responsible."

She should argue he wasn't, because it was obvious he felt guilty. But Annie still harbored resentment. He had brought Nalusa to them; they would never have drawn that spirit's attention otherwise.

"Time apart will do us good," she said, picking up their empty plates and putting them in the sink. She needed time to do some research. Visit Tia again and see if her grandma had any more messages or could help her in her quest. "Hanan said you were behind at work, anyway."

He opened his mouth, and she kept talking, to forestall more objections. "What kind of work do you do?"

"I'm a carpenter," he answered tersely. "There's no reason we can't both do our own thing during the day and then be together tonight."

Annie dropped the forks she was rinsing, and they clanged in the sink.

A chair scraped, and Tombi stood behind her, placing his hands on her shoulders. "I don't expect anything from you. We won't share the same bed."

"Why are you so insistent I spend the night at your cabin?"

He hesitated, as if not wanting to tell her his reason. "Well?"

"It's no longer safe for you to stay alone," he admitted. "Nalusa knows where you live."

Astonished, she turned around to face him, not realizing how close he stood. The nearness of their lips made her throat dry. Annie jerked back toward the sink. "I won't open the door for anyone. I'll be fine."

"I won't take no for an answer."

"I don't care what you do, but I want to stay here tonight, and that's the end of that."

Tense silence settled around them in the tiny kitchen.

"I'll leave you alone, then. For now," he said.

It sounded like a promise to return. She kept her eyes glued to the window and didn't see him leave, only heard the creak of the door as he exited. The door reopened.

"Lock up behind me," he ordered.

Before she could reply, the door shut again, and she obediently locked up. She watched as he strode down the driveway. His golden skin gleamed, kissed by the sun, and his black hair hung past his shoulders, as dark as if it carried the energy of the night.

Day and night. Sun and moon. Hunter and hunted. Tombi was a living veil between this world and the spirit world that he entered into at will.

A dangerous protector. He'd brought her and Grandma Tia danger, but he'd also offered his protection. She sensed he was an honorable man who took his word seriously.

Could he really be the key to her escape from this personal auditory hell, or did he plan on using her? He might be honorable, but he'd set his own code as to what was right and where his duties lay.

Lesson One hadn't gone the way she'd anticipated, but at least it was a start. Annie set about rummaging through Tia's books and papers, gathering them into a pile on the kitchen table. The stack was over a foot high. With a sigh, she opened a grimoire and began leafing through the yellowed paper filled with her grandma's bold handwriting, with its fat loops and exaggerated serifs. An acrid, licorice smell of myrrh and camphor wafted through the old tome. Bits of dried leaves and herbs crumbled into the binding and spilled on to the open pages.

Annie's heart spasmed painfully beneath her ribs. She missed Tia with an ache that tightened her throat. Was her grandma faring any better today? She had to know.

For such a little bit of a woman, Annie sure had a huge stubborn streak. How could she possibly think she could defend herself against Nalusa and the shadow world? And what if she was part of that world, and that was why she was unafraid? He had to make her willing to stay with him in the evenings.

Tombi entered the restored antebellum home. It served as a visitor's center for those interested in touring the bayou for either bird hunting or walking the scenic hiking trail that featured a pier and pavilion where alligators were daily fed. Tallulah was cleaning a glass counter in the museum area that housed a collection of arrowheads, pottery and other Choctaw artifacts from bygone days. Her long hair was severely pulled back and braided, and she wore a red smock over jeans.

A familiar jolt of guilt and sadness pinched his heart. Tallulah should be managing the center instead of working as a combination cashier and cleaner. She'd been studying anthropology in college when Katrina crashed into their worlds.

She leaned against the counter and rubbed a hand along the small of her back. It had to be tough on her when she hunted at night and then had to come work the day job. A job that barely enabled her to eke out a threadbare existence. If he hadn't built her a small cabin on their family's land, she wouldn't be able to eke out any existence at all.

"Backache?" he asked.

She stiffened and returned to wiping the counters. "It doesn't matter." Tallulah slanted him a suspicious glance. "Don't tell me you're here to scold me about that girl again."

Scold? "I'm your brother, not your father."

"Good. I'm glad you remember. Because sometimes I think you forget." She set the bottle of window cleaner so hard on the glass, he expected cracks to fissure the surface.

Tombi inwardly sighed at the chip-on-her-shoulder attitude. Bo's death had made her bitter, as if it were the last straw in a string of tragedies. Something inside her had broken. As twins, they'd had a close camaraderie growing up, but in the past year they had been more like strangers. Worse than strangers, as they each knew just how to push each other's hot buttons.

A phone rang, and Tallulah stalked across the room to answer it.

He leaned his elbows on the counter and idly surveyed the ancestral artifacts while he cooled his infamous temper. *You're as fiery as the sun you're named after,* Mom used to say. Tombi liked to think he'd learned to control it, even if the flames of his anger still blistered his soul and tongue. But Tallulah tried his patience.

A wooden flute caught his eye. It was about twelve inches long and made of river cane. A snake-head design was burned into the tip with its sinewy body wrapped around the barrel. That was a new addition to this collection. It was so well preserved, somebody must have donated it. He shook his head. Too bad it wasn't for sale. He would love to add this to his own private collection. Instruments that harnessed the magical power of the wind held his respect and awe.

His twin returned. "What brings you here?" she asked bluntly.

"I did come to talk about Annie," he admitted. "Can't you cut her a little break? She's been drawn into this whole mess, just as we were years ago."

"Drawn in? What if she was recruited in by Nalusa? We've no reason to trust her."

"Trust or not, we need her. Her aura-hearing can be used to track wisps and to prevent Nalusa attacking us unawares."

"We've done fine without her up till now."

"Not true and you know it. Nalusa's gaining ground, has been for a couple of years. The number of wisps multiplies faster than we can kill them. If this keeps up, he'll soon wander past the bayou boundaries and wreak havoc everywhere."

Tallulah pinched her lips. "So you say."

"You know I speak the truth. Once he slips past us, there will be no hope of containing the evil. He'll blaze a trail of death and misery on a national scale."

"So be it. We've done all we can." Her hands gripped the wash rag like a lifeline.

"That's my point. Now it's time to get outside help."

"What do you want me to do? Bake her a cheesecake and welcome her into the fold? Not happening."

He ran a hand through his hair and sighed. "All I ask is that you be civil. Don't attack her."

"You can't keep me from telling the truth."

"You don't know the truth," he exploded. "Just stay away from her, that's all I ask." He turned and started for the door. The long walk home would do much to cool his anger.

Tallulah ran in front of him, blocking his exit. "Don't be an idiot. Think with your brain and not your dick. This girl could be trouble."

"Her name's Annie, and she could be our salvation. You're the one not thinking straight," he snapped. Tombi took a deep breath. "I don't know who you are these days, Talli girl. And neither would Bo if he were still alive."

Raw pain bruised her eyes, and she sucked in a breath.

He laid a hand on her shoulder. "Sorry. But you needed to hear that. Consider what I said. If you can't treat Annie with any decency, it might be best if you stopped hunting altogether."

"You can't be serious," she said in a strangled voice. "You've known this girl only a few days. Are you completely under her spell?"

He withdrew his hand. "Leave Annie alone, or I'll exile you from the hunters."

Grandma Tia had been unchanged from yesterday's visit, as if any moment her eyes would flutter open. Annie could picture that moment. Her grandma would blink in confusion at the sterile, strange surroundings and then jolt out of bed, demanding to go home.

She had to believe that would happen. Had to believe that, despite her bad heart, her grandma had many months left. Peaceful months that would allow her to approach the end of life among her altars and herb garden and where she could sleep in her own bed at night. Months of entertaining friends and helping customers with her root workings.

Despite all reason, Annie had hoped her mother would come down for a visit after informing her of the stroke, even though she swore she'd never set foot in Bayou La Siryna again. But even with Tia hospitalized, Annie's mom was still being stubborn and heartless about not coming down. Grandma Tia never talked about it, but Annie knew the rift between them hurt her deeply.

She lit candles everywhere, and the glow was comforting. Although only late afternoon, the sky was a pewter gray and the sun hidden behind dark clouds. She hadn't paid attention to the news, but no doubt a hurricane brewed somewhere over the Atlantic Ocean. That or tropical storms always resulted in the Gulf area darkening and churning, making normally stagnant air whip with a briny bite, and the birds, even noisy seagulls, retreated in silence and out of sight.

The candles weren't just for atmosphere. If the upcoming storm were severe enough, the power would likely cut off.

Annie sat at the kitchen table and gripped her hands together. Excitement and fear chased in circles in her gut, percolating like a storm of their own.

Magical Musings, page forty-three.

The title and page number had flashed in her mind when she visited Grandma Tia earlier today. Annie sorted through the papers. She even knew what the book would look like: a brownish-yellow bundle of papers tied up with raffia, a sprig of marjoram in the bow.

At last she began going through the stack of books until she found *Magical Musings*. The aged, frail papers trembled in her fingers like bedsheets flapping on a clothesline. Page forty-one…forty-two…page forty-three. There. *Communing with the Dead or with Animal Spirits*.

Eagerly, she ran a finger down the ingredient list and began gathering the needed items, grateful for Tia's wellstocked pantry and hoodoo supplies. Lightning cracked, and the air sizzled with the smell of ozone. One Mississippi. Two Mississippi. Three Missis—

Thunder crashed. The lightning had struck only three miles away.

A frisson of unease chased down the nape of her neck to the base of her spine. Which was ridiculous. Grandma Tia wouldn't have sent such a specific message if she hadn't meant for her granddaughter to try the spell. Still, Annie wavered and shifted on her seat. *Maybe the timing is wrong?*

No. She wasn't going to let a thunderstorm give her the heebie-jeebies. They were a dime a dozen during the Alabama summers. She'd been seeking an answer for years to stop the music, and now she couldn't stand to wait another evening. With great care, Annie dressed the candles, lit the incense and began her petition. And waited.

And waited.

A great swell of silence numbed her brain. A silence so utter and profound it might as well have been a banshee screaming in her ears. A single word over and over: *no.* Disappointment sliced through the numbness. Surely, after all the signs, there had to be something. *Try harder.* Annie squeezed her eyes shut and strained to hear something—anything.

A great flapping beat the air, a stir of energy swooshed by like a freight train. She gasped and opened her eyes.

Whatever connection she'd made was instantly severed. Outside, the rustle of leaves in the wind and a scrape of limbs clawing the windows. A distant rumble of thunder. Whatever had made itself known had vanished.

Not fair. She stood and paced the room, hands fisted by her side in frustration. She'd try again before bedtime. And she'd keep trying the spell until spirits in the Great Beyond responded—if only to get rid of her and her constant petitions.

The lights died.

Gee, thanks, Alabama Power. This night just keeps getting better. Best thing to do with the little light that still oozed through the windows was to fix something to eat and get a bath.

Twin blazes of light pierced the den. Tombi? She hurried to the front door and opened it. Rain soaked his long black hair, and his jeans and T-shirt were soaked.

"Where's your umbrella?" she called out as he rushed up the porch steps.

He lifted his head and stared her dead in the face.

That wasn't Tombi.

Numbness froze her lips and limbs. "Hanan?" she asked dazedly, leaning against the door frame for support. "What are you doing here?"

He smiled, but the severe angles of his face and the sharp beak of a nose failed to lighten the overall impression of harsh cunning. "I came to clear the air between us. Tombi told me what you heard. What you *imagined* you heard."

Annie calculated the viability of how swiftly she could shut the door and lock him out versus Hanan's speed and agility to block the move.

She wasn't optimistic. *Play along. Play it off. Play it cool.*

She returned his smile, smoothing her features to betray no concern. "We're good. Tombi explained you must have been dreaming. A nightmare, maybe."

Or maybe the sneaky Tallulah was the betrayer. She could only imagine how Tombi would take that news, seeing as how he got all defensive about a friend.

She tried to be fair. Tombi's explanation was rational.

A couple of beats of awkward silence passed. She raised a hand and gestured at the open doorway. "Come in, if you'd like."

He swooped in at once, and she tried not to wince as he brushed by her side and into the cottage. Annie listened intently, but not a single note escaped his tightly controlled body and mind.

She looked longingly at the yard. Her car was in the driveway, mocking. It might as well have been a mile away. She had a wild idea of grabbing her car keys and making a run for it. Just leave Hanan alone in the cottage.

And look like a complete fool for running off. Tallulah would have a field day. Reluctantly, Annie shut the door and faced Hanan. "Would you like something to drink?"

"No. I won't be long." He went to the sofa and sat, one leg bent, resting an ankle on the opposite knee. "That's some special ability you have," he said, getting straight to the point. "As a hunter, my senses are enhanced. I can see, hear and smell better than other humans. But I've never heard of anyone able to judge a person by hearing their energy."

Was there skepticism in his tone? Hard to tell with his poker face and silent aura. Annie never realized before how much she used her extraordinary hearing to glide through interacting with people—anticipating another's thoughts and motives before engaging in conversation. And always working on an exit strategy if the music became too disturbing or uncomfortable. She nodded slowly, unsure how to respond.

His gaze moved deliberately around the room, taking in the candles and altars and saint statues. The air smelled of patchouli and frankincense. "Feels like I'm in church. I expected Hoodoo Henrietta's place to have the opposite atmosphere."

Annie found her voice. He could put her down but not her grandma. "What did you expect? Broomsticks and skeleton skulls everywhere? A simmering cauldron? A black cat?"

He shrugged, seemingly unfazed at her anger. "Anybody would. Easy to judge someone on little to no evidence. Right?"

A clever trap. She'd fallen right into it. Heat scalded the back of her neck. "Point taken," she conceded. She'd been willing to condemn him on what may have only been a dream.

A loud, staccato hammering erupted at the door. Annie jumped.

Hanan smiled slyly. "I know who that is."

Chapter 9

Tombi didn't wait for permission to enter. He burst into the room. The only light came from candles lit everywhere. A romantic tableau if he'd ever seen one. His veins throbbed with anger. Some friend Hanan proved to be. Bo would never have gone behind his back and visited his girlfriend.

Girlfriend.

The word was like throwing ice on fire. His hot anger melted. Annie was *not* his girlfriend. Not his lover, either.

And he still didn't like her being alone with Hanan. "What are you doing here?" he demanded.

Hanan slowly stood. "Just saying goodbye." He offered his hand to Annie. "Are we cool?"

"Sure." She stood as well and shook his hand.

Her eyes were downcast, and Tombi couldn't decipher her mood. Embarrassed? Distressed?

"Why is it so dark in here?" Tombi asked, ever suspicious.

"Power's out." Hanan nodded at him and swept past.

"Be back in a minute," Tombi said curtly to Annie.

He followed Hanan onto the porch. "What did you say to upset her? Did you confront her about what she heard?"

"*Confront* isn't the word I'd use," Hanan drawled. "I pointed out that I shouldn't be condemned on so little."

"Nobody condemned you. If I believed you were a traitor I wouldn't have told you she pointed a finger your way. You had no right to come over here and upset Annie." The anger boiled up again. He shouldn't have left her alone—not even during the day. His rush to finish the Anderson carpentry job on deadline had tainted his judgment.

"You would have done the same had the positions been reversed. Both of us hate to have our integrity questioned."

True. He couldn't argue against that.

Hanan pushed off from the porch and started down the steps. "See you later," he called over his shoulder, with no rankle in his voice.

Tombi watched his friend drive off in the rain. He'd just acted like a complete ass, bursting into Annie's cottage and demanding explanations. As if she owed him one. He stuffed his hands into his pockets and returned inside. An unfamiliar feeling of sheepishness weighted his shoulders.

Annie stood at the rear window, back to him.

"Sorry about that," he mumbled.

"Don't be." She turned and walked to him with a shy smile. "I'm glad you came when you did. He chastised me." She hurried on at the sight of his frown. "But in a gentle way."

"He did the same with me outside," Tombi admitted.

"You're all wet." She ran her fingers down his hair, and his breath caught. "I'll go get you a towel."

Her ass swayed in her tight cutoff jeans, and he'd never seen anything hotter. Just being in the same room with the woman had him knotted up in sexual tension. Tombi peeled off his wet T-shirt and ran a hand over his wet locks.

"Here ya—" Her voice faltered. She stood in the darkened doorway, holding a towel and staring at his chest, as if mesmerized.

Tombi shifted uncomfortably in his suddenly tight jeans. He wanted to peel out of them, undress her and make passionate love. But he didn't want to scare her. Wasn't sure if she had any experience in lovemaking.

"Bring the towel to me," he said huskily.

She obeyed, as if in a trance. She walked so slowly to him that he was conscious of the rain beating against the windows and the smell of something earthy in the air. A cozy intimacy of the two of them against the rain-sloshed world outside.

Annie lifted the towel and began rubbing his skin. He wished it were her hands instead of fabric. Satisfied with her work there, she ran the towel through his hair.

Tombi abruptly pulled her to him and kissed her thoroughly, smothering her gasp of surprise. Her arms went around his bare back, and her hands traveled the length of his spine. He pressed his manhood against her core, and she arched into him, silently asking for more.

"Annie?" he asked hoarsely.

She gazed up at him with hooded eyes. And then blinked and took a step backward. Tombi swallowed down a groan of frustration.

"Not yet," she whispered. "I'm sorry. It's too soon for me."

He ran a finger down the side of her delicate, heart-shaped face. "Never apologize. A lady has every right to say no."

Annie nodded and cast her head down, her dark wavy hair obscuring her face. "Thank you," she mumbled.

He needed space. Space to cool his lust and dispel the awkwardness. He strode to a window. Rain washed against the panes in sheets, but at least the thunder and lightning had grown distant. With any luck, the storm would pass within the hour.

"Why did you come back?" Annie asked from behind.

"I felt uneasy leaving you alone. Especially now that the power's out." He faced her. "Come back to the cabin with me. I'm not asking you to sleep with me. I have an extra bedroom."

"Or you could stay here tonight. No sense in you driving home in this weather. I can't offer much in terms of dinner, but I can always scrape something together."

He'd rather be at his own place, in his own bed, but he'd take what he could. Staying in the cottage beat camping out in her backyard or sleeping in his truck to keep an eye on things. "Deal."

She smiled, the awkward shyness dispensed. "Have a seat and I'll be back with food."

Tombi sank into the sofa, listening to Annie bustling about the kitchen. The domesticity of it settled warmly in his gut. How long had it been since someone fixed him a meal? Too long. Strange, he'd never noticed before how solitary, how lonely and stark his existence was at the cabin. He devoted his life to hunting during the full moon and the rest of his days to running his carpentry business. Always focused, always doing everything with a purpose and sinking into bed at night, exhausted.

He propped his legs on the coffee table and crossed his arms behind him, head relaxing into his palms. Inside was soft candle illumination, and outside the rain and storm were contained. He closed his eyes. Relaxed. He was exactly where he needed to be, and all was well in this moment. Tension drained from his body and flowed down to the ground, where it was absorbed.

A soft touch jiggled his shoulder.

He bolted upright and took in the unfamiliar surroundings.

"It's okay. You've been asleep." Annie's face was calm and a soft smile lit her eyes. "You've been out a couple of hours at least. But I couldn't wait to eat any longer and didn't want to dine alone."

She sat across from him, and he set his feet down. A tray on the coffee table was filled with apples, grapes, cheese and bread. He was starving. Even though it was late in the day, the pewter clouds had been rinsed clean by rain, and it was lighter now than before he'd fallen asleep.

"Sorry I couldn't do better. Power's still out."

"This is perfect. I can't believe I slept so soundly." Highly unusual. If he'd eaten before falling asleep, it would have made him wonder what Annie had slipped into his food unawares. Instead, he'd completely let down his guard. Was he a fool as Tallulah accused? He watched as Annie poured iced tea from a pitcher and handed him a glass.

She pointed to the dishes and silverware. "Help yourself."

He dug in and bit into a sweet, crisp apple, quickly downing fruit with slices of tangy cheddar cheese. She nudged over a wicker basket full of biscuits. Even cold, they were delicious smothered in real butter.

"Thank you," he said at last, fully sated. He leaned back in the sofa and crossed his arms against his chest, studying Annie.

"For what? Dinner wasn't much of anything."

She might not think so, but Tombi hadn't been so relaxed in weeks. And to have someone else fix and serve a meal, no matter how simple, was a novelty. His loins stirred. It had been a long time since that, too. He wondered if it was the same for Annie. "Have you been seeing anyone in Bayou La Siryna?" he asked. Subtlety was not his strong suit.

"As in…a man? No." She shook her head, dark hair spilling over her shoulders. Her eyes shuttered. "Not interested," she added in a flat voice.

Somebody had been burned. Fairly recently, judging from Annie's expression. "So, how long ago did you break up?"

She opened her mouth, as if to deny it, but then shrugged. "Four months."

He raised his eyebrows in an unspoken question.

"His name was Evan." Annie tapped a knife against the edge of her plate. "He's from North Georgia, where my mom and stepdad live. We dated over a year. Until he decided I was too weird…and someone better came along."

"He's an idiot." The words slipped out, unbidden. But at Annie's sudden smile, he didn't care.

"What about you?" she said.

That was the trouble with asking direct questions. Now she felt free to interrogate him on his past love life. He'd set himself up for it. But fair was fair.

"It's been over a year since I've seen anyone seriously. Her name was Courtney."

Annie raised her brows in a parody of his earlier gesture.

"She broke it off, complaining that my priorities were screwed up and that I cared more about the hunt than I did her."

"So she knew about you. About your supernatural tracking."

"No. I saw no need to tell her. She just thought I was

into hunting with friends. But it didn't sit well with her. Courtney accused me of being secretive."

"You should have told her the truth. If you really loved her, that is."

"That's what she said." He'd thought about it and come close a few times, but something had always held him back.

"At least we're honest with each other," Annie blurted. "About what makes us different. Not that we're in a relationship or anything," she added quickly.

"No way." Relationship? It hadn't worked before, and it certainly wouldn't work now, not with Nalusa gaining power. He didn't have time for a relationship. Especially not with a woman like Annie. Sex? Sure. But her hesitation made him realize she wouldn't view it casually. He shifted uncomfortably, aware she looked offended.

"What I mean is, I don't have time for a real relationship."

"Just some sex on the side with a woman who's convenient? Hmm? Someone always underfoot anyway because you watch her closely to see if she's in league with your enemy?"

He wasn't fooled by her deceptively sweet voice. Annie was furious. "When you put it like that..."

"I put it truthfully. Praise the saints I turned you down earlier." She jerked to her feet and gathered up the uneaten food on to a tray.

"Annie, wait. I didn't mean that the way it sounded. I wouldn't sleep with a woman I didn't care for."

"I no longer give a damn." Her chin lifted, and she refused to meet his eye.

He stood beside her. "I can't think of having a serious relationship now. All my energy and focus need to be on Nalusa and doing the things I must to keep up the cabin and put food on the table."

"Your life sounds as miserable as mine." The anger melted, replaced with tears brimming her eyes.

He'd take her wrath any day over this. "I'm not miserable, and you shouldn't be, either."

"Really? Sounds to me like you have no life. All work, all grim responsibility, with no room for love and happiness."

Strange, he'd never given it much thought. Maybe at first, when he began hunting all those years ago. Somehow over the years, the hunting had taken over everything. But it wasn't as if he had a choice. To quit wasn't an option. "I do what I must."

"What are you—a machine or a man?"

Her words cut deep, and he struck back. "Are you saying I should be more like you and run away from everything? Close my eyes and stick my fingers in my ears?"

"I don't…" She clamped her lips into a thin line.

He'd gone too far. "I'm sorry."

She stepped backward and regarded him stonily, the food tray a fortress between them. "Go away and leave me alone."

Damn. He'd really made a mess of everything. "You're upset. Just let me sleep on the couch tonight to make sure you're okay. We'll talk in the morning when you've calmed down."

"Don't you dare tell me to calm down or how I'm supposed to feel."

He sighed. It was going to be a long night sleeping in his parked truck.

The sizzle of a rising sun, the pure notes of a Native American flute and an unidentifiable whooshing.

Annie squeezed her grandma's hand. "Are these sounds connected?"

Tia Henrietta remained immobile, her olive skin tinged with gray. The faintest vibration passed through Annie's fingertips where they rested in her grandma's palm.

Yes, a sign.

Somehow, everything was linked, connected by a thin gossamer thread she couldn't see.

The first two noises she associated with Tombi. The whooshing only started once she'd cast a spell to find a spirit or animal guide. So it might have been an ancestor spirit or an animal passing nearby, stirring the air.

Micro pressure tingled in her hand. Annie hardly dared breathe, awaiting a new message. She stared intently at Tia. A flutter of the eyelids and a twitch at the corners of the mouth passed over the remote, beloved face, a sign of presence.

"I'm here, Grandma. Squeeze my hand if you can hear me."

A gentle press upon her fingers, and Annie gasped, suffused with hope. She lifted Tia's frail, weathered hand and brushed her cheek against the arthritic knuckles. If tears could heal flesh, Tia's hand would be rejuvenated.

Should she call a nurse? Annie pushed the call button on the side of the hospital cot. "You're going to be all right, Grandma. We need to get you home soon. Would you like that?"

Again, a slight twitch at the corners of her mouth. And this time her eyes opened a fraction, revealing nothing but white. Her mouth soundlessly opened and closed.

"You're trying to speak." Annie stood and leaned over the hospital bed, bending over until her ear was inches from her grandma's mouth.

"Go to him." The whispered command was no less authoritative than when Grandma Tia was up and about, issuing orders.

"I can't leave you. Not now. You need me."

"She said go."

Startled, Annie whipped her head around. Miss Verbena stood in the doorway, frowning. "You heard Grandma way over there?"

"I heard you arguing and guessed the rest." She stepped forward and rubbed Annie's shoulder. "What's happened today? She talking?" Miss Verbena pulled out a chair and sat next to Annie. She withdrew a skein of yarn and knitting needles from her basket and took up her usual knitting. The needles clicked over the monotonous, background buzz of hospital machinery.

"You're not surprised?"

"Not a bit. Last night I dreamed that Tia would be a walkin' outta here by the end of the week."

"I never guessed that—"

A nurse bustled into the room. "What do you need?"

"My grandma just spoke." Annie grinned. "She's coming out of the coma."

The nurse frowned and stared at Tia's inert form. "You sure about that?" she asked suspiciously.

Miss Verbena winked at Annie. "She'll speak again when she gets a mind to. Meanwhile, I think it's time for you to skedaddle, young lady."

Annie shook her head and pinched her lips together. She wanted to be here when Grandma Tia opened her eyes again.

"I'll be right here," Miss Verbena promised. "You mind your Grandma, now. She ain't gonna rest comfortable until you do like she said."

The nurse shot Annie a curious look. "I'll get the doctor." She exited with the same bustle as when she entered.

Miss Verbena made a shooing motion with her hands. "Go on, now."

Reluctantly, Annie left, moving down the corridor as if her feet were mired in quicksand. She didn't want to leave Grandma Tia, and she certainly didn't want to see Tombi. *Go to him.* As if Tombi needed anyone, especially her. He'd as much as called her a coward. *Always running away from everything,* he'd said. The man acted as if he had no feelings outside a bloodthirsty need for revenge.

Last night, she'd scarcely slept, peeking out the window and seeing his truck in the driveway. She hoped his night was as miserable and sleepless as her own. In the morning, she'd gotten into her old car and left, deliberately ignoring Tombi and his truck as she drove for the hospital.

Shattering chords of pain assaulted her ears from opened patient doors. Annie quickened her step, skipping the elevator and opting for the stairs—less chance of running into others and their leaking auras.

She skipped along, heartened at Grandma Tia's minuscule awakening. Not only that, but Miss Verbena had dreamed she'd come out of the darkness, and her dreams always came true.

As far as Tombi, she'd show him she was no coward. At least, she'd try to. Annie bit her lip, picturing Nalusa in snake form. But Tombi had promised to stay by her side. She'd cling to him so tight, he wouldn't have an opportunity to escape her if he tried. Strengthened by her decision, and comforted at the thought of lunch and some downtime alone at home before she contacted Tombi, Annie prepared for a quick exit past the ER waiting lounge.

She took a deep breath and pushed open the door from the stairwell to the ER area. Misery wailed like a herd of banshees while an ambulance's real wail reverberated in her brain like a shotgun blast in a canyon. The trick was nonresistance, to let the sound flow in and out and not let it get trapped deep within. Annie focused on her breathing and kept her eyes on the lobby door leading to freedom. The siren echoes decreased in decibels. Another dozen steps and she opened the door to fresh air.

Oomph. Her elbow hit something hard.

"Hey, watch it, lady." An ambulance driver in an all-blue uniform scowled and jerked the gurney away.

Annie shrank back. "Sorry," she mumbled. "I didn't see—" Wait. She knew this man lying on the gurney with blood seeping down the side of his scalp from a head wound. Where had she met him before?

Two more EMR workers started past, with more patients. One of the men on the cot stared at her, recognition lighting his face.

"Hey, you're that Annie woman Tombi brought to camp." The man struggled to an upright position, pushing his dark hair from his face. He held his right arm in his left, and Annie fought nausea at the crooked, unnatural bent of his injured arm.

She recognized him now. Her gaze shifted to the other cot, to an unconscious, bleeding man.

"What happened?" she asked.

The EMR started to wheel him away.

"Hold on a sec," he told the guy. He grabbed her arm and pulled until she was eye level with him.

"We were attacked in the woods," he said in a low, fierce voice. "Ambushed."

"In broad daylight?" she asked. Horror weighted her down. "Where's Tombi?"

"Gone. Kidnapped. The wisps are delivering him to Nalusa as we speak."

Chapter 10

The shadows expanded and contracted into phantasmagoric shapes as Tombi stumbled along the path, squinting at the images. *Something is very wrong.* The miasma of evil was thick as clam chowder and as stifling as the Southern sun. He tugged at his bound hands, staring stupidly at the black cloth tied and knotted at his wrists. How had this happened?

The last thing he remembered was screams and rushing, colored orbs surrounding him and the other hunters. They had surged forward and converged upon him, their colored, swirling forms cloying and pouring acrid smoke into his nose and mouth. Through the smoke, he had made out the figure of a short, bowlegged man with a weathered, gnomelike face.

Hoklonote, no doubt. A bad spirit capable of temporarily shape-shifting to human form. Tombi had glimpsed him over the years, seen his face peeking out from the underbrush or gazing down from a tall tree, ready to pounce. He'd seen him run away on occasion with a queer, wobbly gate that led Tombi to suspect his feet were misshapen, ill-equipped to give chase.

Hoklonote must have been the one to bind his hands. The wisps were formless vapors surrounding the heart of their dead, entrapped victims. But they all were in league together with Nalusa.

When he was a young boy, his parents used to tell him if he didn't stay close to home or if he stayed out too late at night, the evil spirits would get him. Growing up, he'd made sure to be home before dark. As he grew into a teenager, he'd scoffed at the old tales and believed them merely a ploy to keep children from straying too far in the woods and to coerce them into minding their elders.

The Choctaw version of the boogeyman.

Much later, he'd learned there was more than one boogeyman, that they were real and that they had names and roamed the bayou grounds at night in search of prey.

A sharp poke on his lower back startled him out of his stupor. Tombi reined in his wandering thoughts and concentrated on Hoklonote. He sniffed experimentally and smelled an odor of damp and decay, like rotting leaves or globs of worms surfacing above ground after it was saturated by heavy rains. He sensed Hoklonote's physical form only rose to the midpoint of his back.

Tombi took a deep breath. No point being led like the lamb to the slaughter. Even drugged, he should prove a match for the stunted spirit. Pride stiffened his spine. The least he could do was leave the world fighting like a warrior, same as Bo. Tombi screwed up his fists.

"You forget the wisps," the voice from behind cackled. "You're outnumbered."

"So the old tale is true, then?" His voice was slurred,

his throat dry. Yet he pushed on. "You can read people's minds?"

"Sure can." The spirit's voice was high-pitched and tinged with glee. "Won't be taking me by surprise."

Damn. But he could still die trying.

"Quit them death thoughts," Hoklonote said. "Could be you can work out some kind of deal with Nalusa. Same as me, same as the wisps and same as other hunters over the years."

To hell with that, you little, stunted pygmy—

"Stunted, huh?" Hoklonote kicked him in the ass. "Better guard your thoughts."

Tombi gritted his teeth against the crack of pain at the base of his tailbone and continued the labored trek in the woods. He wanted to see Nalusa, face-to-face. If nothing else, he'd like to get a lick in on the beast, whatever form Nalusa chose to assume for their meeting.

"Foolish, foolish thoughts," Hoklonote grunted.

Tombi tried, yet he couldn't sense anyone else's presence but Hoklonote and the wisps. But that could be due to his drugged state dulling his tracking skills. Not that he expected an answer, but the question burned in his mind. "Has anyone else been drugged or hurt?"

Hoklonote didn't bother responding, but again prodded him with a sharp object, probably a stick, that pricked the base of his spine. With every step forward, Tombi felt more disoriented. His skin crawled and itched, and his tongue lay swollen and heavy in his dry mouth, as if he'd suffered a severe allergic reaction. His head was fuzzy, and he wanted nothing more than to curl into a little ball and sleep forever.

The wisps skittering around him were having none of that. Tombi's leaden legs managed to plod along. Again, he worried for his friends' safety. Where had everyone disappeared to? Distress sharpened his mind, which brought a new flood of anguish. Nalusa could kill in so many ways: snakebite, suffocation and entrapment in a will-o'-the-wisp body, or worst of all, a slow, debilitating despair of the mind that led to madness or suicide.

Annie had been absolutely correct. There was a betrayer in their group.

Annie. Her image arose so sharp and clear it felt as if she was within him, alongside him as he struggled to continue. Her hair was soft and brushing against him; he could smell her herbal, floral scent. Her mysterious hoodoo eyes penetrated all his defenses, saw through all his guards into the walled, hardened heart that was scarred and calloused from death and loss.

I'm coming, Tombi.

He could have sworn he felt the whisper of her breath in his ear. He stopped and glanced about, the sharp object in his back pushed deeper, puncturing flesh.

"What the hell was that?" Hoklonote ground out in surprise and outrage. "Ain't never heard the likes of that before."

It wasn't the drugs, then; Hoklonote heard the voice, as well. *Go away,* he urged silently, not sure if she could hear his thoughts like he heard hers.

"Speed it up there," Hoklonote demanded, unease sharpening his tone.

Tombi kept going, knowing that each step brought him closer to Nalusa, closer to death. Best to focus on that fact and block out Annie. He considered the confrontation awaiting him. No way he could win a fight in this weakened, hallucinogenic state. Whoever had betrayed him had won.

He was too drugged to despair. Too drugged to be afraid. Instead, body and brain felt numbed. A sense of fatalism spread through him. He'd tried his best and failed. He'd lost his parents and his best friend. His sister was like a stranger these days. He remembered the destroyed family home, his parents' tombstones, Bo's dead body and Tallulah's angry and shuttered face that masked a grieving heart.

Don't give up. I'm near. Again, Annie's whisper echoed in his ear and filled his body with her warm vibration.

"What's that?" Hoklonote asked. "Who's there?"

As much as it comforted him, Tombi scrabbled to again warn her off. It was too dangerous. *If you can hear me, go away.* Nalusa would love to get his hands on Annie. He could use her gift of hearing to his own advantage. He'd trap her in a wisp and never, ever let her go.

No. Annie's voice was firm. Why did she have to fight him at every turn?

Screams saturated his brain. Something new or a memory of what occurred prior to his being drugged? The painful prodding at his back ceased, and the wisps scattered. Tombi sank to his knees and rested his face in his hands, riding out the waves of screams assaulting his ears. Was this what it was like for Annie every day? And he'd accused her of being a coward, of running away from situations when it got tough. Remorse burned his gut.

And now he'd never have the chance to tell her he was sorry.

Never, ever.

Annie crouched behind a saw palmetto and watched as Tombi fell to his knees, clutching his head. She winced as if experiencing the scraped knees on her own body. A withered, strange-looking man standing behind Tombi raised a stick, poised to deliver a blow.

Hanan, Tallulah, Chulah and several other hunters continued their screaming advance toward the wisps surrounding Tombi. A volley of rocks unfurled and the wisps scattered, but not before a few were struck and disintegrated to ash. The strange man released his stick and ran into a thicket of trees, disappearing from sight.

Chulah dropped to a knee, withdrew a dagger and slit the cloth binding Tombi's hands. Annie scrambled to them and sat beside Tombi, running her fingers through his hair, matted with blood and sweat.

He looked up, eyes as blank and dark as an erased blackboard.

"What have they done to you?" she whispered past the tightness at the back of her throat.

Chulah shot her an impatient look. "The wisps' smoke is a hallucinogenic drug, deadly in a large enough dose."

Hanan emerged by Tombi's other side, and between them, the two men got Tombi to stand, placing an arm over each of their shoulders.

"Going to be a long walk home," Hanan mumbled. "Might not make it back before nightfall."

"I'm joining you, Bo."

Tombi's slurred pronouncement chilled Annie. "Not if I can help it."

"Get out of our way." Chulah scowled as they moved slowly, painfully toward the open field, where a four-wheeler waited.

Annie nervously scooted to the side and followed behind them. Tallulah walked beside her, shooting her dagger glares. As if she had anything to do with what happened.

Annie clutched her mojo bag and purse full of hoodoo supplies close to her chest. She had no idea if any of it worked, but she could try. After seeing the injured hunters at the hospital, she'd rushed home and gathered everything together and then arrived at the hunters' campsite in time to see the inner circle leaving to search for Tombi. They'd reluctantly allowed her to tag along when she promised she could help with any injuries.

She should have done more hoodoo work, and sooner, when her grandma was infected by Nalusa, but it had happened so quickly and she'd been unprepared. This time, she had everything needed for an uncrossing and good-health spell. She had prayed Tombi was unharmed but was determined that if he was injured, she'd go to the hospital and sneak into his room to perform healing rites.

But it might already be too late. Grandma Tia didn't specify how quickly it had to be performed once harm had been inflicted by an enemy.

Hanan and Chulah helped Tombi on to the four-wheeler, and Tallulah and Annie squeezed into the back, Tombi between them.

Hold on, Annie willed him.

He leaned his head against her shoulder, and she began whispering in his ear. "I beseech thee, Archangel Raphael, Healer, Angel of the Son, come now and heal—"

"What's that?" Tallulah cut in sharply.

Annie ignored her. "—Tombi from his enemy's poison. Deliver—"

"Stop that witchy stuff," she demanded, tugging at Annie's sleeve.

"—him and restore his health." Annie withdrew a mojo bag from her back pocket and opened the drawstring. "Provide the breath of life and healing energy." She blew into the mojo bag, infusing its contents with power and intent.

Tallulah jerked her arm. "Stop it!" Bits of dried herbs and crushed plant roots from the mojo bag scattered over their laps and the floorboard. Tallulah pick up the parchment paper and frowned. "What's this? A pentagram?"

"It's a drawing of Solomon's Seal." Annie gathered up the spilled contents.

"Leave her alone," Chulah said, glancing back at the commotion.

Annie shot him a grateful smile.

"All that mumbo jumbo can't hurt anything," he added.

Her smile faded. "It's not…" She sighed. What they thought about her and her root work wasn't important. Only Tombi mattered.

Tallulah handed over the parchment, rolling her eyes.

Annie returned it to the bag, breathed into it once again and drew the string together. "Saints be with us," she muttered, stuffing the bag into the side waistband of Tombi's jeans.

He stirred and opened his eyes. His dilated pupils stared unfocused at the group, then narrowed and sharpened as he turned to his side. "Annie. I heard you."

"I've been right here, talking to you."

His hand claimed one of her own. "Not just now. But before, when I was captured and walking through the woods."

The copper rays in his eyes warmed the sudden chill bumps on her arms. "You heard my thoughts? That's never happened before."

Hanan frowned and peered at them from the overhead mirror. "Impossible. She was hiding behind the bushes, way out of your hearing range."

"How are you doing, buddy?" Chulah asked. "We'll be at the cabin in a few minutes, the hospital in fifteen."

Tombi shook his head. "No hospital."

Tallulah leaned over Annie and thrust her face close to her twin. "Don't be an idiot. Witch spells are bullshit. You need a doctor."

"You should see one," Annie agreed. She lifted his hair away from his forehead and saw swelling with a gash oozing blood. "You might have a concussion."

Tombi winced and jerked away from her touch. "My head is clearing. I'll be fine." He straightened and frowned at Chulah and Hanan. "What the hell happened out there?"

"We were ambushed," Chulah said, a grim set to his jaw. "The wisps were waiting on us as soon as we arrived."

"Betrayed," Tallulah ground out.

They hit a bump, and Annie's insides jostled. She cast a worried glance at Tombi, but his face wore the usual stoic mask. At least he was alert and coming out of whatever fog he'd suffered. A selfish, tiny jab of loneliness pricked her. When he was like this, he seemed so remote and removed— as if he didn't notice or need her.

Tombi kept his eyes peeled on the road ahead but grasped Annie's hand and held tight. Heat diffused over her body. Not even Tallulah's grimace of disapproval could dispel her glow inside. She sucked in her breath, relief and happiness unloosening the tense muscles in her shoulders and neck.

Annie closed her eyes and let the welcoming wind, from riding in the four-wheeler, brush over her face as the others discussed the attack and injuries. No death casualties, although three men were hospitalized and listed in serious condition.

"They weren't there to kill everyone," Hanan said. "Their objective was to capture you." He pulled up to a small cabin and brought the vehicle to an abrupt halt. "I wonder what Nalusa wants with you."

Annie shivered at the mention of Nalusa facing Tombi again. He couldn't be lucky enough to escape with his life on two different occasions.

"He hopes to cut a deal or truce." Tallulah scrambled out of the vehicle. "Either that or kill Tombi, thinking it will weaken all the hunters."

Typical Tallulah. The facts were laid bare with no emo-

tion. You'd never know Tombi was her twin, that they had
once heard one another's heartbeat in the womb.

Tombi stepped out onto the ground with only a slight
wobble. He shook off Chulah and Hanan's offer of assistance and carefully made his way up the porch steps, hand
gripping the railing.

Annie fell in behind everyone, uncertain of her welcome. Too bad, she'd do what needed to be done. Tombi
wasn't out of the woods yet, and she wasn't finished with
her healing ritual. That was—if he allowed her to proceed.
The thought that she still might not have his full trust
slowed her steps and weighed on her chest.

Inside, the spaciousness of the cabin surprised Annie.
She saw now that the cabin was a deep, rectangular shape.
The open den was large, and huge windows on the back
wall framed nature's artwork of oaks and pines. Custom
bookcases lined the side walls, and, ignored by all, she
wandered over to glance at the titles: Choctaw history,
animal spirit guides and archaeology magazines. Interspersed among the books were arrowheads and bits of
pottery. There were also a few corncob pipes and Native
American flutes decorated with feathers. Her mind tickled
with faint piping notes. Could she hear his ancestors from
the past? Instead of the normal dread of her supernatural
sense, the sound filled Annie with awe and appreciation.

She ambled to the opposite wall, ignoring the buzz of
conversation from another room where the others had disappeared. In the center of the largest bookcase was a Native American headdress decorated with colorful beads and
feathers and shells attached with leather cords. A feeling of
pride and majesty settled on her with a formal solemnity.

There were also several framed pieces of art featuring
elaborate, beaded necklaces and collars. The need to create
art in even a simpler, more natural past existence revealed a

deep-felt human desire to express beauty, one that touched Annie. She fancied she could hear the lighthearted, higher-pitched voices of women talking and laughing together, beautifying the life of their community.

Being here was like walking through a time portal in a museum. It felt warm and right, like a secret home, a feeling of belonging and acceptance.

Wishful thinking. She pictured her mother's home in North Georgia, a shotgun-style house that was always cold in winter and stifling hot in summer. Everything in it was worn and shoddy and contained a past history of careless-ness—just like the family who lived in it. Careless and hot and cold with their love.

Mostly cold.

Instinctively, Annie wrapped her arms across her chest. She didn't ever have to go back there again. She was done trying to earn their love. If her mom could shake off Grandma Tia and wash her hands of her own mother and hometown, Annie could do the same. *It's the last time I'll let history repeat itself*, she vowed. Crazy Annie was in the past.

She strode down the oak floorboard, taking in more of Tombi's belongings. It was obvious he was a man who took pride in his heritage and loved family and friends. Near the end of the bookcase was a shelf of framed pictures. Square in the middle was a small, faded three-by-five photo of a man and woman holding a pair of toddlers in their arms. She picked it up and examined it closely. Tombi and Tal-lulah. Tombi regarded the camera with wide, solemn eyes, while Tallulah's mouth parted in a huge laughing grin, a chubby finger pointed at the photographer.

Times had sure changed. Annie carefully set it down and retraced her steps to the headdress. She lifted her hand

and touched one of the white feathers, startled to hear the slight swish sound of a bird in flight.

"Don't touch that."

Annie swirled around at the abrupt command, guiltily clutching her hands behind her back. "Sorry."

"Do you need a lift home?" Tallulah asked, scowling.

The message was clear. She wasn't welcome. "I can walk." Despite the heat in her cheeks, Annie lifted her chin and made for the front door.

"Suit yourself."

Annie refused to look at Tallulah as she left the cabin and fled down the steps.

"Hey! Where are you going?"

Tombi leaned on the door frame, swaying slightly. "I can't chase after you today. Come back."

Of course. How could she have allowed Tallulah to so completely sidetrack her? Tombi needed her. She'd come to do a job, and it was only half-complete. The first whiff of rejection had lanced the sensitive sore in her heart, and she'd run away, mortified.

Again.

Annie straightened her shoulders and went to Tombi.

Tallulah stepped onto the porch beside her brother. "You sure you want her with us?"

Tombi shot her a warning look, and she backed to the door. "Your call," she said, shrugging her shoulders.

"Don't you have some hoodoo juice or herb tea or something for me to drink?"

His smile was crooked, and the unexpected humor lightened the weight in her chest. She lifted her purse. "In here. The tea won't taste any better than the last brew you drank, but it will draw out any poison or toxins in your system."

Tombi held the door open, and she swept past him, back into the cool tranquility of his cabin.

Hanan, Tallulah and Chulah exited the kitchen, ready to leave.

"We'll check out who sent those texts," Chulah promised. "Pisa's a cop and has access to phone records."

Hanan fished the four-wheeler keys from his jean pockets. "And I'll notify everyone to meet here tomorrow. We'll figure out who sent it."

Tallulah stood behind her brother and flashed Annie a slash mark at the throat.

Annie paled. "It wasn't me."

Tombi faced his twin, hands on his hips. "What did you just do?"

"Nothing." Tallulah lifted her chin and smiled sweetly, sweeping past everyone. "Let's go. We all have lots to do before the gathering."

Annie watched them leave with relief. "Point me to the kitchen, and I'll make that tea."

He nodded and made his way out of the room. His gate was stiff and unnaturally slow. Tombi was hurt more than he wanted anyone to know. "Why don't you lie on the couch, and I'll bring it to you when I'm finished."

"I need to show you where everything is."

Stubborn man. Annie followed behind him. The kitchen had gleaming walnut cabinets with a matching island at the center. "Did you make these?"

He nodded, sinking into a chair at the small table in the corner. "Pots and pans are in the cabinet below the oven."

Quickly she set about brewing the tea. Outside the window, the sinking sun was a striking coral. She realized she was ravenous. "Are you hungry? What can I fix for supper?"

"Now that you mention it, I'm starving. You don't have to cook anything. I've got leftover spaghetti in the freezer."

With his directions, Annie got dinner going. She served

him the herbal tea and returned to the stove, warming the spaghetti and buttering French bread. She found a pitcher of iced tea in the fridge and set the table.

The cozy intimacy of the meal restored her good spirits, as well as the sight of Tombi's skin turning from its former ashy color to its normal cinnamon glow. They settled into a comfortable silence. At last, Tombi set down his fork and pushed back his chair. "I feel like a new man." He held her eyes. "Thank you."

The simple compliment had her own skin glowing. "I just warmed up leftovers." She stood.

Tombi clamped his warm hand over her own. "You did more than that."

She screwed up her courage. "There's something else I'd like to do. If you'll let me."

He raised an eyebrow. "What do you have in mind?"

She so didn't want to do this. If only Grandma Tia were here, everything would be so much easier. Her grandma was the one with the real healing touch, the real magic. Her own attempts were weak, more hesitant. But she was on her own. She had to try. Annie took a deep breath, suppressing her inhibitions. If he refused or mocked her, at least she tried.

"I want to do a healing ritual."

Tombi strummed his fingers on the table. "And what would your ritual entail? Because we have our own purification rituals. Unfortunately, I don't have days to seek solitude and stay in a steam tent to purify my blood."

"I don't know that mine's as effective, but it's simpler and quicker. All that's involved is a prayer, lighting a candle and—" she stammered a heartbeat "—an anointing with healing oil."

"Who gets this anointing? Me or the candle?" He was

as still and tense as a crouching jaguar, eyes intent and assessing.

"You." Annie cursed the burn in her cheeks. This was a sacred ritual, purely performed for medicinal and spiritual purposes.

Tombi slowly rose and came to her side, guiding her up by the elbow, until her body faced his, only inches apart. His aura melted into hers with the vibration of a base drum pounding in her ears and in her gut and in the womanly core between her thighs.

"Let's do it."

The deep, hoarse words implied more than an anointing. Tombi cocked his head toward the door. "This way."

Quickly, she grabbed her purse and followed him down a hall into a bedroom.

It was sparse and utilitarian. A large four-poster bed dominated the room, neatly made with green sheets and colorful Native American blankets folded at the foot. A matching wooden dresser and two nightstands. A brightly colored braided wool rug was in the center of the room. The windows were curtainless. Despite the barrenness of the room, Annie appreciated the minimalistic masculine atmosphere.

"We don't have to use your bedroom for the ritual." She stood by the door, clutching her purse.

"I'm going to take a quick shower. Just relax and set up everything."

Relax. Hah, fat chance. As soon as she was alone in the room, Annie walked to the dresser and pulled from her purse all she needed to arrange an altar. She placed a blue candle and a white candle on the table between a small, wooden statue of Black Hawk, a Native American spirit guide called upon in hoodoo as much as the saints.

The sounds of a water spray from the shower, and she

pictured Tombi naked, the rivulets running down that silky black hair, onto his chest, down the lean abs and… Annie swallowed hard and returned to her task.

Carefully, she set out a stick of incense and a vial of sand from the Gulf Coast. She dressed the candles with Van Van oil and lit them with unsteady fingers, the tiny flame dancing between her fingers. Again she struck another match and applied it to the tip of the sage incense stick until it turned ashen, and curls of smoke saturated the air. She inhaled the pungent herbal scent and focused on the coming ritual.

Don't think about his naked body. Don't think about his wet flesh being lathered by soap. Don't think… As if.

She could think of nothing else. Sighing, she withdrew the last ritual item from her purse, a small glass bottle of healing oil. How would she be able to rub it across his chest without molding herself into his arms and kissing the strong plane of his jawline? From there she would be a hairbreadth from his lips, from his chest…and then she would be lost.

Well, it wouldn't be a crime if they made love. They were both single, consenting adults. Annie couldn't deny how drawn she was to his power and strength. Only— she wasn't the kind of woman who had casual sex. Oh, she wished she was. Very much. But for her, it went so much deeper.

Annie sat on the edge of the bed and closed her eyes. What did she really want? Her body yearned to feel Tombi inside her; it had been so long since a man had touched her. And emotionally, she had to admit, she was equally drawn to Tombi. The problem was she had no clue how he felt about her. He wanted her body, that was plain. And he wanted to use her gift to fight Nalusa. He was kind in trying to shield her from his sister and the other hunters' mistrust.

But did he love her?

The question drew her up sharp. Equally important, did she love him? If she didn't, she was close. So very close.

The shower spray ceased, and Annie paced, fighting a desire to flee the room and return home. The urge was strong. She went to the dresser, picked up her purse and flung it over her shoulder.

"Annie." Tombi lounged by the bathroom door, wearing only a white towel knotted at his hips. His long hair was sleek and plastered back from his temples, making his already severe face look harsher, more intense. "Running away again?"

Chapter 11

She was doing it again. Running. Over the years, it had become her go-to method for dealing with difficulty, ingrained since that disastrous kindergarten class with the unbearable, discordant triangle music. *You need to stop running away*, Grandma Tia had warned. *Stand up fo' yerself, girl.*

Grandma Tia was right. Tombi was right. She was sick of the cowardly acts.

No more.

Slowly, Annie pulled the purse strap from her shoulder and set it on the dresser. "I'm not leaving. I came here to do a job, and I intend to do it."

Tombi nodded. "Glad to hear that." He sniffed the air and pointed to the altar. "I smell sage. We burn it, too, for cleansing. Tell me how the rest of this works."

The matter-of-fact voice dispelled some of Annie's nervousness. He wasn't mocking her beliefs. "Sure. We traditionally use blue-and-white candles…" She inhaled sharply as he drew next to her. She smelled soap and some secret pheromone that was unique to him. And so utterly sexy and irresistible.

Tombi picked up the carved statue and examined it, frowning. "What's this?"

Would he take offense? "It's a statue of Black Hawk, an old war chief and spiritual guide we petition for help in battle. In this case, the battle is for your health. I'm worried that when the wisps attacked you, you inhaled some of their form or absorbed it through your skin. The earlier prayer to the saints helped in the emergency, and the fig-tree-bark tea helped revive your strength, but to really get rid of any lingering toxins, I think this ritual is needed. It's what I know Grandma Tia would recommend."

"Your recommendation is good enough for me." He put the statue back on the dresser. "Anything else?" Amusement lit his eyes. "I seem to remember you mentioning an oil rub."

Annie strove to keep her face and voice controlled and smooth. "If you'll sit on the edge of the bed, I'll get to work. I'll invoke Black Hawk in my thoughts while I rub your chest, above your heart, with healing oil."

"Time for the oil massage?" He gave a slow, sexy smile. "I like your witchy ways."

Annie pointed to the bed. "Just sit. And please don't talk while I rub you, because I'll be silently invoking Black Hawk while I do it."

Surprisingly, Tombi obeyed without a word. He sat on the bed and winked. "I'm ready. Actually, I'm a little tired, so I'll lie down instead of sit."

He swung his legs up on the mattress, and Annie blushed at the part in the towel that exposed him for a second.

Did he mean to do that? Sure he did. She should be angry. But instead, her thighs tightened in response. This would be the hardest ritual she'd ever performed. Annie licked her dry lips and went to the dresser again and retrieved the bottle of healing oil, spreading a generous amount in her palm. She rubbed her hands together, releasing the purifying medicinal smell of eucalyptus, allspice, myrrh and thyme.

Annie eased on the bed beside him and placed both her hands on his bare chest. At Tombi's dark look of desire, she closed her eyes, fighting the draw of attraction. The heat of contact was intensified by the slippery oil. Annie rubbed clockwise over his heart, determined to do her duty.

Inwardly chanting the familiar words of the petition eased her nervousness, and a deep calm settled through her body. A drowsing numbness crept into her fingers and palms, spreading upward, tingling unpleasantly.

So this was how Grandma Tia must have felt when she'd absorbed the toxins from Tombi after he'd been bitten by Nalusa in snake form, only it had to have been much more dangerous and intense.

It is done. All is well. The thought whispered through her consciousness, and she withdrew her hands and placed them in her lap.

Thank you, Black Hawk. She took a few deep breaths and opened her eyes, catching Tombi's frowning stare.

"Are you all right?" he asked, rising up on an elbow. "You look funny."

"I'm fine. Only a little tired."

"Damn." Tombi scooted over and patted the mattress. "Lie down and rest."

"Good idea." Lethargy weighted her bones, and she sank down on the bed. "Just a little nap," she murmured.

A large calloused hand gently brushed the hair from

her face. "Are you going to be okay? I couldn't stand it if something happened to you."

He cared. Annie smiled with a secret happiness and curled her knees into her chest. "I'm fine. Just hold me for a little while."

A warm, strong arm planted on the side of her hip. Nice. Passion warred against drowsiness. Sleep won. At last, she became aware that the pressure of his hands against her had vanished. Annie opened her eyes. "Where are you going?"

Darkness had settled in the room, and in the candle glow she watched as Tombi picked up the glass bottle of healing oil and returned to her side.

"Time for me to return the favor. Looks like you need this stuff."

"I'm okay." Black Hawk had reassured her on that point.

"Maybe. But this couldn't hurt." He emptied a dollop of oil into his palms and rubbed them together before sinking into the mattress beside her.

Annie's heart thudded with anticipation at the dark intent in Tombi's obsidian eyes. With great deliberation, he placed his hands on either side of the nape of her neck and rubbed the tight pressure points where skull joined spine. She rolled onto her back and sighed at the pain/pleasure cocktail as he worked his fingers and loosened the tight knots of tension.

The caress lowered to her shoulders, and Annie closed her eyes, relaxing into sensation. Bliss. If only this moment could last forever. A tug at the neckline of her T-shirt snagged her attention.

"This needs to come off," Tombi rasped.

She offered no resistance as he pulled her shirt over her head. One deft movement, and he'd unsnapped her bra and removed it, as well. Annie quickly pulled the bedsheet over her exposed breasts.

Tombi didn't remark on it, but resumed his ministrations on the curve of her shoulders. The oil glided like the liquid, healing caress of warm water. It spread from her shoulder to her collarbone and inched farther down to the round swells of her breasts. Her nipples tightened underneath the cotton sheet, and the friction made her core ache. She kept her eyes squeezed shut, unwilling to break the magic spell of passion.

A tug of the sheet, and she was exposed. Annie instinctively crossed her arms in front of her chest.

"What's wrong?" Tombi asked.

"N-nothing," she lied.

Evan's face filled her mind. She didn't want to think of him, didn't want to remember the feel of his rough hands and the quick thrust of his lovemaking. Or his jeer when it was over, complaining that she was frigid and should be grateful that he put up with her crazy ass.

"Relax," Tombi commanded. He reached across her and poured more oil into his palms.

Right. Relax. She calmed her quick, shallow breathing and concentrated on the cozy candle flames flickering on the walls and ceiling and the uplifting scent of the herbal oil.

Heated hands settled back on her breasts. "Am I supposed to say something special for healing?" he asked.

"Not necessary," she squeaked.

One hand palmed the skin above her heart on her left breast. "I'll pray to my own spirit guides," he murmured.

Peace engulfed Annie like a balm, soothing her skittish mind. Tombi's hands roamed lower, cupping her and teasing her nipples. She moaned and arched into his touch.

"You're so beautiful," Tombi breathed, his hot breath suddenly against her lips. "I love your body."

Surprise and relief bubbled inside. Annie kissed him, wanting to feel his lips, his mouth, his tongue. He kissed her back, settling his weight on top of her, pressing his erection against the apex of her thighs. *More, deeper, quicker.* Annie wiggled impatiently beneath him, inhibitions be damned.

Tombi rolled to his side and cradled her body against his own. The sexual tension between them grew and he pulled off what remained of her clothes. His mouth suckled her breasts and one hand lowered until his fingers probed the opening of her womanhood, and he inserted a finger.

Yes. She moved against it, delighting in the ripples of pleasure spreading all through her body, like a pebble dropped in smooth water.

Tombi moaned. "So damn sexy."

"You really think so?" she asked, seeking reassurance.

He took one of her hands and placed it on his erection. "There's your answer."

Her fingers curled over his long length, and she stroked him up and down, luxuriating in the smooth flesh. She did this to him, turned him on.

"I want you," she whispered, emboldened by the evidence of his desire.

His mouth lowered over a nipple. "There's no rush."

His tongue flicked her sensitive bud and need shot through her like an electrical shock. Annie gasped. "I don't want to wait."

Damn. Why did she say anything? Evan would have been annoyed; he'd taught her to shut up and go along with his tempo and desire.

Tombi raised his head and stared at her. "If you're sure that's what you want?"

His weight again pressed against her as he rolled on top. His eyes scorched her, the planes of his face were harsher and fiercer than she'd ever seen, even at that first encounter in the swamp. The candlelight behind him highlighted the golden undertone of his olive skin, and his long black hair hung loose about his broad shoulders.

She'd never been so sure about anything in her life. "Yes. Now." *Hurry*.

He took his sweet time, teasing his length along the wet folds of her core. Annie arched her hips, and he entered in one deep plunge, filling and stretching her completely. Her breath caught.

"You okay?"

She moved against him in answer.

Still, Tombi proceeded ever so slowly, deliberately, heightening the tension until Annie wanted to scream with passion. The ebb and flow of his advances were as powerful and deep as an ocean's tide. It consumed her, became the epicenter of her world.

"Please," she whispered brokenly.

He thrust deeper, quicker, and their bodies worked in harmony, a dance of desire as old as mankind. Annie was swept up in a thunder of need. Her muscles tightened, and release came, sending her free-falling back to reality. She sank into the mattress, exhausted and stunned. It had never been this way. Ever. She almost wanted to weep for the old Annie who had never climaxed, who'd always been told she was cold, who'd always been just a girlfriend of convenience.

What had he done?

Tombi stood at the window and surveyed the waning moon. The next time the celestial orb revealed its peak would be at the appearance of the Full Corn Moon. A time that had been a critical one for his ancestors as they harvested their maze and other crops for the barren winter ahead.

And he knew that in the weeks leading up to Full Corn Moon, he was preparing for a final battle. The bite from Nalusa, a betrayer revealing information that almost decimated the hunting band, and the gathering power and boundaries of Nalusa and the wisps convinced him that the scales had tipped in Nalusa's favor.

And the Old Shadow well knew it.

Nalusa would strike against them once and for all; Tombi could feel it in every cell of his body. He had only one hope at turning the tide in his favor.

He glanced back at the bed, where Annie lay sleeping. The white bedsheet was bunched up near the slight curve of her hip, leaving her shapely breasts exposed. Her hair fell against the linen in dark waves. She looked so womanly—yet still so young. A woman-child, a healer, a witch, a sound sorcerer—all wrapped up into one extraordinary person who didn't realize how incredible she really was.

Especially in bed.

His blood heated as he remembered Annie's shy but passionate response during their lovemaking. And he frowned as he recalled the drowsy happiness in her eyes afterward, the tender way she brushed his hair from his forehead and kissed his temples.

He couldn't allow himself to fall into her tender mercies, and he hoped she would be a sensible, modern woman about what had taken place between them tonight. He needed her gift of hearing, not her love. An unfamiliar, uncomfortable tug pulled at his conscience—had he used her tonight to further his own cause and get her cooperation in the fight against the shadows?

Tombi hoped he wasn't that kind of man.

As if hearing his unsavory thoughts, Annie thrashed against the sheets and bolted upright. Her eyes were wide and wild, and she clutched the sheet up to her neck.

"What's wrong? Did you have a bad dream?"

"I'm not sure." Her brows knitted. "I heard a flapping noise. Like a large bird did a flyby near my head."

"Must be your animal spirit guide trying to get your attention."

"A bird?"

He laughed at the disappointment in her voice. "Nothing wrong with that. Makes perfect sense, actually. Birds are messengers, just as you have been with Bo."

"I suppose. Secretly, I was hoping it would be a cat. A long, lean jaguar or panther."

"Cats that eat birds for breakfast, huh? Think of it this way—in our culture some of the most revered guides are eagles. They represent freedom, strength and victory."

"I could use some of that. Especially victory. How will I know for sure if the eagle is my guide? How do I communicate with it?"

"Watch when you're outside for a particular bird, or if feathers of a particular bird appear. If you keep looking, it will make itself known."

But he'd lost Annie's attention. Her gaze kept drawing up and down his body. "You're already dressed," she noted, picking at the sheet bunched in her hands. "Don't you want to…you know…come back to bed?"

Did he ever. Yet, Tombi hesitated. If she stayed with him indefinitely here in his cabin, shared his bed, Annie might have…expectations. Best to establish boundaries now. He sat on the edge of the bed. "About last night—"

The happiness in her face melted, the soft, vulnerable shine in her eyes hardened. "Don't worry. I expect nothing."

The reasons why she should do just that—expect nothing—died on his lips. Someone had hurt her badly. "Damn. Who made you so bitter? Evan?"

"He made it clear that a girl like me should be grateful for any attention thrown her way. That sex is just sex. Not to be confused with love." She turned her face to the side, stiff and brittle.

Tombi gently placed a finger on her uplifted chin and drew her face toward him. "A girl like you? What the hell is that supposed to mean?"

"I've told you before, I'm known as Crazy Annie in my hometown."

"You're a beautiful, exceptional woman," he argued.

"Then why—" Her voice trembled, and she took a shaky breath. "Go on and say what you have to say."

"It's not you, it's me." Damn, that sounded lame even to his own ears. Tombi dropped his hand and paced the room, needing his space, needing to find the words that were impossible to formulate while staring into her disappointed eyes.

"It's like this," he began. "My life is dedicated to stopping Nalusa and the wisps and all the dark creatures of the night from taking control of the light, of all that's good in the world. It's been my mission since I was nineteen years old. It's what I was born to do."

"I wouldn't stop you," she said softly.

"You say that now. But when it comes time for me to face Nalusa, you might try to stop me from what I have to do. Guilt me into turning away." He'd seen it with a few hunters, the ones who'd chosen to marry and raise families. Priorities changed.

"No one's ever put me first. Don't worry, I won't expect it now."

The hard edge was back in her tone, in the pinched set of her lips.

"You deserve better than that." Tombi strode to the window, where the first sun rays peeped through the horizon, casting shadows that broke up the darkness. But for him, there was no ameliorating the darkness. He faced the truth, the secret fear he'd lived with for so long.

He was afraid that the darkness would win. Not just in the real, bayou backwaters and beyond, but deep in his soul. Ever since his parents had died, a wound had festered inside that had been fed through a series of subsequent blows—the death of his best friend, the loss of kinship with his twin sister, the growing realization he was fighting a battle he most likely could not win.

If Annie and her grandmother hadn't come along when they did…he'd have surely died from Nalusa's snakebite.

"I've already caused you enough grief," he said gruffly. "Your grandmother may well die because of her effort to save me."

"I don't blame you anymore. For whatever reason, she made her own decision. Grandma Tia's always been that way." Annie gave a shaky laugh. "She's doing better, you know. She's awakened from the coma."

Relief lightened the pressure in his chest, where guilt and worry weighed like a boulder. Unfortunately, it was still heavy from other burdens. "Good to hear."

"Now, if you don't mind, could you give me some privacy to get dressed?"

The hurt in her eyes and the former frost in her voice had disappeared, but she was overly polite, distant. "Annie, I…" He stopped, unsure how to proceed. Wasn't this what he wanted? To put some emotional distance between them?

"I'll say it for you. The sex was mediocre and you aren't

in love with me, so I shouldn't get any ideas that this is some kind of permanent relationship."

"What?" Shock and pain iced the blood in his veins. She was quite the actress if his lovemaking hadn't pleased her. Unfamiliar heat rose up the back of his neck. He'd been accused of being too fierce, too unfeeling and too bent on revenge, but he'd never had any complaints about his sexual prowess. "I could have sworn you were satisfied."

"I was, but you weren't. There, happy now?"

"Who said I wasn't?" Damn, she was confusing as hell.

Her eyes narrowed. "I thought that's what you were trying to tell me."

"Let's start over." Tombi folded his arms. "I only wanted to warn you that my number-one priority right now is defeating Nalusa. The situation is dangerous and headed for a breaking point."

"I already know this."

So far, so good. Annie seemed calm and accepting. If it had been Courtney sitting there in his bed…he'd be paying hell. She'd broken up with him because she wasn't first in his life. She resented the time he spent hunting during the full moon and the allegiance he had to his people.

"It doesn't bother you?"

"I worry about your safety."

"Which leads me to my next point. Nalusa and the shadows grow more powerful every day, and they have an inside track to our whereabouts and strategy, thanks to some informer. It could well be that the next full moon, Nalusa will go after me again. This time, I don't expect to live through it."

"Oh, Tombi." Annie dropped the sheet and climbed out of bed. Her body, only a shade lighter than his own, glowed in the pale dawn light. She approached him slowly and placed her hands on his shoulders. "Don't say that.

Don't even think it. We'll find the betrayer. Together, we can work out a plan. And now that Grandma Tia is coming around, she'll help, too."

He wanted to believe Annie, but the years hadn't trained his mind to expect the best. "I wish I didn't have to involve you or your grandmother. But if there's any chance you could turn this war around in our favor, I need you."

"I'll help you."

Annie rested her head against his bare chest, and he stroked her hair, humbled at her willingness to stand with him and his people. "Thank you," he murmured in the comforting warmth of her scalp.

"I've never been needed before."

"Hard to believe." If he wasn't careful, he could grow to need her too much, could bask in her kindness and healing nature and let her brighten the dark, warring evenings.

She lifted her face. "It's true. I've always been the afterthought, never normal enough or smart enough to fit in with my own family, much less a boyfriend."

If he could, he'd erase every painful memory she suffered. Would kiss away every tear and chase away all her doubts and insecurities as mercilessly as he tracked down every wisp leading to Nalusa.

"Their loss," he ground out. Damn it to hell, if there was any way to keep from hurting her, he would.

Don't fall in love with me, Annie. He should tell her, warn her. But he couldn't bring himself to say the words. He bent down and kissed her full lips, hungry for her touch, her feel. As if last night hadn't been enough.

Tombi feared it would never be enough. There weren't enough days and nights in his lifetime for making love with Annie. He pressed his hands on the sides of her hips, marveling at her soft skin, at the way her body melded to his own, seeking oneness. He was selfishly taking all she had to offer. Eternal spirits help him, he couldn't caution Annie to guard her heart.

Because much to his chagrin, he needed the warning more than she did.

Chapter 12

The clear, pure melody of the flute danced in the breeze. As if a flock of birds warbled in the same octave, with high notes that trilled in a soaring ecstasy, tempered by a deeper undertone of mourning. And blended between was all manner of feeling: lyrical, haunting. Weeping whistles of warring hope and despair.

Tombi stopped playing, and the silence echoed in Annie's brain like a sudden death. "You're up early," he commented, his rigid back to her. His shirt was off, and the golden skin on his chest glistened with sweat. The red bandana on his forehead was wet.

It was one hell of a sexy sight.

Annie continued across the yard toward him, carefully maneuvering between workbenches and piles of wood and cabinet frames. The air smelled of cut pine.

She faced him, trying to evaluate his mood. Yesterday he'd been aloof, despite the previous night's closeness. He'd spent most of yesterday out speaking with other hunters and planning a meeting. All afternoon and into the evening, he'd worked his carpentry job, claiming to be behind schedule. But last night… She blushed, remembering their intense lovemaking. "Enjoying your break?" she asked.

"I was." He nodded at the pocketbook hanging from her shoulder. "You going to visit your grandmother again today?"

"Yes. Unless you're ready to give me another lesson."

He picked up a piece of lumber and placed it on the workbench. "Why don't you go ahead? The lessons can wait."

"Maybe for you," she answered sharply, frustrated with his aloofness during the day. He acted as if he wanted to shut her out of a large part of his life.

He raised a brow. "Problem?"

"Seems like you've been avoiding showing me how to control my hearing. We had a deal. Remember?"

He frowned. "Is that all that's wrong? I've been a little busy. Give me a break."

Annie tried another tactic. "I thought you said time was of the essence, that things were heading to a showdown between you and Nalusa."

"I have no way of knowing for sure, but that's my gut feeling."

"And you said you needed my help. So why aren't you putting me to work for you? I feel like you're shutting me out." Except when he wanted her body.

"All I need is for you to come with us during the next hunt to let us know when you hear something that we can't. Especially if Bo tries to communicate again."

"There must be something we can do between now and the full moon."

A knowing smile broke through Tombi's inscrutably

calm face, and his pupils darkened. "I can think of a few things," he said with that deep gruffness she remembered from last night's bedtime talk.

"Well, there's always *that*." She cleared her throat. "My grandma's expecting me to eat breakfast with her at the hospital. Want to come with me?"

He picked up a saw and shook his head. "Not now. I have a couple client appointments today. Tell her I'll drop by again this evening."

"Suit yourself." Annie headed to her car, conscious of him watching her. She turned her face slightly to the side. Sure enough, he stood, saw in hand, staring at her ass. Her own lips upturned in a knowing smile as she climbed into her vehicle. She had the power to break through his remote facade whenever she wished.

Was it wrong to hunger for more? There must be something she could do to gain his respect, to make him see she could be a stronger ally. Some way to defeat Nalusa. As long as Nalusa lived and controlled the wisps and the birds of the night, Tombi wasn't free to live a normal life. His need for revenge consumed him.

"Be careful," Tombi called out.

Annie started the car and headed for the county road, her mind filled with possibilities. For starters, she could return to the cottage and study the grimoires she'd culled from Grandma Tia's collection. Maybe there was something there. She glanced at the dashboard clock. She had time for a little reading before visiting her grandma. Annie gunned the motor and arrived at the cottage quickly, filled with optimism. Must be some reason Grandma Tia communicated about the grimoires while she was in the coma, even if she didn't now remember why or how she'd done so.

Inside, she lit candles and settled at the kitchen table. She pulled the top one off the stack and opened it. Metallic ink shimmered on the pages with its flecks of crimson, forest green and ocean blue. The crinkling as she turned the page seemed an unnaturally loud rustle, as if a pile of dead leaves were stirred by a stiff breeze.

A sudden scent enveloped her awareness. An earthy, bitter greens top note sweetened with rich, dark undertones. Annie inhaled and analyzed the enticing mixture—it contained licorice, vanilla and myrrh. She'd noticed it before around the cottage, often when Grandma Tia performed a ritual calling on the guidance of an ancestor.

"Who are you?" she whispered, her skin tingling. The scent grew stronger, as if a spirit drew closer. Annie waited, hardly daring to breathe, but no other sign was offered. "Thank you for coming," she said, louder, more confident this time. She'd asked for help, and it looked as if she was getting it.

She ran her fingers down the cracked spine of the old grimoire. This book was the one. It whispered promises and answers. The strong premonition settled in her gut while her heart raced.

Primitive music sounded—so faint she wasn't sure she heard it at first. Annie strained and deciphered the vibration of a drum that provided a base to a flute. The music was subtly different from what Tombi played—there were fewer notes, less range of pitch, less sophistication. But instead of deterring from the sound quality, it made it more unique and poignant.

The pages began turning without any assistance, like an invisible hand leafing through the tome. It was like the time when she was twelve and playing with her grandma's Ouija board without permission. An unseen force had moved the planchette across the alphabet, spelling a slightly sinister message. Even now, Annie preferred tarot cards and crystals to seek help from beyond.

This time felt different, not sinister at all. As if the unseen hand was pointing toward a solution. Besides, an ancestor was in the room with her, one that smelled of strong femininity grounded by the earth.

The rustling stopped. Reverently, Annie pulled the grimoire closer and started reading. Excitement charged her body like an electrical shock at the story of an old Choctaw tale involving Nalusa Falaya and how his spirit was bound in an ancient ritual performed by the strongest warriors in the tribe.

Why had Tombi never mentioned this ritual? Annie tapped an index finger against her lips and gazed out the kitchen window, deep in thought. Maybe he hadn't heard of it, or maybe he did know about it and didn't believe it would work. Worry wiggled into her consciousness. Or maybe he knew there was a ritual, and he hoped to enlist her cooperation to perform it with him. And if that was the case, perhaps he didn't mention it hoping that in time she would become so bound to him through their relationship, she wouldn't refuse the request when he made it.

Annie shook her head, refusing to let negativity cloud her brain with such questions. If Tombi was trying to control her through a relationship, he'd be telling her he loved her and promising her the moon instead of keeping his distance.

She continued reading. In order for the containing ritual to work, the tribe leader needed to summon Nalusa with their sacred flute, crafted with the spirits' help. It was ancient, originally created at the time of Nalusa's first rise to power.

Chills tingled up and down Annie's spine. It all came together. Bo's words to find the music contained in the wind. The image of a flute Grandma Tia communicated from her bedside at the hospital.

Find that flute, and they would have the key to defeat Nalusa and his shadow creatures.

Kee-eeeee-ar. A hoarse screeching erupted as a large, rust-colored bird flew close against the windowpane and then jettisoned away in a flurry of beating wings. *Kee-eeeee-ar.*

Beating wings. Just like in her dreams. Annie jumped up and ran to the front door and down the porch steps, but the bird flew into the woods and disappeared. Some animal spirit guide; it did nothing but startle her. A small glint of dusty red and a shiver of movement by the kitchen window caught her eye. She walked across the grass and picked up a feather lying on the sill, fancying it still felt warm to the touch.

A memento from her bird, her guide. She held it in her hands, awed at the physical evidence left behind. Maybe it was like a courtship—every day it would draw closer and reveal more of its nature. Was there some way to thank it for appearing?

She scurried inside and returned with several pieces of bread. She crumbled them in her hands and cast them on the yard. "A little something for you," she called out toward the woods. She liked to think the bird was out there, watching—watching and protecting her from the birds of the night and snakes that crept nearby unawares, coiled to strike with deadly venom.

Annie spun in a dizzy circle of happiness, her heart lightened with optimism and hope. Even if Tombi was consumed with revenge and headed for a showdown with the bayou shadow world, she had not only an ancestor spirit guide, but also an animal guide helping her seek a way to defeat the evil. First, she would conquer evil and prove her trust and worthiness, and then she'd make headway into Tombi's heart and future.

She might just discover a real love.

Over halfway to the hospital, it struck Annie that she hadn't even considered her own need to control her hearing. If she hadn't already lost her heart to Tombi, she was damn close.

Annie burst through his door and found him in the kitchen. Her eyes glowed with excitement, and her aura burst with energy. "Let's go on a hunt tonight."

What the hell had gotten into her? She hated hunting, the stumbling around in the dark and the fear of encountering a snake. Not that Tombi could blame her; she'd witnessed the worst of the worst after Nalusa had almost killed him and her grandmother. He set his glass of tea on the counter. "What brought about this change of heart?"

"I may have found a way to defeat Nalusa." She lifted up an old, thick book with aged, yellow paper poking out of its sides, and rocked on her tiptoes, grinning as she awaited his reaction.

Yeah, right. She'd never heard of Nalusa until last week, and now she had a plan to defeat the king of the shadow world? After he and the other trained hunters had been trying for years with no success? He crossed his arms and leaned against the counter. This should be amusing.

"Aren't you dying to hear?"

"Shoot," he said, lips curving into an indulgent smile.

"It's true. Grandma Tia and my great-great-great-great-grandmother, Belle Hamilton, led me to a possible way."

"I think you added a couple of extra *greats* in there. It would make her close to a couple hundred years old."

Annie blinked. "I didn't say she was *alive*. Anyway, we need to find the ancient flute that your ancestors used to keep Nalusa's power contained."

"Ah, so you heard that old tale. Surprising, though—

it's not a generally known story." He nodded at the book she clutched in front of her. "I guess the story's in there."

The sparkle in her chocolate eyes dwindled. "You already knew about it," she accused. "You might have mentioned it."

"What's to tell? I've never figured there was any truth to it."

"But...but why not? It's a recorded legend by the Choctaws."

"And so are stories of the *Kowi anuskasha*—knee-high fairy creatures said to roam the bayou and play tricks on humans. I don't believe in them, either."

"It's worth a try."

"Only one problem. There is no such flute. Or if there ever was one, it's long since vanished."

"There must be. I heard it playing."

His heartbeat pounded in his ears, like the roar of a million insects on a rain-dampened summer night. This couldn't be. "Say that again."

"I heard the flute. Remember the grimoire Grandma Tia told me to find when she was in the coma? Well, I started reading it when all of a sudden I smelled this distinctive scent that was familiar. I couldn't place it, but when I visited Tia at the hospital she said it was my great-great—"

"Great-great-grandmother," he cut in impatiently. "Tell me the part where you hear the flute."

She frowned but continued on. "Anyway, as I was reading about the legend, the notes of a Native American flute drifted up from the pages. It sounded more primitive than yours. I even know what it looks like." She tapped the aged book. "There's a drawing and a description in here."

Excitement buzzed along his spine. "Let me see."

Annie opened it to a page marked with a red thread and pointed. "Right there."

He carefully took the book, afraid the fragile tome would crumble at rough handling. Tombi scanned the elegant cursive handwriting with its unusual glimmering ink and the dried brown bits of old flowers stuffed in its pages. Halfway down the right page was a drawing of the flute. A design was burned into the cane wood, but a long turkey feather tied at the base obscured the carving.

"Do you have it here in your bookcase?" she asked breathlessly.

He frowned at the description—it could belong to almost any of the reed instruments he'd collected over the years. Of course, the feather would have rotted away by now or have been switched out over the years. Tombi made his way to the den and stood in front of his music collection. Each one had given him so much peace over the years, had inspired him to learn to play and even craft several of his own flutes.

"Did you find these yourself?" Annie asked by his side.

"No. Tallulah works at the local museum, and she alerts me whenever they host a fund-raising auction. That's how I got most of these artifacts, except for the odd pottery shard or arrowhead."

Four of the flutes were made of cane wood and about the length described in Annie's book. He picked them up and showed them to Annie. "Do you think it could be one of these?"

Annie closed her eyes and lifted cupped palms. "Hand me each of them, one at a time."

He did so, despising the flash of hope that flared in his gut. *It's going to be another dead end.* But his gut didn't listen to his mind, and it burned on with unrestrained optimism. He carefully placed one of the flutes in her palms. Annie slowly shook her head "no," a gesture she repeated until he placed the final one in her hands, his hope at last in tatters.

Seconds—or an eternity—passed. "No. This isn't it, either."

Told you so, his inner voice mocked. Tombi put the flutes back on the shelf. "Well, that was fun."

"Are you giving up that easily?"

"You got any other ideas?"

"For starters, we can go to the ancestral land where it says the artifact is stored, see if we can find it."

"It's been tried, not just by me, but also many other hunters over the years. Face it, the flute is long gone—if it ever existed. I think it's all bullshit."

"You're wrong. I know it. I wouldn't have been sent messages if it weren't real. The least we can do is search again. Maybe it's mysteriously turned up?"

Annie was so enthusiastic, so full of optimism. He'd been like that once, so many years ago he'd forgotten what it felt like. Life would crush her spirits eventually, too, but he wouldn't be the one to do it. "Okay. We'll go look. But I'm warning you that the chance of it turning up is extremely remote. But hunting together at night will be good practice for you."

"Part of my training for the next full moon's hunt?"

"Exactly. Plus, it's an opportunity for Bo to speak with you again."

She clasped her hands together. "He might know where the flute's hidden."

"We'll go. I hate to put you in danger, but I promise I won't leave your side."

"I believe you, especially if you keep your other promise to me."

He raised a brow. "Which one?"

"I want you to teach me to control my hearing. I know

you're busy with your work, but surely you can spare an hour every day."

It was only fair. "Let's do it now."

Annie bestowed a dazzling smile. "You don't know how much this means to me."

"Again, don't think this will be easy or a guaranteed success," Tombi cautioned. "I've never tried to help anyone this way, so it's all an experiment."

"I have faith in you."

Unease twisted him inside. *Damn, please, let this work.* Couldn't something go right for once in his life? "Normally, I'd do energy work outside. I have a circle set up with conch shells in the backyard. But right now is too risky. Not when there's a betrayer in the group and not when Nalusa's power's grown so strong he's been active during daylight."

"Inside is better for me anyway," Annie said. "More sound insulation. All the birds and insects drive me nuts, not to mention the rustling leaves and the tide."

"You hear the ocean way out here?"

"Yes, but it's not too bad—it's like a background sound, a white noise that's with me even in dreams." She clapped her hands and glanced about the den. "We can set up a circle right here. You do that, and I'll run upstairs and bring down my altar materials."

"The witchy stuff isn't necessary," he objected.

"I'm so excited right now I can't even get mad at you for that stupid comment." She ran up the stairs, paused halfway and leaned over the railing. "Besides, what could it hurt?"

True. He would need all the help he could get. Tombi walked to the backyard, braving the wave of heat, and gathered the conch shells. Back inside, he pushed the furniture to the walls and formed a circle with the shells. At the center, he unrolled a woolen rug woven by one of his cousins years ago. Amid an indigo background, a large golden sun was woven in the middle. The edges of the rug featured a series of intertwined pyramids.

As he lit a sage smudge stick, Annie returned with an armful of candles and statues and arranged them within the circle. Tombi walked to all four corners of the room, calling on his ancestors for their assistance and driving away any negative energy. He was as ready as he'd ever be. He settled on the rug and watched Annie.

She silently prayed at the altar, kneeling, moving her lips. After finishing, she picked up a spray bottle and walked on the outside of the circle, spritzing. The sweet herbal scent of sage melded with a strong floral scent.

"What are you spraying?"

"It's called Florida Water, one of the oldest hoodoo concoctions. It has bergamot, lavender and clove. I also mixed in a few drops of orange, ginger and pine for extra spiritual power."

They sat across from each other on the floor, cross-legged, letting silence settle in the room. At least, for him, all was quiet. "Do you still hear my energy field sometimes?" he asked, curious.

"Not often. Mostly whenever you let your guard down. Like when you're asleep at night or…" She blushed. "When we make love."

Fascinating. "Do I always sound like the flute?"

"No. When we make love you sound like a drum vibrating with the rhythm of your heart."

He could feel it pulsing now, as it always did when he was close to Annie. The familiarity of having her at his cabin did nothing to dispel his body's immediate reaction to her nearness. If anything, the link between them grew every day.

"We haven't talked about it, but the day I was drugged by Nalusa, I heard you in my mind."

Her eyes widened. "You did?"

"You told me to hold on, that you were near and help was on the way."

"That's what I was thinking."

"There's an energetic bond between us. My parents said they shared one, and Bo and Tallulah shared one. But it's a rare thing."

Annie interlaced her fingers with his own. "I'm honored." She leaned forward and rested her forehead against his.

He felt oddly vulnerable as he absorbed the tenderness through their contact. "That bond will probably grow much closer after this," he warned. "Do you still want to try?"

Annie pulled away and nodded solemnly. "Yes. I trust you completely."

"And I trust you." Somehow, some way, she'd infiltrated his mind and body and…heart. He cared way too much for Annie. Worry about her safety and concern for her future weighed him down, at a time when he should be totally focused on Nalusa.

Her eyes clouded with tears. "Thank you."

"And now we begin. First—"

"Oh, wait, I forgot something that might help us." Annie withdrew her hands from his and stood. "My great-great-great-great-grandmother wasn't my only supernatural visitation today."

He watched as she went to the sofa and rifled through her purse, at last producing a feather. "You were right—my spirit guide is a bird. He made contact with me and left this."

"Some bird." He laughed. "I thought for sure it would be along the lines of a robin or a starling." Something feminine and petite like Annie. But the cinnamon-red tail feather was one he instantly recognized. "This is from a red-tailed hawk. Your bird is a highly intelligent raptor known for its hunting skills and partnership with humans through falconry. An excellent animal guide that will offer you its protection."

"It's huge. A little intimidating even. But I'm sure we'll become great friends. Maybe the feather can help us with the ritual."

"Absolutely." He laid it between them as she resumed sitting across from him.

"All hunters have the skills of night vision, extraordinary hearing, a keen sense of smell or an intuition when the shadows arrive. We can even discern the marks and signs of shadow creatures. And some of us are better at various skills more than others. My specialty is blocking."

"Blocking?"

"I can prevent certain sensations from entering or exiting my energy field. When hunting, it allows me to maintain intense focus while at the same time I can stop others from sensing me. To a degree, that is. It's not like I'm invisible. If a shadow draws close enough, they will hear, smell and see me. But I have a definite edge no one else has. It's why I've been an unofficial leader of the group."

"That's not the only reason," Annie objected. "You would be a leader no matter what. You're smart and courageous and fair. The other hunters recognize those traits in you."

She had too much faith in him. He should warn her off; there was a certain ruthlessness to him that grew sharper from every contact with Nalusa and the wisps. He hated to imagine how much that ruthless nature would have overcome him after Nalusa's bite if Annie and her grandmother hadn't been there. She was truly his savior, although she was too insecure to recognize it.

"At any rate, I'll try to show you how I block sound. I'm not sure you'll be able to do it. I don't know if this is something I inherited, but I do know that over time I've been able to perfect this ability, so maybe some of it is learnable."

"It will be, I can feel it."

A smell of fresh-cut grass quickly followed by a flower aroma wafted through the air. "What the hell is that?"

"Ms. Belle, the great-great-great-great one. She's lending her support and approval."

Would he ever get used to this hoodoo witchy business? Then again, she'd adapted quickly to his fight against the shadow world. If she could deal, he could do the same.

"It's like this. During a hunt, when I'm blocking noise, I visualize sound waves floating toward me in slow motion. At the instant I hear a note, I picture a golden shield of light covering my entire body. As the waves advance toward me, I filter each note through the shield so that the noise is muted. If the will-o'-the-wisps are trying to fill my mind with negative messages, I can entirely block their attempt."

"That's so cool," Annie whispered.

"Let's try something. Describe any sounds you hear now."

She closed her eyes. "I hear the electrical hum of the air conditioner and the refrigerator. Far away, I hear the tide and the screech of a few children playing tag. I hear the whirr of the ceiling fan above and a car passing by on County Road 143."

"Can you hear my energy field?"

She shook her head. "Not at all."

He took a deep breath. He was about to open himself

to someone as deeply as he'd ever allowed. He dropped the normal protective barrier that was his walking-around daily existence. Let it all go in a swoosh that felt like a boulder rolling off his shoulders.

Annie gasped.

Had he released too much? Quickly, Tombi blocked the flow. "Are you okay?"

She inhaled deeply. "Yes."

"What did you hear?"

"It's hard to explain, but the music from your aura was rich and deep and melancholy. I heard the flute, drums, a chanting, a rush of flooding waters, a snake's hissing and rattling, and the music of the wisps, only it was distorted. Instead of alluring, it was frightening and demented."

Rushing waters. Always, his parents' death weighed on his heart and mind. "You nailed it." He shook off the sad memories. "Let's try something. I'm going to play a few musical notes on my cell phone, and you try to picture the sound waves and block them with a golden shield." Tombi withdrew his phone from the back pocket of his jeans. Ready to try?"

Annie nodded.

He hit Play.

Annie screwed up her face. A minute passed.

"Annie? Are you okay?"

She waved him off. "I'm concentrating."

"Sweet Home Alabama" rocked on. When it ended, Tombi shut off his phone.

"Any luck, Annie?"

She opened her eyes and grinned. "Yes! Dammit, it freaking worked. Only for a few seconds, but it worked!"

What a relief, it actually worked. "Good. With practice you can do it for longer periods of time. Don't do too much at first, or you'll get exhausted."

Tears rained down her cheeks. "I can't thank you enough."

"I can think of a few naughty ways you can express your gratitude," he said with a wink.

Annie smiled. "Okay. I'm ready when you are."

"Right here in the circle? Right now? Suits me fine."

Annie sat up, resting on her knees and placing her hand on his shoulders. "Making love to you feels natural and right, whether in a sacred circle or not." A grin swept her face as she tilted her neck upward. "If you're still around, my dear great Ms. Belle, I suggest you leave immediately."

Chapter 13

Tombi pulled Annie's body against him so that his face nestled in her cleavage. For such a petite woman, her breasts were full and luscious. He knew she wore no bra, had been eyeing the peak of her nipples beneath her cotton T-shirt ever since she'd come home from the hospital and changed clothes. He liked that, with him, she was comfortable enough to let loose. Hell, he'd love Annie to loosen up enough that she'd want to parade naked whenever they were alone.

He cupped his hands beneath her breasts and turned his face into one of the ample mounds, kissing her through the thin cotton, until the fabric was wet and rough in his mouth.

Annie groaned and squeezed him tighter, reaching down and pressing her hand against his manhood. It bulged and chafed against his jeans, straining for release. She obliged by unbuttoning his pants and unzipping the jeans.

Reluctantly, he withdrew from sucking a nipple, stood and hastily stepped out of his pants. He bent his knees to sit back down, but Annie had other ideas.

Her mouth was on him, taking in every inch. Tombi placed his hands on her head and ran his fingers through her soft hair.

Sweet, sweet Annie. It felt so damn good. This was what he wanted. Needed. To experience her in every way. But if she didn't stop… Tombi tugged at her hair, and she withdrew.

"What's wrong?" she asked, her voice rough and deep with passion.

"Not a damn thing. It's just your turn." He nodded at her clothes. "Take them off," he demanded.

Annie gave a slow, seductive smile and stood, taking her sweet time as she lifted the shirt up over her breasts and then her head.

He could never get enough of this woman. Ever.

Even slower, Annie hooked her thumbs over her pink gym shorts, taking her lacy panties down with them. She stood before him naked. The sun streaming through the rear window cast beams on her slim figure, as if she were an angel sent from heaven.

Maybe she was.

Her hair cascaded around her shoulders and hips like a curtain. She was the epitome of everything feminine and mysterious. "You're so beautiful," he said, knowing the words were inadequate, but hoping she'd glean the strong emotion behind them.

A blush stained her cheeks, and he even found her sudden modesty touching. Soon, very soon, modesty would have no place in what they were about to do. Annie ducked her head, dark hair falling over olive skin.

Tombi took her hand and tugged. Gracefully, Annie

sank beside him, fluid as water, and stretched her lithe body against the woven rug, covering the sun design at its center. She was a goddess. A witchy goddess, and he was completely under her spell. She affected him like no other woman he'd ever known.

He allowed some of his tight reserve to break free. He wanted to give, to share everything with Annie. With time and practice, he might be able to completely relax his tightly held energy field that separated him from others. One which he donned every morning like an armor.

Tombi parted her thighs and pressed his face into the folds of her hot core and tasted her soft essence. And now she was the one with her hands on his head, pressing him deeper and deeper. His tongue lavished her folds until she writhed against him.

"Now. I want you now," she complained. "Please."

He couldn't wait, either. Tombi lay beside her and lifted her hips so that she straddled him. He entered her, and they moved together in the ancient dance of humankind.

It was an electrical storm of passion, as need rumbled in his heart and manhood. His blood pounded faster, straining and crackling in the tempest that was Annie. Her high-pitched moans roared in his mind, but he held back his own release until her thighs and core convulsed, signaling her climax. He let go all restraint, exploding like thunder deep within Annie.

She sank her body on top of his, and he ran his fingers through her hair, utterly sated.

"Am I getting heavy?" She slipped off him and folded herself against his side.

"Not at all." He rested his hand on the slim curve of her hips and ran his fingers over the small of her back.

Annie yawned.

"Why don't you take a nap?" he suggested. "It's going to be a long night."

"Does that mean we're going to go look for the flute?" She propped up on her elbow, eyes aglow.

"It does."

"This will be fun. A treasure hunt."

Huh. When was the last time he'd had an *enjoyable* hunt? Never, actually. He vowed not to get his hopes up about finding the flute. He could just enjoy the night with Annie and help her practice blocking skills and the ability to maneuver in the darkness together.

Tombi gently kissed her cheek. "Sleep well. For tonight, we hunt."

Kee-eeeee-ar. Three seconds elapsed. *Kee-eeeee-ar.* Another three seconds of silence.

Her hawk followed them as they went deeper into the woods, and after the initial surprise, Annie found the bird's calls reassuring. He was guarding her, offering his protection. She took it as a good omen. A sign that something special would take place this evening.

Annie gripped Tombi's hand firmly, determined to match his long strides. The waning moon didn't provide much light. Not even will-o'-the-wisp smoke glowed in the forest, not that she could see much at any rate.

Tombi stopped abruptly, and she realized she was on the muddy bank where she'd first met him and where Bo had first appeared. So much had happened since then, it seemed like months ago instead of a mere week.

"This is where my ancestors once prayed and petitioned the great spirits. And it's where they imprisoned Nalusa."

"Do you know which tree to check for the flute?" she whispered close to his ear.

"There's only one that has a hollow in its center."

Annie kept walking beside him and almost ran into the towering oak a few feet in front of them.

"This is it." Tombi dropped her hand and peered into the opening.

Suspense shivered along her spine. "Well? Do you see anything?"

He straightened. "Nothing. It's empty."

Shock doused her faith. "But… I don't get it. We were led here." She forgot to whisper, so deep was her disappointment. "Are you sure there's nothing in there?" She peered down the tree hollow for herself but couldn't make out anything in the darkness.

"Positive."

Annie kicked the tree, angry tears of disappointment welling under her eyelids. She hadn't realized how much she'd depended on the legend being true. She'd wanted to be a help to Tombi, especially after all he was doing for her. Instead, she looked like a fool. An optimistic, mystical idiot chasing unicorns. "Damn it. Why'd they even bother making contact with me if it's all nothing but a myth?"

"Hey, it was worth exploring," he said gently, wrapping his arms around her waist. "I didn't expect anything tonight. No harm done."

"No harm?" She laughed bitterly against his chest. "Feels like our last chance was snatched away."

"We'll keep trying to contact Bo. If he can identify who's destroying us from the inside, we might be able to regroup. And it's still possible you might pick up a sign around one of the hunters during an unguarded moment."

"I'll do anything," she promised.

Tombi pulled away and regarded her sternly. "Nothing risky. There's still much you have to learn."

"Then teach me. Now."

He looked around the woods. "Not here. Let's head home."

Home. The sweet sound of the word rumbled inside her with longing. *Don't make too much of it.* Tombi hadn't said he loved her, and he clearly had no designs for long-range planning, other than to do his duty by his people.

If only they could have met under different circumstances. Well, she wasn't giving up yet. There must be something she could do, some way to help Tombi, other than being with him on a hunt in case she heard Bo or an approaching wisp before he heard it. She vowed to find a way. She'd come out alone and find Bo, ask him what had happened to the flute. She'd work spells to find the betrayer, ask her hawk to lead her to the flute, if there was one, and visit every single hunter on her own in the hopes of catching them off guard—especially Tallulah. And if Grandma Tia came home soon, she could be a powerful ally in sorting out this dilemma.

Black shadows lightened by degrees to silver and ash. Perhaps Tombi was right that, with practice, her night vision would acclimate, or at least not be so dismally poor. There was so little time left, and she needed to work every second to hone her own skills and prepare for the next shadow encounter.

His battle had become her battle, as well. They were a team. No matter what happened the next full moon, Annie knew she'd never leave the bayou, would never leave Tombi and this dangerous, mysterious, haunting bayou world.

It was in her blood. Her crazy, mixed Cajun/Native American/Caucasian blood that fit in nowhere but Bayou La Siryna. Crazy Annie could live here in this crazy swampland. And she wanted to share this life with Tombi.

She loved him.

And she'd take what time they had together, whatever Tombi was willing to share, whatever the number of weeks before the shadow world might smother the light and capture their souls. Annie gripped Tombi's hand as they walked in the dark woods, aware of his hot body, his energy expanding to include her in a protective shield.

Back at the cabin, Tombi lit the fire pit on the deck. "I'd hoped not to frighten you too much, but if you're going to go in the woods at night, you need to know about all the night's creatures."

"You mean, there's more?" Annie shuddered, remembering Nalusa as a giant snake.

"You've seen the worst, but there are others besides Nalusa, the wisps and the birds of the night. If you hear a fox bark or an owl screech, others of their kind will bark and screech in reply. You already know that these animal sounds foretell bad news. But if an animal makes a noise and there's no like response, it means that the *shilombish* is imitating the animal to cause trouble and grief."

"The *shilombish*?" she asked.

"A restless spirit who roams the earth."

"What do they look like?"

"They have no shape or form, but are merely spirit. They can't hurt you. Their only power is to frighten and confuse people."

She shook her head, bewildered at the news that the dark force was even stronger than she first realized. "Why don't the wisps capture these spirits?"

"Because they are the outside shadows. The wisps can only capture the *shilup*, men's inside shadow, which is supposed to cross to the land of ghosts after death."

"So the spirit that helped me that night was a *shilup*."

"Right. You have nothing to fear from them. They long to leave the bayou as quickly as they can. And there are a few other supernatural beings who won't harm you, but it's best if you know of their existence."

Wow. Annie wondered if her grandma was aware of all this. If so, she'd never even hinted at it.

Tombi poked the fire with a stick, and an arc of sparks crackled. "There's Kashehotapalo, who's a combination of man and deer. Even though he's frightened hunters in the past, our people admire him for his speed and agility. He's harmless unless you rouse his anger. In that case, he will find your enemy and warn them of your presence."

Such a creature was hard to visualize; it sounded so far-fetched. "Have you seen him?"

"I caught a glimpse of him once. Otherwise, I would never have believed he existed and put the legend down as a fairy tale."

"Like you do the fairies. Maybe you just haven't seen them yet. Are they said to be dangerous?"

"No. Their worst trick is to throw stones or rocks at people as a joke. Supposedly, they're only a couple of feet tall and dwell in the deepest recesses of the bayou."

"They don't sound so bad. Anything else?"

Tombi hesitated.

"Go on," she prodded. "Nothing could be stranger than the half-man, half-deer creature."

"Just in case you're ever roaming the woods and decide to take a dip in the waters to cool off, be sure not to swim anywhere there's a white patch, because that's where the *Okwa Naholo* live."

"Underwater creatures?"

"Yep. The translation is 'white people of the water' be-cause they have light flesh like the skins of trout."

Annie tingled inside. "Mermaids?"

He gave a crooked smile. "Exactly. And if you invade

their territory, they'll capture you and turn you into be-ings like themselves."

"Pretty cool, actually. Not getting captured—but the idea that mermaids exist. Most little girls dream of being one. I think they represent the epitome of feminine power and beauty."

Tombi shrugged. "It's another one of the tales I'm skep-tical about." He leaned back in his chair. "Anything you believe I should know about hoodoo?"

"Not really. We try to bend the natural laws for heal-ing and to bring us luck in love and money." She laughed self-consciously. "Not that my life is an example of either."

Tombi regarded her soberly. "Your luck could change."

Annie's heart hopscotched along her rib cage. Did that mean he loved her? Secretly, she believed her fortune *had* changed. Despite the setbacks, she knew what it was like to love a good man. A man worth fighting for. A man worth risking her heart, her pride, her life.

Pop. A large ember from the fire flamed and jumped in the air, breaking the moment.

"I still can't believe we didn't get the flute," Annie com-plained.

"More than likely, it never existed."

She couldn't believe it. There was some reason Ms. Belle and the hawk had arrived at the moment she read about the legend. Some reason that Tia had visualized the grimoire while in a coma.

"All that was in the book was that the flute helped con-tain Nalusa and where to find it. Is there more to the leg-end than what I read?"

"It's said our ancestors used it whenever Nalusa grew too strong and disrupted the balance of light and shadow. If that happened, the tribe would gather for a full-moon ritual and play the flute. Nalusa would be drawn to the music, but could only appear in his visible, half-human form and not sneak up on them like a snake."

Annie shuddered, wondering if that version of Nalusa was less scary than the snake. "What does he look like in this half-human form?"

"He's named after his half-human form. In Choctaw, Nalusa Falaya literally means a 'long black being.' It was said he resembled a man but had tiny eyes and long, pointed ears."

She couldn't picture it. "I'm thinking of snake eyes and donkey ears, and the two don't seem to go together."

"Is it any harder to imagine than the religious tradition of a pitchfork-carrying devil with a red body, hoofed feet and horns for ears?"

He had a point.

"But why would your ancestors want to draw Nalusa to them—no matter what shape-shifting form he chooses? Personally, I don't ever want to see him again."

"According to legend, while he's exposed in human form, he's vulnerable. The legend also says that only in this form can we force him back into his resting place and bind his power."

She remembered the tightness in her chest as they approached the tree, the lingering miasma of evil. Some of his malevolent energy had marked his former prison. "He was trapped inside the hollowed oak, right? I felt a heaviness there, the way misery feels when it crushes you inside."

"That's his mark. He feeds on human grief and misery. It's what makes you vulnerable to his will. It weakens your fight and warps your thinking."

"Like it has the betrayer in your group," she said softly. And who among his circle had suffered the most?

Tallulah.

She'd been grief-stricken over Bo's death. And the mourning had left her susceptible to Nalusa's voice whispering in her mind, murmuring dissent as poisonous as his venom injected in a blood vein. Couldn't Tombi see the obvious? But Annie kept her mouth shut. *Blood's thicker than water.* He'd known her a week; he'd known his twin since the womb.

Time to pay Tallulah a visit. Maybe invite her over for dinner and slip a little hoodoo concoction in her drink. Once her guard was down, Annie would listen in on her aura. Not something she was looking forward to. Annie imagined the noise from her damaged aura would be akin to nails scraping chalkboard—times a million. And how could she ever break the news to Tombi?

His mouth pressed into a grim line. "Whoever it turns out to be, I'll have no sympathy. A warrior's mind and body never breaks."

"Not everyone has your strength."

"I would expect any of the hunters to confide in me if they were in danger of succumbing to the shadows."

He was in for a huge disappointment. "Could be they are too ashamed. Or maybe the darkness in their minds crept up on them so gradually they didn't realize the danger until it was too late."

"He should know better."

Or *she* should know better. But Annie wasn't brave enough to speak the words aloud. Tombi had been angry before when she'd suggested Hanan—how much more upset would he be if she suggested his sister? His twin, no less.

"Enough talk of Nalusa," he cut in, his voice as rough as oak bark. "We've done all we can do for tonight. Tomorrow will be here soon enough with its worries and duties."

Annie reached out a hand and touched his knee. "And

whatever comes, I'm here to help. Anything you need me to do."

His mouth twisted. "If there's any way possible, I'll shield you from seeing Nalusa again."

"Don't even think it. You need me with you, and you know it."

Tombi stood and stretched. "We won't speak of it anymore tonight." He took her hand and lifted Annie to her feet. "We've better things to do."

She couldn't agree with him more. Tombi might skirt expressing his feelings for her, but his body had a language all its own. And his body said he loved her, too, even if his lips never formed the words.

Chapter 14

The dark of the moon settled into the night, smothering the bayou like thick fog. Annie lit every candle she'd gathered from her grandma's cottage, until Tombi's cabin glowed as if a thousand stars were contained within its rough-hewn walls.

The past two weeks had been filled with training sessions as Tombi, true to his word, initiated her more deeply into blocking external stimuli as well as containing the amount of energy she released into the world.

Too bad she and her grandma didn't call on the questionable, seamier side of hoodoo, since amoral spirits were more accessible at the New Moon. She'd been so tempted last week during the dark-moon phase. She could use some extra supernatural help—if the old tales were true that she'd overheard in whispered conversations behind closed doors.

Don't go there, Grandma Tia had warned a hundred times, wagging a finger. *The ends never justify the means*.

You start dabbling in that mess, you might get sucked into their evil forever.

As a child, whenever Annie had heard those warnings, she'd pictured a giant hand rising up from the swamp and curling its fingers toward her, beckoning her to come and sink into the murky depths from which it supernaturally emerged. A quicksand of destruction for the unwary.

Frightened the hell out of her.

For the second time in her life, Annie considered the consequences of calling on a dark spirit. Only a few weeks earlier she'd also contemplated the same—desperate to stop the blaring music that assaulted her mind. But the childhood nightmare of the beckoning hand always stopped her from such invocations. Better a quick death from a venom-filled fang than the agony of a slow drown in the swamp.

Pick your own poison, Annie-Girl.

The choice was easy.

Annie frowned at the kitchen window. The gleaming black pane seemed like the core of a pupil in a giant eye that watched her and waited. If Tombi had bothered with curtains, she'd have drawn them over the window like an eyelid, sealing shut the outside world. She quit stirring the large iron pot and rubbed her forearms that prickled with unease.

"Something wrong?"

Annie spun around. "I didn't hear you come in."

His smile was quick and warmer than the heat emanating from the stove. "I'm known for sneaking up on wisps, but for *you* not to hear me is quite a feat."

"All your lessons are helping me block sound for longer periods of time."

"Good." He sidled up beside her at the counter and

peeked in the oven. "Chicken's done. Another fifteen minutes on the huckleberry cake."

"Hominy's ready and water's boiling for the banaha."

"I'll take care of the bread," he said, giving his hands a quick wash at the sink, before mushing together the cooked field peas and cornmeal.

Annie watched his dark, muscled forearms as he shaped small rectangles from the mush and set them to the side on a dish. Quickly, she removed the roasted chicken from the oven and put the dirty mixing bowls in the dishwasher. "I can help with that," she said. "Let me finish the patties while you wrap them."

They fell into a companionable silence as Tombi enfolded the rectangles in dried corn husks and dropped them in boiling water. She'd been skeptical at first, but the traditional Choctaw bread, banaha, was surprisingly good. Tombi had explained that for centuries, hunters had eaten this bread for the sustained energy provided by the complete protein.

"We make a pretty good team," she remarked.

Tombi shot her a slow, sexy smile that made her insides flame. A smile that promised another night of passion and enchantment. Heat chased across her neck and cheeks.

"Still shy?"

Tombi playfully slapped her ass, and she laughed.

Annie had never been this happy—so long as it was just the two of them alone in the cabin. Each day, Tombi let go of his reserve a fraction and spoke to her of happier times before Nalusa had broken his confinement and began wreaking havoc. Each day she'd opened up more on her difficult relationship with her mother. And each night they made passionate love, interspersed with such moments of tenderness that Annie felt sure of his affection, even if he hadn't professed his love—yet.

But to Annie's frustration, she could never catch the sly Tallulah unawares. They were no closer to naming their betrayer. As usual, she pushed the reminder aside, determined to enjoy their shared meal. Every moment they spent together was precious. In her heart, she tried to impress every detail to memory, wanting to remember everything in case… No, it didn't help to dwell on the possibilities of everything that could go wrong at the next full moon.

They sat down to eat the mini feast. Tombi eagerly eyed the golden and purple huckleberry cake throughout dinner. Annie delighted in his pure enjoyment of her cooking whenever he spooned in mouthfuls of the baked berries crusted in a butter and flour pastry.

"How's your grandma doing at rehab today?" he asked.

Annie swallowed a spoonful of the hominy. She still preferred grits but accepted hominy as its grainier cousin. "Grandma's giving the physical therapists hell. Which means she's feeling a whole lot better. They told me she can come home in another two or three weeks."

"When I visited yesterday, she was barking orders at the staff, saying all she needed was to go home and pray at her altar and drink her special tea. The staff thinks she's a bit of a crackpot."

Annie laughed. "I can't see her staying more than another week there before the doctors gladly sign off on the release papers just to stop hearing her fuss."

"She can complain all she wants," Tombi said firmly. "I'll never forget that she saved my life. If there's a way to repay her for—"

A heavy thud bumped against the kitchen window where a ruddy-colored ball of fur rustled. *Ker-thump.* Annie dropped her spoon and watched as it whacked against the window again. A scraping of talons against glass made her entire body wince and curl in upon itself.

"What the hell?" Tombi pushed away his plate and jumped up. "Your hawk's here."

The raptor had drawn closer every day while she hunted with Tombi and had appeared with increasing frequency in her dreams, but it hadn't been this close since it had made its first appearance at her grandma's cottage.

"What do you think it wants?"

"Only one way to know for sure." Tombi hurried to the den, grabbing his knapsack filled with rocks and sling-shots.

"Don't you dare hurt him," she said, following close behind.

"Of course I won't. I'm bringing ammo in case he's alerting us to trouble outside."

Trouble. Her stomach roiled, but she needed to buck up and go out there with Tombi and face the hawk. *Her* hawk. Annie sighed as she quickly slid into her shoes by the front door. Why couldn't her animal guide have been something friendly and nonviolent like a cute little chipmunk?

Kee-eeeee-ar. The screech erupted the moment they opened the door. The hawk beat its wings and flew toward the woods, glancing back at them in a command to follow. *Kee-eeeee-ar.*

Tonight, its squawks were higher-pitched and the cries closer together. Annie didn't need Tombi to explain that this signaled distress. Something was wrong.

Everything raced—feet, heart, mind—as she sprinted through the field after Tombi. Had Nalusa struck again? Had the wisps killed and captured another's soul?

The world darkened a shade as they entered the woods. Annie tried to keep up with Tombi as he forged ahead, chasing the hawk's cries. The crunch of twigs and dried leaves underfoot was a symphony of disaster. Over the jarring sounds of brokenness, musical notes clamored for attention. Annie halted and put her hands on her knees, panting. "Stop!"

Tombi came to her at once. "Out of breath?"

"Do you hear music?" she asked, holding a finger to her lips.

He cocked his head for a moment. "I don't hear anything."

The notes tantalized her memory. They were familiar, haunting… Excitement inched up her spine. "It's the flute!"

Tombi's expression was blank.

"*The* flute," she explained eagerly. "The one I heard through the pages of the grimoire. The one of legend. My hawk's leading us to it."

"How can you know it's the same flute?"

"It has a more primitive sound, with a reedy kind of twang. I'd recognize it anywhere."

His face tightened. "Who would have it? And why would they summon Nalusa? This might be another trap."

Annie shook her head. "My hawk wouldn't draw us into danger. He's trying to help us."

"Maybe."

A whoosh of wings, then a cry, bleated above them.

"We should go." Annie tried for a smile of encouragement, even while the thought of Nalusa made her lungs freeze with fear.

Tombi remained rooted to the spot, frowning. "I hate exposing you to danger."

Every cell in her body screamed *run*, but Annie overrode the scared demand. "You need me. Besides, this could be your chance. Get the flute, and Nalusa is yours."

He squeezed his eyes shut and nodded. "I know. Stay close behind me and let's try to be a little quieter."

Annie lifted her neck and stared at the piercing eyes upon her. *Quiet*, she mouthed, placing an index finger on her pursed lips. She placed a hand on Tombi's shoulder. "If you're planning a sneak attack, I'll lead since I'm the one tracking the sounds."

Tombi's mouth twisted in a grimace, but he nodded his acceptance.

Hesitantly, Annie walked forward, pausing every few steps to listen to the faint music. Above and in front, her hawk flew low, giving her confidence that she was headed in the right direction. On she plowed, heart hammering in anticipation. Tombi didn't say it, but whoever was playing the flute must be the betrayer. Any of the other hunters who came in possession of it would have alerted the group immediately, and they would have rallied together to fight Nalusa and his shadow creatures.

And if the betrayer was playing it, why did he want to speak with Nalusa? It could only be to share more damning information on the tribe's secrets and plans.

The flute grew louder, and she recognized where they were—the ancient tribal ground said to house Nalusa. Slowly, stealthily, they made their way to a parting in the trees. A person sat on the felled oak, elbows lifted and crooked, a flute held to their lips. A long black braid fell down their back, which could have been any of the hunters.

Annie studied the figure. As the betrayer shifted their position on the log, the profile gave away the identity. *Damn. Why couldn't it have been anyone else?*

Tombi's swift inhalation from behind meant he recognized the betrayer at the same moment she did.

Tallulah.

Na haksichi. The rogue, the betrayer.

His very own twin, the only one of two people in the world who had heard their mother's heart beat from the womb. Pain flayed inside Tombi, a vivid crimson that burned and coated his retinas like an infrared filter, obscuring his normally keen vision.

He plunged through dense saw palmettos, uncaring of the noise. Let Tallulah see him, let her view his full fury, let her know that he found her utterly despicable.

"*Aholabi!* Liar!" he shouted, brushing past Annie's outstretched hand.

His sister jumped up and swung to face him, freezing like a cornered deer ready to take flight.

"It was you all along." He lobbed his words like darts. "*Na haksichi.* Betrayer. Why?"

Her eyes narrowed, and she gripped the flute tightly in her fist, holding it out with a defiant lift of her chin. "You would never understand."

"Tell me." He stopped before her, hands fisted at his sides. If this were anyone but his sister, he'd pummel the truth out of the man.

"I did it for Bo." Her voice was like torn strips of paper shredded from her soul.

"Bo?" Dread was a boulder weighting his feet to the earth, anchoring an urge to walk away from Tallulah's confession. He'd lost his parents and discovered his sister was a traitor. Was it too much to ask that the memory of his best friend be preserved? "Bo has nothing to do with this," he ground out.

"He has everything to do with this." She nodded at the flute. "This can bring him back to me."

"Where the hell did you get a crazy idea like that? You've no idea what you've done."

Annie stepped between them and cast worried glances around the woods. "Aren't you worried Nalusa is here? Tallulah's been playing it for at least a few minutes."

"Let him come. If he's hiding behind a tree, it's because

he's vulnerable." Tombi raised his voice. "Come out, you coward. I'll take you on right now."

Annie shook her head, eyes wide with fear. "Stop. This isn't the time or place. Remember the legend? Wait for the full moon. Wait for the other hunters to be with you."

Tallulah laughed. A mad, eerie laugh fit for an insane asylum. "That old legend? This flute has no power against Nalusa."

"Give it to me," Tombi said between clenched teeth.

Tallulah snatched the flute to her chest, like a child protecting a toy. "No. It's mine."

Not for long. Tombi stepped forward. Sister or not, he *would* get that flute. "I said, give it to me."

Annie's slight head shake drew his attention. What was she about?

She turned to Tallulah. "If you don't believe the flute has power, why do you want to keep it?"

Her voice was calm and soothing. A mother placating an unreasonable child. Tombi wanted to shake sense into his sister, but maybe Annie's approach was best.

"I didn't say it was powerless." Her eyes watered. "Although it's done nothing for me yet."

Annie stepped a little closer to Tallulah. "What do you expect it to do?"

Tallulah dropped her head. A wailing, ruined cry spewed from deep within her.

He couldn't help it, pity snuffed out the worst of his rage. Tombi had seen her like this only twice before, at their parents' funeral and at Bo's death side.

"It's supposed to...to..." She swallowed hard. "I thought that if I stole this from the museum and played it in the woods, Bo would find me."

She raised her head and gave Annie a hard look. "But

he never came to me. Only to you. Why would he do that? I hate you!"

Annie winced and took a step backward.

"Stop it, Tallulah," he ordered. His sympathy dried up at her treatment of Annie. "I can't believe you let Nalusa's shadows warp your mind this way. You betrayed us all for nothing."

"I knew you'd turn on me. You've never loved anyone in your life. You're a heartless robot. All you care about is fighting."

Indignation left him speechless. Tallulah had betrayed them all, and *he* was the bad guy now?

"That's not true," Annie said quietly.

In his anger, he'd almost forgotten she was there.

Annie gazed at him with a soft radiance lit within her brown eyes, like candle glow in the night. It warmed him inside. "Your brother is capable of great love," she said, a soft smile trembling on her lips.

"What do you know?" His sister's voice cut like broken glass. "So what if Tombi sleeps with you? Nothing's more important to him than his battles with the shadow world. You're just a…a…diversion."

Tombi sucked in his breath at the stark cruelty of his twin. Annie didn't deserve her vindictiveness.

Tallulah faced him. "That's what Courtney, your last girlfriend, told me."

"Is that so? And what is Hanan to you if nothing but a diversion?"

Tallulah gasped.

"You don't think I know about your late-night visits in his tent? Don't give me this crap about how much you loved Bo."

"Please, don't, you two." Annie looked back and forth

between them, distress lines marring her face. "You're family."

Tallulah sank to her knees, sobbing. This was the worst he'd ever seen her.

"If you knew what it was like to love—really love somebody—you'd understand. Hanan helps me forget when the pain and loneliness are too much to bear. I would trade my soul to speak with Bo one last time."

"That's exactly what you've done. Traded your soul. But the worst part is that you placed us all in jeopardy by keeping the flute for yourself. Every day, Nalusa and the shadows grow, and yet you selfishly said nothing about the flute. How long have you had it?"

"A few weeks. It's worthless."

So quickly, he could do nothing but watch, Tallulah stood and flung the flute into the air with all her strength. The wooden reed twirled and spun in the treetops, blending into the brown-and-green canopy of oaks and pine.

And then it began its inevitable fall back to earth. The fragile, ancient instrument that was the only hope of containing Nalusa. His heart fell along with it. Surely it would crash and splinter on the ground upon impact.

Kee-eeeee-ar. The hawk swooped down and gathered the flute in his beak.

Relief washed over him in a wave—until the hawk ascended back to the treetops, taking the flute with him. *Damnation.* Tombi hastily pulled the knapsack from his shoulders and opened it, gathering his slingshot.

"What are you doing?" Annie asked in alarm.

"Getting the flute back."

He placed a rock in the sling and drew back the elastic band.

"No!" Annie launched herself at him.

Just as he released the band, she grabbed his arm and

changed the trajectory of the rock. It harmlessly thudded against a tall pine, several feet from the perched hawk.

Its loud screech thwacked the air, and Tombi could have sworn it mocked him. He shook off Annie's arm to try again, but the hawk flapped its massive wings and flew off, taking Tombi's last hope with him.

"We're doomed," he said flatly.

"We always have been," Tallulah lashed out. "I don't care, either. Not if I can't be with Bo."

Annie hugged her chest, wide eyes on him. "I'm sorry. I…I couldn't let you shoot the hawk. He's my animal guide."

"I only meant to have the stone be a near miss. Enough to scare him into dropping the flute." He wanted to reassure her, to lie and say everything would be okay. But the lie died on his lips. To have had a chance, to be so, so close, only to have it snatched away at the last second. It was all too much.

Tombi turned to his sister. "You have no idea what you've done," he said harshly. "Hunters have been injured and placed in jeopardy, all because of your treachery."

Her tears dried up. "I had nothing to do with that."

"Liar. I don't believe anything you say. I'll never trust you again."

His sister's lower lip trembled. "I'm telling you the truth. I would never help Nalusa in an ambush. I was going to give you the flute eventually. I just wanted to contact Bo first."

"Always thinking of yourself and what you want." Tombi pulled his knapsack back over his shoulders. "From now on, you'll have all the time in the world to be selfish. You are no longer one of us. Don't embarrass yourself and show up at the next hunt."

Her eyes widened. "You're banishing me?"

He hardened his heart. After all, the lives of others depended on them working together as a team. As such, absolute trust among them was needed. There was no room for someone like Tallulah. He turned his back on his sister.

"Wait!"

Her anguished cry squeezed his heart, but his feet never hesitated. She had left him no choice.

Two more steps and he halted. "Annie?" Why wasn't she by his side? He didn't turn around, not wanting to face Tallulah again.

A rustle of leaves and pine needles, and Annie stood before him.

"You were pretty harsh back there."

He stared at her incredulously. "I can't believe you—of all people—would care. Tallulah's given you nothing but grief."

"It doesn't matter. She's your sister, your twin. You can't disown her."

The anger and frustration erupted once more. "I can do what I damn well want. You don't know what you're talking about."

Annie stiffened. "Stop being an ass."

The insult cut to the bone. After two weeks of staying together at the cabin, he thought of them as one, united. But at the first opportunity, Annie took the side of a woman who had shown her nothing but scorn. A woman who had betrayed him and the other hunters in the worst possible way. Annie had gone too far. "Fine. Stay here and let Tallulah cry on your shoulder. She won't thank you for it."

"I will stay."

Her stubborn streak surprised him. "Look, don't let her fool you. She's put all of us in danger, you included."

"Can't you bend a little? Show forgiveness?"

"Not on this. She's destroyed my hope."

"Don't you mean I have?" Annie asked with a gentle stillness that ripped at his conscious. "It was my hawk that flew away with the flute. Do you blame me, as well?"

The word *no* wouldn't come. He stood mute, unable to say it. Unable to give Annie the reassurance she wanted. Logically, he couldn't blame her; she didn't control the hawk. But something in him had snapped, was beyond reason.

At the prolonged silence, Annie flinched as if he had struck her.

"I see," she drawled. "I feel sorry for you, Tombi. Hate and revenge have consumed your heart. Tallulah's right about that. There's no room in it for love."

"Wait." He placed his hand on her arm, dismayed at the tears swimming in her dark eyes. "She's wrong."

Annie waited.

"It's just—I can't make any promises. The situation is too bleak. It wouldn't be fair to either one of us."

"I'm not afraid to say how I feel. I love you, Tombi."

No. Not now. He couldn't think about it. To fall in love would weaken his focus. How could he organize and fight Nalusa while worrying over a loved one's safety? "Don't," he said harshly.

"Too late." She attempted a smile and a light tone, but the hurt in her brown eyes muddied the light that usually gleamed in them.

He was responsible for that.

"I'm—"

She shook her head. "Don't say you're sorry. If you don't feel it, you don't feel it. At least you didn't lie to me."

She walked back to Tallulah, and he trudged back to the cabin. Alone. The weight of his aloneness smothered his hope even more than the loss of the flute and the betrayal of his twin.

They were right. He'd lost his capacity to love. Tombi shivered in the muggy heat. Nalusa had as good as won the battle.

Chapter 15

"Why did you come back?" Tallulah frowned and narrowed her eyes. "Go on. I don't need you."

Tombi was right. There was no winning with his temperamental sister. Annie sighed. She longed to run after him. But she had her pride, and she wouldn't beg someone for their love. He either felt it or he didn't. She had deluded herself thinking Tombi felt something stronger between them. Oh, she was convenient, and he liked her well enough, but Crazy Annie had struck out once again.

Tallulah swiped a hand across her cheeks and sniffed.

Annie couldn't help but sympathize. She was close to tears herself. "Come to my grandmother's cottage with me, and I'll fix you something to eat and drink."

"I'm not hungry." Tallulah frowned again, but her eyes threatened to spill tears.

An unexpected smile broke across Annie's face.

"What's so funny?" Tallulah asked suspiciously.

"You. You're just like your brother. So prickly." And so proud. Too proud to admit they ever needed anybody.

"What do you see in him? That relationship will never go anywhere. You know that, right?"

Annie's smile wilted. "Bet no one ever accused you of being a Little Miss Sunshine. Ever."

Tallulah snorted.

"That's what I thought. Stay here and cry your eyes out, then. I'm leaving."

Annie started down the path in the opposite direction of Tombi. To hell with both of them and their damn arrogance. She had her own dignity, and her temper was at a breaking point. She marched on, seething at fate. Useless, but it kept her heart from breaking at Tombi's silence after she'd spilled her guts. And why had her own animal spirit even betrayed her trust? Maybe she was as deluded and deceived as Tallulah by placing her faith in the wrong place.

Annie stomped through the path, crushing pine needles and twigs beneath her feet. Sweat steamed on her sticky flesh as she pressed on in the gathering twilight. Damn mosquitoes would eat her up before she arrived home.

A stinging pain whiplashed across her jaw and neck. She'd carelessly run into a thick, jutting limb.

A snicker sounded from behind. Annie turned, surprised to find Tallulah a mere ten feet away. Annoyance prickled her burning welt. "Are you following me or heading in the same direction?"

Tallulah shrugged. "Guess I could use a bite to eat after all."

Annie's temper melted at the admission, but she hid her smile. "Suit yourself." On she went until she reached the clearing. No light shone in the cottage. It wasn't the same without Grandma Tia. She longed for the light and warmth of Tombi's cabin. Instead, she was stuck with the cold Tallulah and an empty house.

"Is that your place?" Tallulah asked, stepping to her side. "It's so tiny."

Yep. A real ray of sunshine that one was. Annie kept walking, Tallulah close by.

"What does your name mean in Choctaw?" she asked, more to keep her mind occupied from Tombi's rejection than a burning urge to know more about his twin.

"Leaping water. Why?"

Annie thought of bubbling brooks, gurgling streams and effervescent bubbles. Happy, excited sounds and movement. Tallulah's name fit her about as poorly as Tombi's representing a warm glowing sun.

"Just curious."

Tallulah shot her a suspicious look. "Are you named after someone? *Annie* is so common."

"Meaning that I'm also common? You really shouldn't insult someone about to feed you."

"Whatever."

Annie retrieved the spare key from beneath a flowerpot on the porch and unlocked the door.

Stale incense and dust tickled her nose as they entered. "It smells funny in here," Tallulah complained.

"Yeah, well, no one's been here in a couple of weeks." Annie flipped on lights and turned up the AC. "Let's go in the kitchen."

She was conscious of Tallulah's damning assessment of the cottage. Her face puckered in disapproval as she pulled out a chair and sat at the kitchen table. "Guess all the candles and herbs are for y'all's witchy stuff."

Annie didn't bother replying but retrieved a couple of glasses from the cupboard and poured tap water into them.

"Here." She plopped one in front of Tallulah. "You hungry?"

"I could use a bite if you're eating, too."

"Tombi and I already ate." She pictured the simple meal they'd shared. How contented she'd felt a mere two hours earlier. That would teach her to think life had turned around for the better. Annie opened the freezer. "I can offer you a fried chicken TV dinner or a pint of salted-caramel ice cream."

"Ice cream."

Figured. Annie had wanted that for herself. She handed her guest a spoon and the pint, thinking longingly of the huckleberry cake at Tombi's. Resolutely, she turned on the stove burner to heat the teapot. A good cup of rosemary and mint tea to refresh their spirits. Annie mixed together some herbs into a sachet as Tallulah ate.

"Hey, what are you doing there?" Tallulah asked around a mouthful of ice cream. "I want plain black tea without that herbal stuff. Or coffee."

Suspicious as her brother. "You'll drink what I'm fixing, and I need this concoction."

Tallulah sniffed, but when the cup was placed in front of her she sipped it experimentally. "It's actually pretty good," she admitted grudgingly.

"So, how did you come in possession of the flute?" Annie asked, sitting down and leaning back in her chair.

"Does it matter? Your stupid hawk flew off with it. Not my fault it's gone." She bent over her cup and gulped down more.

Apparently, nothing was ever Tallulah's fault. Annie held her tongue. Tombi had been so angry, he'd neglected to get the details. But she wanted some answers.

"It's important we figure out everything together so

we can get the flute back and find out who's really the betrayer."

Tallulah's neck snapped up. "You don't think it's me?"

"No."

"Why not?"

"I think you were duped. You weren't out seeking Nalusa and trading information for your own benefit. I believe what you said, only wanting to conjure Bo."

Tallulah set her cup down. "You're right," she answered softly.

"Tell me who put you up to it."

"Nobody. One of the archaeology crews found that old flute on a dig, and they brought it to the Cultural Center to be archived. I always guessed that it held powerful magic. Then yesterday, when everyone went home after five, something came over me. I *had* to have that flute. I can't explain it."

Annie nodded. "Go on."

"That's it. I went out to the woods, and this crazy notion wouldn't get out of my brain that if I played it, Bo would magically appear."

"Nalusa must have planted that idea in your brain, then."

Tallulah's brow furrowed. "But the flute makes Nalusa weaker, forces him to appear as himself and not in snake form. Why would he want me to play it?"

"Because, even weakened, Nalusa could take you on, one-on-one, without interference from the other hunters. Then he'd grab the flute and take it back into his possession. Your tribe would lose its best chance to capture him at the next full moon."

Tallulah nodded slowly. "Makes sense. Wish my brother had reasoned everything in his mind before jumping to conclusions."

"He's too close to the situation to react logically. He'll

come around." Tombi might forgive his sister for bad judgment, but the fact remained that he didn't love her. Nothing about their relationship would change for the better.

"Don't hold your breath," Tallulah mumbled.

Annie stiffened in the chair, back to pondering the mystery. "I'm disappointed that it wasn't another hunter who gave you the idea that you had the power to contact Bo. Because if it had been one of them, we'd know the real betrayer."

They sipped their tea in glum silence until Tallulah spoke again. "Not only did the flute fail me, but if anyone at the Center finds out it's missing, I can kiss my job goodbye."

Well, she *did* steal the flute from her employer, but Annie bit her lip. Who was she to judge? Nalusa's influence must be a powerful thing. And at least Tallulah was opening up to her a bit.

Tallulah regarded her thoughtfully. "Why won't Bo talk to me? We were in love. He never even met you."

"Don't take it personal. I hear things no one else can."

"Can you try to contact him again?" Tallulah grasped Annie's hand. "And take me with you. Please?"

That was exactly what she'd do. Initiate contact. Many nights she'd wanted to sneak away into the bayou and try to find Bo, but Tombi wouldn't hear of it. They had sought him together, but no luck. Secretly, Annie thought Bo wasn't able to risk talking to anyone but her.

"I'll try to reach Bo tonight, but alone. You can't come with me. It won't work with you around. You're a distraction to him."

Tallulah's eager expression fell to one of resigned misery. "Okay." She gulped. "Thank you for trying and… thanks for believing in me when my own brother didn't."

So the seemingly unbreakable warrior woman wasn't

all badass. She had a heart that had been broken and bludgeoned. A feeling Annie knew all too well. "You're welcome," Annie said softly. She rose and gathered up the dirty cups and saucers.

Tallulah placed a hand on her arm. "Tombi is a fool if he doesn't love you."

He was a damn idiot.

Tombi stood on the porch and stared out at the night. Where was Annie? Was she okay? He pulled out the cell phone from his jeans pocket and then angrily stuffed it back in. There was no need to call. She'd told him she loved him, and he'd just stared at her and said nothing. He'd lost the right to know where she chose to spend her evenings.

The cabin was silent and empty without Annie. How quickly he'd grown accustomed to her presence.

A spherical beam of light turned from the main road onto the dirt road leading to his cabin. About time Hanan and Chulah showed up.

Tombi pushed off from the railing and paced the porch. Telling them the news wasn't going to be easy. They would be almost as torn about Tallulah as he was. Hanan especially. He didn't know how deep their feelings for each other went. Or, as Tallulah implied, if they were merely friends with benefits. Ugh. Not how he wanted to think of his sister.

The old Chevy truck doors squeaked as the hunters jumped out of Chulah's pickup. Hanan's silver sheriff's badge glinted like a miniature star. "What's up?" Hanan asked, direct as always. His eyes were as sharp and focused as the eagle he was named after. Once he swooped in on a problem, he never let go until he was satisfied every stone had been turned. It made him an excellent officer.

"We have a problem," Tombi answered.

Chulah bounded the porch steps, face crafty and search-ing. "Where's Tallulah? She should be here, too. We al-ways meet together when there's trouble."

"Tallulah *is* the trouble."

Fear danced in Chulah's brown eyes. "Is she okay?"

Best to just spit it out. "Tallulah's our traitor."

"No way. She'd never do that," Chulah said, voice pitched low and fierce.

Hanan stuffed his hands into his uniform pockets and frowned. "Hard to believe. How can you be sure?"

"The ancient flute that we once searched for and couldn't find? Turns out, it's a real thing after all. Tal-lulah has it. I caught her playing it in the woods today."

Shock registered on his friends' faces.

"But that's great news," Chulah protested. "She found it for us, and now we can use it to capture Nalusa."

"You say you caught her," Hanan said slowly. "Did she admit to revealing our secrets to Nalusa?"

"Of course she didn't admit anything. But she's desper-ate. Somehow she got it in her head that the flute would help her contact Bo's spirit. Tallulah would stop at noth-ing to hear from Bo." A kind of madness must have eaten away at Tallulah's mind. Her grief over Bo went far deeper than Tombi had realized. And someone suffering such grief was a target for Nalusa and the shadows. It made a person easy prey to whisper false promises. A seduction to the mystery of the night.

Chulah's face crumbled, and he stumbled down the porch steps, no doubt needing distance until he regained his composure.

"Where's the flute now?"

As usual, Hanan cut to the heart of their situation. His friend hid his emotions well, buried them under logic and a determination to attack problems. Tombi didn't see the attraction between Hanan and Tallulah, but there was no accounting for sexual chemistry. Personally, he'd rather Tallulah had chosen Chulah, an honorable man who'd quickly become his closest friend in the past few months. Hanan was honorable as well, but in a detached, intellectual manner.

Tombi sighed. "My sister threw it in the air, and a hawk flew off with it."

"You didn't have the opportunity to kill it?" Hanan asked.

"Annie stopped me. The hawk is her animal guide. Or so she believed."

Chulah jerked around. "Where's Annie now? I bet she's behind everything. Not your sister." He stomped onto the porch, warming to his theory. "That's it. She's been the one whispering in Tallulah's ear about the flute, knowing Tallulah's grief. And Annie knew Tallulah gets to examine artifacts as soon as the archaeologists bring them in from their digs. She's the real traitor."

Tombi winced. No. Not Annie. It couldn't possibly be Annie. The porch tilted beneath his feet, and a rushing whirled like a tornado in his mind. Chulah had a point. A damn good one. He couldn't be so duped...or could he? What if it were true? What if his sister were innocent?

Shame pounded through his veins. He'd brought Annie into their inner circle, had come to completely trust her and taught her all he knew. Worse, he'd accused his own sister of being the traitor.

So which was it: Annie or Tallulah? Lover or sister?

Both choices were unimaginable.

"Let's not jump the gun," Tombi said.

Chulah gritted his teeth. "Oh, but you were quick to accuse your own sister."

True. Tombi didn't defend himself. He needed proof.

"Have you found out anything yet from the computer records?" he asked Hanan.

"Not yet. Pisa says the tech expert he trusts to be discreet in reviewing the phone records is still on vacation for a few days."

"Isn't there anyone else that can look at them to see who sent the text messages?"

"No one we trust. Besides, if the person was smart, they'd use a throwaway cell phone that's untraceable."

Tombi slammed a fist into the railing. "I suppose you're right about that." How was he going to figure this out before it was too late?

"Isn't there anything you can do?" Chulah asked Hanan.

"Nothing. We could interrogate Annie and Tallulah, of course. But Pisa can't do it in his official position as a sheriff's deputy."

"I'll talk to Tallulah," Chulah volunteered.

Some interrogation that would be. In Chulah's eyes, Tallulah was an innocent.

"Might be best if I did it," Hanan said calmly.

Tombi studied his friend. Just what kind of relationship did he have with Tallulah? You would think that the news the woman you're sleeping with was a possible betrayer and could have killed you by sending information to the enemy would illicit a strong reaction. Yet nothing fazed Hanan, not even this.

Chulah, on the other hand, was distraught. Not for the first time, Tombi wished his twin had chosen Chulah. The man cared for her and was loyal in his defense of her character.

"I'll talk to both of them," Tombi said.

Chulah shot him a hard look. "I don't see how you can be fair. Considering you've been sleeping with the enemy for the past two weeks."

Heat burned his skin. "Careful, Chulah. My relationship with Annie is none of your business."

"It *is* my business when she's blinded you to the truth and disrupted our circle. What's the matter with you? Our tribe comes before all else. Are you going to throw away your family and our bond and duty for...for...a piece of ass?"

Tombi stepped up to Chulah, got in his face. His fisted hands twisted by his sides. "Don't you ever call her that again."

Chulah glowered, and anger crackled between them.

"Stop it." Hanan pushed them apart with both arms. "We have to work together."

He was right. Damn it. Tombi stalked off, needing distance between him and his friends before he landed a punch or said something unforgivable.

Everything was falling apart. The beginning of the end unraveled before Tombi. Nalusa was winning the battle before it even started. For all he knew, Hanan or Chulah might be the real betrayer. Maybe Chulah was emotionally unstable and Hanan a little too cool and calculating. His inner circle had collapsed.

"Where are you going?" Chulah called.

"To find the truth."

"We'll go with you," Hanan offered. "No sense in you walking in the woods at night by yourself. We can drive to Tallulah's place in the truck."

Tombi faced them. "I need to do this alone. Don't follow me."

Hanan nodded, and Chulah frowned but made no move to join him.

Tombi turned away from the faces of his closest friends, from the light and comfort of the cabin he'd built with his own hands, and marched into the gloomy darkness of the swamp. His arms prickled with a chill that defied the Alabama heat. He plodded forward, his heart hardening to stone—so hard it could be ripped from his chest and used to sling at a will-o'-the-wisp.

The fall of footsteps sounded behind him, but Tombi didn't bother turning. He recognized the vibration of the footsteps, as familiar to him as a voice.

"Here." Hanan thrust something large and heavy against his right shoulder. "Don't be stupid."

Tombi grabbed the leather straps of his knapsack that was loaded with rocks and other hunting supplies and armored himself. How many times had he entered the woods laden with pounds of stones on his back? Too many to count. And yet he and the other hunters barely made a dent in fighting Nalusa and the night's shadows.

He kept moving forward. It was all he could do. Just keep showing up in the face of the odds stacked against him and his people.

"I put your phone in there," Hanan said. "Call me if you need backup."

Tombi flipped an arm in the air, acknowledging that he heard. But this was something he needed to do on his own. No one else knew Annie or Tallulah as well as he. Surely, whichever of them was lying, he'd be able to extricate their deception.

He stepped onto the path and into the woods. Cicadas and frogs chirruped and harrumphed in a bayou symphony. Mosquitoes buzzed by his ears and nipped at the unprotected skin of his neck and forearms. He swatted at them absently, eager to question the two women at the heart of the treachery. He could believe Tallulah had succumbed to grief, thus allowing herself to be in a weakened, vulnerable state that Nalusa preyed upon.

But Annie?

Sweet, sweet Annie. Memories flashed in his mind—the soft curve of her naked hips, her eyes darkening with passion, her fingers tracing his lips and jaw. Her sunny smile as she learned to block sound for the first time, her sorrow at her grandma's ill health, the special tea she brewed when he was hurt, the sound of her voice in their kitchen as they cooked together in the evenings.

Their kitchen. He'd come to think of the cabin as their special place. A mysterious, sexy, caring, complicated woman who had become a part of his life. Yet, he had to question her. Had to be sure she hadn't deceived him right from the start.

Chapter 16

The candle flame danced a red-hot tango, dipping and swerving to its own unheard music, leaving in its wake a hissing and popping of spent passion. Miss Belle was in the house, tripping the light fantastic. Annie knew it before she smelled the licorice and myrrh scent. She placed the grimoire on the altar top, opening it to the middle. She untied the strings of her mojo bag and placed it on the exposed pages marked with handwritten magical root-working recipes.

"Bless these herbs and infuse them with holy power. May they draw Bo's spirit close to me and help him speak this evening."

The pressure of a warm hand patted her shoulder. *It is done.*

Weeks ago, a physical manifestation of a long-dead ancestor would have sent her screaming from the room, but now, Annie welcomed Miss Belle's reassuring contact.

Tonight, she would speak with Bo and get the name of the betrayer. After that, it was a matter of convincing her animal spirit to return the ancient flute. Her hawk wouldn't desert her and betray her trust. He just wouldn't.

A sharp rapping blasted the cottage's quiet. Annie glanced at the clock in the den: eleven thirty. Tallulah had cried herself to sleep in Tia Henrietta's bedroom over an hour ago. The muffled sobs from her grandma's room wouldn't have been audible to anyone but Annie. She and Tallulah might never become the best of friends, but Annie recognized there was some good in Tallulah. She was capable of great love.

Too bad her twin wasn't.

It had to be Tombi making that racket. Knocking in an arrogant, haughty way with no regard for the people inside. What did he care if she was asleep? He'd decided to talk at last, and that was all that mattered to him.

Annie worked up a righteous indignation. Better that than be a whining, pining fool who'd laid bare her soul. She jerked open the door. "What do you want?"

Tombi glowered, face set in harsh, grim lines. His brown eyes appeared hard as blackened, burned coal. What the hell was *he* mad about? He hadn't had his love thrown back in his face. She was the injured party here.

"We need to talk."

"Well, I don't want—"

He pushed past her and strode into the middle of the den, filling the feminine vibe of the cottage with a bit of the dangerous night that cloaked his aura. He smelled like smoldering wood chips and damp peat and moss and cypress. Intoxicating but dangerous.

Annie didn't budge from the doorway. "Say what you want and then leave. I was getting ready to go to bed."

A flicker of something—passion?—chased across his

face, and Annie winced at her choice of words. *Bed* conjured up images of snuggling in Tombi's arms, of his skin golden in the moonlight, naked and smooth beneath her touch. Tangled bedsheets and groans and whispers and... Annie bit the inside of her mouth to stop the memories. "Why are you here?" she asked, knowing the hoarseness of her voice tipped him off to the passionate direction her mind had leaped to.

"Annie." He came to her and ran a calloused hand over her face, brushing back a curly lock of hair. "You're as much a mystery to me as the night we met," he whispered.

"There's nothing mysterious about me," she denied. "You know me better than anyone. I shared everything with you."

"Everything?"

"There are no secrets between us."

Tombi abruptly dropped his hand to his side. "I want to believe that."

"Why shouldn't you?" Annie countered. "I've been open. I've held nothing back." She swallowed painfully. She'd been too open, too trusting with her heart. And Tombi had crushed it.

He hardened his face and crossed his hands. "Tell me the truth. Are you in league with Nalusa? Does he have some kind of hold over you? Because if he does, I can help you break free."

"What?" Annie rubbed her temple, confused at the questions. "Why are you asking me that?"

"Because I believe the betrayer is you or Tallulah."

"Oh, yeah? On what evidence, you...you jackass?"

He ignored the gibe. "Ever since we met, the shadows have grown more powerful, Nalusa has infiltrated our ranks, and the inner circle has crumbled. No one trusts anyone else."

A cold fury tingled along Annie's spine. "I'm not in league with anybody. And neither is your sister."

"I want to believe you."

The anguish in his eyes softened her temper. "I understand that you have to suspect the worst of most people. But I thought we had something special."

He drew her to him, resting his chin on the top of her head. "We do."

The warm, husky voice made her tingle inside, and her thighs tightened. This part, the physical attraction, was so easy between them. If only everything else could be.

"Come back to the cabin with me," he urged, pressing his need against her core.

Annie's breath caught. She wanted to so much. To bury her heartache and disappointment in his kisses, to feel him inside her, pulsing, their bodies electric with desire. It took all her strength to step out of the warmth and safety of his arms.

"No."

"Why not? It's so damn good between us, Annie."

"In bed. But I want more than that. If you can't love me, I at least want your trust. One hundred percent."

"I'm working on it. Isn't that good enough for now?"

No. She'd tried to make Evan love and respect her, but it only ended with her doing all the giving. She wanted Tombi, but only if he could love her as she was. Nothing less would do.

"Don't hurt me any more than you already have. The longer we're together, the more I need to know you love and trust me. I'm done with one-sided relationships."

He gave a reluctant nod. "Best we end it now. There's nothing more I can teach you about blocking sound anyway." He started to the door and then stopped. "You'll let me know if your hawk brings you the flute, won't you? The full moon is in two weeks. We'll need it."

"I'll do my best to get it back," she promised. "I'll still help you any way I can. That hasn't changed."

He opened the door and stared into the night. "Will you be safe?"

"I managed twenty-seven years without your protection," Annie pointed out. "And at least for tonight, Tallulah's staying over."

"If you need me, call me."

Annie followed Tombi and shut the door behind him. She leaned her back against it and closed her eyes. It would be so easy to stop him, to go back to his cabin and enjoy his lovemaking. No, she'd done the right thing. Too much had been either said or left unsaid between them.

The rattle of his truck engine faded.

He was gone.

Annie took a shuddering breath. If Tombi knew what she'd planned for the evening, he would have never left. Quickly, before she lost courage, Annie went to the altar and picked up the mojo bag she'd infused with power. She tied it to a belt loop on her jeans and blew out the candle. On the way out, she grabbed a flashlight from the bookshelf near the entryway.

The black night was sticky with humid moisture as she gently shut the door, not wanting to wake her guest. But if Tallulah hadn't awoken when Tombi came over, she wasn't going to get up now.

Good. Best to proceed on this task on her own. Bo had never come to her while she and Tombi sought him together. She suspected his strength to communicate while trapped in a wisp was a difficult feat, easier attempted when he only had to concentrate on one human gifted to hear his voice.

With each step to the woods, Annie relaxed her mind and opened her hearing. The buzz of mosquitoes and the guttural music of bullfrogs were an instant, familiar backdrop. Amazing how the weeks training with Tombi had allowed her to adjust her supernatural hearing at will.

The elliptical beam of the flashlight guided her steps. Between its light and her night walk training with Tombi, her steps were quick, and the dark didn't impede her as much as before.

The smell and taste of salt tickled her nose and the back of her throat. Strange how often taste was enhanced by a stronger sense of smell. She didn't just absorb scent through her olfactory glands without it also arousing her taste buds.

Darkness descended further as she entered the woods. Annie stopped and leaned against the rough bark of a pine tree, switching off the flashlight. How far would she have to go in? She fingered the smooth flannel of her mojo bag.

The slightest snap of a twig and her breath seized. Was she being followed? She hardly dared breathe, straining to see or hear anything else in the silence of the swamp. Must have been a porcupine or squirrel. She shook off the fear and inhaled deeply.

"I'm here, Bo. Come to me," she whispered.

A faint blue-green light skittered from afar.

"Closer, Bo. It's okay, I'm alone."

The orb streaked through the forest, leaving a comet tail of sparkles that illuminated the twisting tree branches above and tangled vines and saw palmettos beneath. It stopped and hovered several feet away, its inner heart pulsing, breathing color.

It worked. She gripped the mojo bag, crushing the herbs and releasing more of the scent, bolstering her confidence. The glowing light twisted its shape, the upper half bending and pointing westward. Figured he would want to go back to the Choctaw sacred grounds where they'd first met.

"I'll follow you."

The wisp's glow made the flashlight unnecessary. A blue-and-green haze coated the air, painting teal brush-strokes everywhere. It felt like entering a strange, beautiful fairyland. She trudged along until the path grew less firm beneath her feet and became sludgy, the salt smell grew more pungent and her mouth puckered, briny as a pickle.

The light stood still.

"You came back," Bo said, his voice faint but clear. He sounded weaker than their previous encounter.

"Yes. Tombi wants to free you. But first we need—"

"Such a good friend," Bo said mournfully. "And Tallulah, my love, is nearby. She's followed you."

Aha. So that was what she'd heard earlier. "I thought I heard something. She's desperate to talk with you."

"No. It would only make her healing that much harder. I'm dead to her forever, and she must move on with her life."

"I'll give her your message. Knowing you care might help." Annie hesitated to bring up the purpose of her visit, but she sensed their time together was brief. "Please, can you tell me the name of the person who's been telling Nalusa the hunter's plans and secrets? If we don't find him soon, Tombi fears that they have no chance of winning. That, with the next full moon, Nalusa and his shadows will make a bold move to eliminate all of them."

"Tombi's right. *Na haksichi* is—"

"Bo!" Tallulah burst through from the path, long black hair streaming behind her, silver-streaked with moonlight. Her eyes were wild with a combination of grief and hope. "Is it really you?" She cast wild eyes on Annie. "What is he saying?"

The teal heart flame within the smoky wisp heated to an incandescent red that roared and cackled like an erupting forest fire. Annie took a step back from the wall of heat that singed her clothes and hair.

Tallulah dropped to her knees and held her hands out, imploring. "Take me with you, Bo. I only want to be with you."

Annie's own heart broke at seeing the proud woman so humbled and vulnerable. The woman warrior's loss was so intense, and seeing Bo trapped as a spirit had to be devastating.

"No!" Bo's voice rang out so loud it vibrated the earth beneath Annie's feet.

"It *is* you," Tallulah whispered in awe. "Even I heard you just now."

Annie knelt in front of Tallulah. "I need to talk to Bo. We have to find out the name of the betrayer."

"He approaches now," Bo warned. "Run!"

Annie scrambled to her feet and looked behind her. But this time she could make out nothing in the darkness. Except a stealthy footfall advancing toward them, one she had heard before. It teased the back of her brain like a spider crawling up her arm. "We have to go," she said, tugging at Tallulah's arm.

Tallulah didn't spare Annie a glance. She was transfixed by the fire that was once her lover, had eyes only for the conflagration burning at the wisp's center.

"C'mon," she urged, pulling harder.

The vibrations underfoot grew stronger, faster, more sure. *Na haksichi*, the traitor, was near. Annie dropped Tallulah's arm and stood, slowly turning around, dread prickling her spine.

Hanan's eagle eyes pierced the night, the topaz glints in his pupils like ground star chips.

"You," she breathed out, past the lump of fear in her throat. "You are the one."

His smile emphasized the sharp beak of his nose, and his white teeth were prominent as a chomping wolf's. "Just as you suspected at the start."

"Tombi had so much faith in you."

"Tombi." He spit out the name in apparent distaste. "He's leading us down a path of sure destruction. We are outnumbered. He should have compromised with Nalusa long ago."

"What kind of bargain have you struck with the devil?"

"One that allows me to live."

"And to hell with your friends? Your family? What kind of life is that?"

The wisp moved between her and Hanan.

"Be gone," Hanan commanded. His voice screeched like the talons of an eagle scraping glass. "You have no power here, Bohpoli. I killed you."

Tallulah shrieked, her banshee wail echoing through the swamp. She rose to her feet and stumbled past Annie. "You killed my Bo? Why?"

"Because he caught me with Nalusa. And because he was the most skillful hunter, the best shot."

Tallulah leaped at Hanan, screaming and clawing. He shoved her, and she tumbled several feet away.

"Stupid woman," he hissed. "You're weak. So weak you were in my bed only weeks after Bo's death."

The fire orb popped and hissed.

Hanan cast it a sharp glance. "By Nalusa's power, I command you to be gone, wisp."

The elongated smoky form of the wisp expanded, grew more dense and gray, smothering the light of Bo's trapped spirit. It skittered away in a heartbeat.

"Don't leave me behind," Tallulah wailed after the fleeing wisp.

Hanan said, face scrunched in contempt, "Shut up."

Annie stepped between them. "Why are you doing this?"

"The reign of Nalusa and the shadows is imminent. Might as well join them and share in the power. Tombi is an obstinate, stupid fool."

Anger burned in her gut. "He's not. He's a decent, honorable man."

"Who will die a horrible death." Hanan advanced slowly and deliberately.

"And so will you. Nalusa has no use for you. He'll kill you when this is over."

"I've worked out my deal. I'll be a rich man. All I have to do is provide him the flute." Hanan swooped upon her, grabbing her arm and clutching her, digging into her flesh, past muscle and to the bone.

Annie clenched her teeth, not wanting to give Hanan the satisfaction of hearing the whimper clawing at her throat.

Hanan's breath was hot on her face, and the topaz glints glittered like the eyes of a wild predator. "Call your hawk. I want that flute. Now."

So he knew. He probably knew everything, had hung back in the shadows and watched and waited for this opportunity.

"No," she ground out.

"Yes."

He shook her until her head bobbed like flotsam on the wave of a storm. "Do it," he growled.

"Or what?"

"Or you die. Tonight."

"You can't kill me. Without me, my hawk will never return the flute."

"Listen to me, witch. Call the hawk now, or you'll deal with Nalusa."

"And you won't get your reward," she shot back.

Hanan abruptly let go of her arm. "I don't have Nalusa's power, but I can give you a taste of what you can expect if I don't get your cooperation."

The screeching of a flock of owls and eagles erupted between her ears, a squall of birds of prey caught in a storm wind. Annie clamped her hands over her ears and bent at the waist, staggering backward. The sound stopped abruptly.

"It can get so much worse," Hanan warned.

Tallulah roused herself and came to Annie's side. "Leave her alone."

"That's rich," he sneered. "Only a couple of days ago, you hated Annie, said she was a witch who couldn't be trusted. You're a fickle lover and friend, Tallulah."

Fury wiped out the grief still evidenced by the tears on her cheeks. "And you're a bastard," she spat.

Hanan shrugged. "You're no longer important." He turned his eagle eyes on Annie. "Back to business."

Tallulah wedged between them, her back to Hanan, and raised her arms as if to hold him back. "Run, Annie! Go, get Tombi."

How she wanted to. Every cell in her body screamed *flee*. But she couldn't leave Tallulah alone with the enemy. Still…they would both be better off if one of them escaped and got help.

"You go," Annie urged.

Hanan laughed. "Run home, little girl. By the time you get your big, bad brother it will be too late."

Tallulah raised her eyebrows at Annie in a silent question.

Annie nodded.

Tallulah sprang from them and disappeared into the night.

A sardonic smile perched the corners of Hanan's thin lips. "Like I said. Fickle."

Her palms and underarms itched with sweat. What would he do now? "Even if I wanted to help you, I can't," she said calmly, hoping to reach some rational part of his mind not contaminated by Nalusa. "I've never tried to command my animal spirit. I don't know if I can."

"For your sake, this better work," he said quietly.

The kind of quiet that meant business.

The kind of quiet that was the whisper of the wind before the swooshing gale.

Infinitely more menacing than the noisy whirlwind he'd stirred moments before in her brain.

Some good her special petition and mojo bag had been. Annie's lips numbed with dread. She was alone and powerless in the midst of the most forsaken swampland on earth, alone with a heartless hunter who'd turn his own mother over to the devil if it meant gaining power.

"You left her alone out there in the woods?" Tombi slammed his fist on the counter and glared at his twin.

"I'm more help to her as a messenger than if I had stayed behind." Tallulah raised her chin. "Hanan would have taken us both hostage, and you would never have known until it was too late."

Hanan. Someone he'd known since childhood. Tombi remembered playing baseball with Hanan, their initiation into the hunter's world on their nineteenth birthdays. The friend who'd attended his parents' funeral, and the one who had helped him cut wood and hewn logs for the cabin he'd built.

His sister pulled out her phone. "I'm calling Chulah

and the others. They can meet us here in fifteen minutes. Together, we might have a chance."

"You stay behind. I'm leaving now." Tombi rushed to get his knapsack and slung it over his shoulders. He had to get to Annie. Visions of Hanan torturing her clawed at his guts. He should never have left her earlier. Tallulah had been no protection.

"Don't be stupid. What difference can fifteen minutes make?"

"Every second I'm apart from her is agony," he answered shortly.

Tombi rushed to the den and grabbed his keys from the fireplace mantel. If he drove his truck through the field to where the path started at the edge of the woods, it would save a couple minutes. More important, he wouldn't waste energy. He'd need every last ounce of strength to save Annie.

"Give me the keys," Tallulah snapped. "I'll drive you to the path and come back. You don't need to drive in your condition."

"Then move it." Tombi flew down the porch stairs and climbed into the truck.

Tallulah acted just as quickly, revving the engine and then slamming her foot on the accelerator. Headlights framed a square, narrow tableau of shadows and masses of swarming mosquitoes. The old truck bounced up and down on the uneven, rough soil, enough to make his teeth chatter.

And still it wasn't fast enough. "Hurry," he urged.

"I'm going as fast as I can. When I left they were on the edge of the salt marsh, near where Bo's body was found. You remember the spot?"

As if he could ever forget. "Yes. Anything else I should know?"

"No. Only…" She hesitated.

"What?" he asked brusquely. Could this situation get any worse?

"I have to give your lady credit—she insisted I leave. She stood her ground with Hanan. Never would have believed that tiny slip of a girl had it in her when we first met."

"She's not a girl, she's a woman." How many times had he said that same thing? Appearances were deceiving. Annie had depth and talent and compassion…and didn't even realize her own worth.

"And you love her," his sister stated matter-of-factly.

Love? Tombi scowled. Now wasn't the time nor the place for thoughts of love. He gripped the door handle, ready to pounce as soon as the truck slowed.

Tallulah raised a brow. "It's okay to be in love. It doesn't make you weaker."

"So you say," he grumbled. The truck came to a shuddering halt at the path, and he prepared to leap.

His twin laid a hand on his shoulder. "And she loves you, too. I can tell."

He didn't want Annie's love. She'd be better off without him and his problems. Especially now that she'd learned to control her sense of hearing. There was nothing more he could offer Annie. Tombi shrugged off her hand. "Bring everyone as soon as you can."

He leaped out of the truck and hit the ground on a panicked run. *Must save Annie. Must save Annie.* The refrain echoed with every footfall, forming a rhythm of urgency. Heart and breath raced in despairing accompaniment.

Tombi wanted to kill Hanan. The rat bastard. After everything they had been through together. If the traitor harmed Annie, he'd pay with his life.

Chapter 17

Annie's arms, shoulders, back and legs dug into rough pine bark. Rope burned into her wrists like a bracelet of thorns. The more she struggled, the more it tightened, as if the cords were the sinew of a boa constrictor squeezing opportunistically with its victim's exhale. So this must have been what it felt like hundreds of years ago for women accused as witches and bound to a stake.

Hanan walked around the tree, inspecting his handiwork with the precision of a mechanical engineer. "That should hold you."

Annie bit her lip, struggling to hide her fear. Worse than the physical pain was the terror from being at Hanan's mercy. She was totally vulnerable, and he could do anything with her that he wanted. For as long as he wanted.

Had Tallulah gotten to Tombi yet? Her sense of time was as warped as an antique mirror. Every second dripped like a dollop of molasses. Tallulah could have been gone twenty minutes or twenty seconds for all she knew.

Defend yourself. Miss Belle's scent of myrrh and licorice teased the back of her throat. *I'm not alone.* She grabbed on to the belief as if it were a lifeline at sea.

What would Tia Henrietta do if she were in this position? Annie took a deep breathe. First, her grandma would admonish her to calm her mind, to find that quiet place deep inside that was still and peaceful and ever-present, an inner lagoon of peace and tranquility. There, she would find guidance—or the endurance to weather this ordeal. As long as her hawk possessed the flute, Hanan and Nalusa needed her alive.

He stood before her and crossed his arms. "Call your hawk."

She wouldn't outright defy him. Not tied to a tree. "I'll try." Annie closed her eyes and moved her lips in a flow of mumbo-jumbo words. It helped not to look at his eagle eyes dissecting her every move, watching for the slightest misstep. On and on she continued the charade, knowing each moment that passed brought Tombi closer.

Hanan interrupted her almost hypnotic reverie. "How long is this going to take?"

"I have no idea. This is new to me."

A sudden pressure pinched her chin, and Annie's eyes snapped open. Hanan's face was so close to her own that his hot breath fanned across her eyelids. His fingers dug into her flesh. Slowly, he increased the pressure until she feared he would break her jawbone. Tears stung her eyes, and a low whimper escaped her mouth.

"We don't have all night, witch."

"I'm…I'm doing my best." Her words were distorted from his grip on her chin.

"Try harder. I'll give you another minute. If it hasn't appeared, you'll force me to use other means to persuade you." He ran a hand down her breasts and painfully squeezed a nipple.

Bastard.

Annie clamped her teeth together to keep from crying out. Hanan would like that. She guessed he was the kind of man who would find rough sex a turn-on. What had Tallulah seen in him?

He took a step back and lifted his head, searching the night sky. She couldn't keep putting him off with the fake incantation. Perhaps the wisest course was to try to summon the hawk after all. Just because it came didn't mean it would bring the flute.

Come to me. If you are my animal spirit, meant to guide me, I need your help. Fly toward me. I ask this by the power of all the saints and by all that is sacred in our bond.

From a great distance, the swoosh from a spread of wings brushed against the synapsis of fear pounding inside her body. The hawk had heard her petition and would soon be here. The beating of its feather upon liftoff fluttered in her chest, and she sagged against the tree in relief. "My hawk's on the way," she whispered.

"Excellent." Hanan unloaded the leather backpack from his shoulders and withdrew a rounded stone.

Annie's breath caught. "What are you doing?" But she knew. She tugged against the ropes binding her wrist and ankles but only succeeded in further abrading the raw skin. Liquid trickled down her fingers. That blood would soon be a mosquito magnet.

"And now we wait," he said coolly.

"Please, can't you loosen these ropes a little bit? I'm bleeding."

"As soon as I have the flute, you'll be free."

Liar. She'd be trapped forever in a will-o'-the-wisp. Just like Bo. With the flute, Nalusa would defeat the remaining hunters, and there would be no one left to free trapped souls. And what would happen to Tombi?

Be careful, Annie urged the hawk. *Hanan is armed and means to kill you.*

Ca-ca-caw came a faint screech. The hawk understood her silent petition! There was still a chance to escape this disaster.

"What are you smiling about?" Hanan growled, his attention back on her. He stared up and down her body, slowly and deliberately.

She hadn't realized she was smiling. The blood drained from her face at this new menace.

Hanan abruptly grabbed her hair on both sides of her face and thrust his body against hers so hard she could feel his need pressed against her core. "You planning something, witch?" he growled into her right ear.

"N-no."

As suddenly as he'd been upon her, Hanan withdrew, and she gulped in fresh air.

"What the hell? Something's burning me." He slapped at the front of his jeans, and his brows knit as he studied her. Rough hands reached for her again, yanking and ripping the mojo bag from her belt loop. Smoke drifted through the cloth, and he threw it on the ground, shaking his fingers from the hot contact.

Annie smiled. This time a deliberate curling of the lips, a taunting. Hanan wasn't invulnerable against her hoodoo powers. He might hurt her, but she wasn't entirely defenseless.

"We'll have our fun later," he promised.

A flurry of feathers and wings beating in the wind sounded from above, so loud even Hanan heard it.

Thank the spirits.

Her relief was short-lived. Hanan gripped a rock, and his thin lips set into a predatory line.

"Look out!" she screamed.

Hanan rounded on her so swiftly she didn't see the blow coming. Pain slashed her left cheek and cut her bottom lip—white heat pulsed and burned. A metallic taste tinged her mouth. Annie braced herself for more of the same, but Hanan's attention was directed upward.

The casual violence of the assault churned her stomach. This man would have no mercy in reaching his goal for more power and money. It was as if his soul had already blackened to match the pitch of the night.

A flick of the wrist, and his round stone was propelled upward. It pinged against a tree branch and fell harmlessly back down to earth. Hanan loaded his slingshot and attacked again.

Ca-caw. The hawk drew near enough she could make out the reddish-brown feathers spread in flight from one tree top to another. *Be careful*, she warned silently. *He's trying to kill you.* But her animal guide could probably see the enemy from afar better than she could only a few feet away.

Or so she hoped.

Another stone missile rustled through leaves and again fell harmlessly down.

"Damn it," Hanan muttered, loading another stone in the sling. The weapon whizzed in the night.

A sickening thud of rock hitting bird flesh rent the thick, humid air. *Ca-ca, ca-caw.* Its cry high-pitched and tattered. Wings fluttered and the sound of dead weight descending.

No! Not her hawk.

"Bingo." Hanan smirked, his voice pregnant with satisfaction.

Damn him. If she could escape her bindings, she'd make him pay for this.

A brown clump of feathers and claws appeared a few feet above Hanan's head, a motionless heap of dead weight.

"What the—" Hanan began.

The clump of bird stretched, wings spread open, feet and talons extended.

It lived.

Hanan flung his slingshot to the ground, one leg moved forward, set to run.

Her hawk swiped the man's forehead, ripping flesh. Hanan screamed and batted uselessly at his attacker. The hawk clung mercilessly to the top of Hanan's scalp, even as Hanan ran.

She was alone. Annie sagged with relief, muscles grateful for the reprieve. If only she could untie the bindings at her wrists. Her hawk would take care of Hanan, and Tombi should be along shortly. At least she was safe. Unless… Annie cast a nervous glance at the nearby underbrush. Unless Nalusa saw her predicament and decided to pay a visit.

She shivered in the sweltering darkness.

Tombi stilled at the unexpected scream. Could it be Annie? He pushed away the paralyzing terror and ran toward the sound. If it was her, at least she was alive.

For the moment.

He cut through to rough, less-traveled shortcuts on the main path. Limbs smacked his torso and scratched his face, but nothing mattered if it shaved microseconds in getting to Annie.

He'd never leave her alone again. Not for a second. Not for a chance to reclaim all the trapped souls in Bayou La Siryna. Not even for a chance to kill Nalusa. Tombi ran on, not bothering to consider the ramifications of his thoughts.

Still no sight of anything but the familiar, accursed swamp. "Annie?" he called. "Where are you?"

"Here!"

Relief jellied his knees for two seconds. The cry was weak but near. He pushed on with even greater determination. The path widened, and he rushed into the Choctaw sacred land by the marsh.

And found the most unholy sight—Annie tied to a tree, blood oozing down her bottom lip, the left side of her face discolored and bearing a hand imprint. Her eyes were wild and frightened.

"Be careful," she warned. "Hanan might be back any moment."

Tombi wished he'd show his traitor face. "Let him." He walked to her and reached out to touch her swollen cheek. "How bad did he hurt you?" Despite his intention to be gentle, his voice was rough, and he choked down bile. Hanan dared do this? He would pay with his life.

"I'll be okay," Annie whispered. "Untie me and let's get out of here."

Tombi rounded the tree, and anger gushed like a geyser at the sight of the blood-soaked rope. Grabbing the knife from his backpack, he made quick work of cutting the ropes binding her wrists and ankles. "Don't try to walk just yet," he cautioned, returning to face her.

"We have to hurry." She took a step forward, and her body collapsed.

Tombi caught her and lifted her slight frame in his arms. "I'll carry you. It's going to take a few minutes for the blood to recirculate in your feet."

She nodded, and he hurried down the path, holding her in his arms. "You're a dead man, Hanan Sheffield," he yelled, itching for a confrontation. But first, he had to get Annie to safety.

"He tried to kill my hawk."

Tears ran down her cheeks, salty as the bayou breeze. He stopped abruptly and kissed her tenderly on the forehead. "Everything's going to be okay now," he promised.

She smiled in spite of the swollen, disfigured lips. "I know. You're here. I knew you'd come for me."

Her trust humbled him. And to think he once suspected her as the *Na haksichi*. She deserved a man so much better than he. But he would never let another man touch her. Not now. Not ever.

"Always," he said, voice near breaking. He frowned. This wouldn't do at all. The battle was near, he knew the enemy, and it was a time for courage, not weakness.

"I love you, Tombi. Take me home."

"I can't leave you alone at your grandmother's cottage," he apologized, deliberately ignoring her declaration of love. "Come back to my cabin, where you'll be safe."

"Your cabin is my home," she said softly.

Her words felled him, touched the cold, dark spot deep within his heart. Resolutely, he resumed walking, intent on getting her to the safety of his cabin. Tallulah could protect her while he sought Hanan.

She laid her swollen cheek against his chest. Her absolute trust, after all he'd put her through, was his undoing. He might keep silent with Annie's declarations, but he could no longer deny the truth to himself.

He loved her. Loved her passionately, loved her tenderly, loved her with mind and body and soul.

Forever.

Violet-and-coral streaks radiated from the east, although the risen sun was merely a promise of the golden glory to come.

Annie snuggled in Tombi's arms, inhaled his unique

scent. "Aren't you tired of carrying me? I can walk this last little bit."

"You aren't heavy." Vertical lines marred the bridge of his nose. "How are you feeling? You look like hell."

"Gee, thanks." She tried to smile, but her swollen bottom lip pulled and cracked at the motion. "Oomph," she mumbled.

Tombi's frown deepened. "Soon as we get home, I'll put some ice on it to stop the swelling."

"Perfect." They entered the clearing, and light glowed from the cabin. Tallulah and Chulah stood on the porch, watching them approach.

"Let me down," she insisted, wiggling out of his arms. She and Tallulah may have drawn a truce, but Annie didn't want to risk again being viewed as weak, as someone who needed her brother's attention and distracted him from his duties.

Her feet made contact with the earth, and her knees buckled. Some of the numbness had left and in its wake left sharp nerves flagellating in protest at bearing weight. Damn. She was about to fall and humiliate herself. Tombi slipped an arm around her waist, and she gratefully sagged against the support he offered. She might look a bloody mess, but at least she stood on her own two feet. Sort of.

Tallulah shoved off from the porch steps and approached, Chulah close behind. "You look like shit," she proclaimed.

Tombi stiffened. "Tallulah, what did I tell you—"

"I'm fine," Annie said hurriedly. "A hot bath and a good night's sleep is all I need."

Tallulah stepped to her side and wrapped her arm around Annie as well, lending her support. "Any of your special witch's herbs you want me to brew?"

Her words were brusque but not unkind. A cup of chamomile tea would be just the thing. "Sure. I'll go in the kitchen with you and show you how."

"Not necessary," Tombi said. "I've watched you make it, and I know where everything's at."

They slowly made their way to the porch, and Chulah stepped in front of them to hold the front door open. He regarded her with—could it really be?—concern in his warm brown eyes. "I'm glad you're okay."

"Seriously?" Annie clamped a hand over her mouth as if to call back the word, wincing at the contact with her tender lips. "Thanks," she mumbled, feeling foolish. Of course he and the others were glad she'd survived; they needed her to get the flute.

She hobbled to the kitchen table and sank into a chair, bones heavy and eyelids even heavier. One cup of tea and then it was bath and bedtime. She closed her eyes and sank her head in her hands, feeling the smooth oak of the table. Cabinet doors and low murmurs, the clanking of a teapot, the running of water—cozy sounds that invited slumber and a cocoon of safety.

Warmth pressed into the middle of her back.

"What—" She sprang up, dizzy and confused. The kitchen was packed with men. The hunters had come together, and they each stared unwaveringly at her.

Tombi set a mug of tea in front of her. "Drink this."

The heat singed the raw flesh on her lips, but she drank and cradled the warm cup in her hands as if it were a magical elixir. She took dainty sips, conscious of everyone watching.

It was evidently too much to ask that she be allowed some peace and rest. They were set on hunting Hanan, and they would want to know everything that had taken place earlier. Tombi kept his hand possessively on her shoulder. For all she knew, some in the group still suspected she was the traitor. That would be much easier for them to accept—a witch infiltrates the group, charms their leader and casts blame on one of their closest friends. So much more acceptable than the truth, that the evil sprang from one of their own.

"What do you want to know?" she asked wearily, setting down the empty cup.

Chulah spoke for the group. "Tombi and Tallulah have filled us in on what happened. The only question remaining is—can you summon your hawk to bring us the flute?"

"I can try. I was able to contact him earlier. I don't see why I couldn't do it now, too."

"Not right now." Tombi's grip on her shoulder tightened. "She's been through enough. We'll summon the hawk tomorrow and hold our ritual next week when the full moon rises. Our best chance to defeat Nalusa once and for all is to have that flute and use it at the right time. Together."

"At least agree to let us track Hanan tonight," Chulah argued. "He's injured, and the odds of all of us against him are in our favor. We'll find him and keep him under lock and key until this is over."

Tombi's heartbeat grew stronger, faster, an angry tempo exploding sound waves.

"Go with them," Annie said, looking up at his tight, set face. He wanted to be with his friends, wanted to help capture the traitor. "I'll be fine."

"I've left you alone before, and it never turns out well. I'm staying."

Astonishment washed over Annie. He chose her instead of his men, instead of his duty. "You are? Really?"

"Of course."

Tallulah jumped up from the table. "Good choice, brother. I'll make sure that bastard pays for what he's done."

She plucked a feather from her braid and held it out to Annie. "You showed great courage tonight. You insisted I run to get help, and you faced *Na haksichi* alone. And you had enough presence of mind to summon your animal guide and escape."

Annie accepted the feather and nodded, too overcome with surprise and gratitude to speak. Tallulah nodded and marched out. One by one, each of the hunters stopped before Annie and gave her a feather, until the wooden tabletop was hidden beneath a pile of feathers in every dark earth and rainbow shade. When the last one had exited, she let the tears fall. This was the closest she'd ever come to feeling like part of a family. She hadn't even known how much she'd craved this until the sense of belonging and acceptance built to a crescendo of emotion.

"Be right back." Tombi withdrew and walked his guests to the door.

Annie dropped her head on the table, and feathers tickled her nose and cheeks. She heard a chorus of birds, each feather a note in a melody, as lovely as any she had ever heard. Sweet notes of love and home and family.

And she lost it. Totally lost all self-composure. She'd survived the ordeal with Hanan, but the acts of kindness were her undoing. If only Grandma Tia were here to see it, all would be perfect.

Strong arms enfolded her, encouraging her to stand.

"This has all been too much for you. Let's get you cleaned up and into bed."

She struggled to her feet, quelling the sniffling. Tombi smiled tenderly. He gently removed a blue feather stuck to her cheek with salty tear paste.

"Our tradition is to wear the feathers in our hair and not on our face."

"I thought y'all should start something new."

Annie shuffled to the back bedroom, leaning heavily on Tombi's arm. The sight of the familiar four-poster bed with wool patterned blankets folded at the ends and the handmade, sturdy furniture felt like an oasis in a storm.

"It feels like I've been away for weeks," she said with a sigh.

"It does. I've missed you."

The admission glowed her heart and numbed the pain in her wrists and ankles and face. It wasn't *I love you*, but she'd take it. In a heartbeat. Annie put her arms around his neck and kissed him enthusiastically.

"Ouch," she gasped as her cut bottom lip protested the deep kiss.

"Passion can wait." Tombi quickly guided her to the bathroom. "I've already drawn the water for you."

The scent of chamomile and sweet orange emanated from the Jacuzzi tub. "You even added my favorite essential oils," she marveled.

Tombi flashed a rare grin. "I pay attention," he boasted. "Now take off your clothes."

Annie mock saluted. "Yes, sir." She slipped out of the dirty, sweaty T-shirt and jeans, bra and panties. Hanan had touched her through these clothes. The whole lot should be burned. If she ever wore them again, she'd remember him.

Quickly she slipped into the warm, scented bath, ready to wash away the unsettling memory of Hanan's promise of more to come later. Impulsively, Annie dunked her whole body, face included, and let the water completely submerge her—a self-baptismal ritual to symbolically wash away all thoughts of *Na haksichi*. The raw skin on her wrists and ankles stung like a bitch, but they needed cleaning to prevent infection.

Tombi's face was above her own, its harsh, dear form and features rippled and blurred through the transparent liquid wall between them. His frown meant he was concerned. Annie immediately sat up, pushing through the water. She clasped her wet hands on his forearms and tugged. "Join me."

Tombi peeled off his shirt, and Annie smiled at his haste. No way was passion waiting until the morning. The sound and sight of him unbuckling his belt and unzipping his jeans wiped the smile from her face. This was what she needed. Him.

His erection popped loose from his briefs, and she swallowed hard. She squirted some body wash in her right palm, and when he sank into the tub opposite her, she massaged the wash onto his broad chest. White scars crisscrossed his golden flesh, and she lightly ran her fingers over them. "How did you get these?"

"Ishkitini. Horned owls known as shadow birds. They will sometimes attack if we slip past the wisps and get too close to Nalusa."

She shuddered to think of Tombi being sliced by the birds of prey. And she pictured her hawk carving Hanan's forehead and attaching his long talons into Hanan's scalp. "My hawk attacked Hanan today. Do you think my spirit guide might have once been on the dark side?"

"No. Once you've crossed, you can never go back. Any being, human or animal, is forever tainted." Tombi grasped her shoulders with his calloused hands and lowered his head to her level. "Now that we're alone, tell me…what did Hanan do? The swelling on your face and lips is proof he struck you at least once." He reached in the soapy water and raised her right hand. "And he cruelly bound you too tight. That was overkill."

"He only struck me once. Let's leave it at that."

Tombi placed his palm over her left breast. "You are bruised here, as well."

Annie hung her head. "Please. I don't want to talk about it."

He tried to gently lift her chin, but Annie jerked her head to the side.

"It will do you good to open up. We only have to talk about it this once, if you'd like." He paused a heartbeat. "Did he force himself on you?"

She shook her head, still refusing to meet his direct gaze. "It didn't get that far."

Tombi remained silent, and she rushed to fill the void. "Once I was tied to the tree, he kissed me and…and then shoved himself against me and…pinched my breasts."

"You must have been so scared." Tombi wrapped her in his arms. "I'll never let him hurt you again," he said with fierce tenderness.

"I know," she said, her voice muffled against his chest. "Just hold me a minute, okay?"

"Always."

The steady drum of his heartbeat vibrated in every cell of her body, pulsing a message of love. He might not realize it, but he did love her. She knew it as certain as she knew she was the granddaughter of the most revered hoodoo practitioner in Alabama.

She soaked in every sensation, Tombi's heartbeat, the warm water a liquid caress against her bare skin, the sweet scent he'd so thoughtfully provided. Annie used her newly found abilities to block out the rest of the world—the distant noise of cars, the humming of electrical appliances, the birds beginning to awaken and stir, welcoming in the morning. By focusing on the here and now, the intimacy was more profound.

For the first time, she was thankful for her special gift of hearing. This moment obliterated the childhood pain of being an outcast. She'd been born and fashioned for this man, just as he had been destined for her.

He had to feel it, too. The stubborn man. Even if this were their last night together, her heart and soul had irrevocably linked to his.

"Annie, are you ready for bed?"

She opened her eyes and blinked. "Huh? Did I fall asleep?"

"Just for a moment. Let me wash your hair and then tuck you into bed."

She didn't feel like bothering, but it seemed to please him to take care of her. "If you want."

He climbed out of the tub and pulled the plug, turned on the faucet. "Stick your head under."

A splat of shampoo landed on the top of her scalp and expert fingers massaged it in, kneading her temples and working back down to the tight muscles at the base of her neck. Heaven. And to think she had wanted to pass this up. Tombi could wash her hair all day if he pleased. Satisfied, he rinsed away the suds and then wrapped her head in a warm towel.

"That was amazing," she said with a tired smile. "Thank you."

His face darkened. "It's the least I can do after failing to protect you."

He helped her out of the tub and rubbed a thick towel over her body to dry her off, taking care to avoid the abraded skin.

"Don't do that to yourself. Guilt is a terrible thing. It can destroy your spirit."

"Easy for you to say," Tombi grunted. "You're an angel."

Annie laughed until she caught his eye. He wasn't smiling; he'd meant it. She flushed, thinking of all the times she'd been angry with her grandma for not instantly curing her of her hearing gift. "Not true. I can be quite self-ish. You're the one who's always sacrificed everything for your family and friends."

Tombi ruffled through a vanity drawer and produced a white tube. "Antibiotic cream," he explained.

"That's not necessary—"

"Lie on the bed, and let me dress your wounds."

He was in full master-doctor mode, so she followed him to the bedroom and obediently lay down. Tombi sat beside her, squirted a dollop on his fingers and, with incredible gentleness, took one wrist and applied the cream.

It still hurt like hell. Annie pursed her lips, determined not to make a sound. No reason to make him feel guiltier than he did. With gentle precision, Tombi applied the cream to all the raw flesh.

"Anything else I can do for you?"

She flashed a wicked grin. "Really? Do you need to ask? You're beside me in bed—naked. I can think of some naughty things you can do for me."

Tombi's eyes darkened, and he slowly leaned over and kissed along the side of her neck. She turned her head slightly, allowing him access to the sweet spot. He kissed the nape of her neck that always sent bursts of pleasure along her spine.

Right there. His warm breath tingled her nerve endings, just like he knew she liked it. Annie moaned.

Tombi pulled away. "Am I hurting you?"

"Quite the opposite," she assured.

He lowered his head and kissed the hollow of her throat. The man knew her weaknesses, had explored every inch of her body with intensity and curiosity. And she'd enjoyed every second of it, as much as she had loved learning every contour of his muscled frame, where scars crisscrossed his chest and shoulders, his long fingers and toes, his smooth flesh and solid jaw and cheekbones. Every detail thrilled her, made him more desirable each time they made love.

She pressed her hips against his erection, and his breath grew stuttered and harsh. She took delight in knowing she pleased him as much as he pleased her. It was as if there was no space between their bodies, no barrier between their souls, as they explored one another.

Tombi placed his mouth over one of her nipples, his tongue lathing the sensitive bud. His hand felt her core, and he inserted a finger. Annie bucked against it, her muscles contracting. The roaring in her head was like that of an incoming train—a powerful force bearing down and that couldn't be stopped.

She fondled his erection, and Tombi groaned. He entered her, and she squeezed her thighs and core, desperate for release from the building crescendo.

It came, crashing like the Gulf tide at high waters. He plunged in and out, advancing and retreating, dominating and surrendering, until together they climaxed. She held on to his muscled back, an anchor in the passionate maelstrom. Her breath gradually slowed down, and her heart returned to a normal rate.

Tombi rolled beside her, a soft music of flute and drumming played like a lullaby. She was so tired…slumber beckoned. Before she surrendered to it, an unexpected quiet filled her mind and body.

A perfect silence blanketed her world for the first time—blissful, peaceful silence. And all because of Tombi. Annie sighed and snuggled under the crook of his arm, knowing she was safe and loved—even if he didn't know his own heart yet.

Chapter 18

Tonight was The Night. Two weeks had passed since Hanan had tied her to the tree, and her wounds had scabbed over.

Morning rose with twin orbs gracing the sky—the bright sun to the east and the pale slip of the full moon visible and awaiting its hour to usurp the heavens.

Annie had glanced fretfully at the moon for hours, knowing that with each minute that passed, she was either a step closer to a future with Tombi or a step closer to losing him forever. Various hunters had come and gone throughout the day, conferring with Tombi on tonight's battle strategy.

Annie shyly moved among them, her hair adorned with two skinny plaits at the front, the hunters' gifted feathers braided in the strands. She gleaned from snatched conversations that in the prebattle ritual, she was to summon her hawk for the heirloom flute to defeat Nalusa.

Talk about pressure. If only Grandma Tia were here, but she'd be in rehab a few more days.

She fully understood what Tombi had dealt with for years; the weight of responsibility pressed down, smothering her lungs until her breath grew shallow and her stomach leaden. What if the hawk had been injured or killed? The hunters had found no trace of Hanan, no clue as to who had been the victor in that skirmish.

The murmur of voices grew louder in the cabin's den as the whisper of twilight approached. A furtive glance behind, and Annie snuck out the back door, certain no one saw her. The heat had cooled from near one hundred degrees to the low nineties. Tolerable. Nothing like the cool night air of the North Georgia Mountains, but she'd been a summer visitor to the bayou ever since she was a baby and had acclimated to the heat and humidity, as much as humanly possible.

Not to say she enjoyed it. Annie grabbed the front of her T-shirt and fanned the cotton cloth back and forth in a futile effort to dry the perspiration gathered in her cleavage. Quickly, she scurried down the back porch steps, eager to reach the patch of trees that would shelter her from human eyes. There she could beckon her hawk without the prying...

"Where do you think you're going?"

Caught again. Annie's shoulders sagged, and her head lowered. Slowly, she turned around to face Tombi. "Just getting a little air," she called nonchalantly over her shoulder.

"Nice try."

Annie sighed and faced him. "I thought you were absorbed in business."

"I'm never so busy that I don't notice where you are."

"So I see."

"Why do you keep sneaking off? You're welcome to join us. I just didn't think you'd be interested."

Might as well tell him the truth. Annie kicked the toe of her sneakers in the red clay dirt. "We've tried every day to summon my hawk together, and it hasn't worked. Let me try to do it alone without everyone watching. It might work this way." She sighed heavily. "I feel like such a failure when my summons don't work."

"No one will consider it a failure if the hawk doesn't ever show. You can't control an animal guide. He'll show or not, depending on its own will. We all know that." Tombi walked to her and held out his hand. "Come back inside where it's safe. I don't want the distraction of worrying about *you* on top of everything else."

Annie folded her arms under her chest. "Y'all don't stand much of a chance without the flute. Everything depends on my hawk. And me."

Tombi dropped his outreached hand. "This wasn't your battle to start with."

"Well, it is now."

"No. It's too dangerous." He ran a hand through his long hair. "I won't lie. That flute could be crucial, but not at the risk of putting you in more danger."

"I'm already in danger," she pointed out. "I overheard you telling the others that I'll be included in the ritual dance and that we'll try to contact the hawk as a group. But I need to do this on my own."

"No. We do it before the battle, and then you'll stay here in the cabin with one of my hunters on guard."

Anger scraped the back of her throat. "And when were you going to tell me this? Right before the ceremony? It's already dark, almost time for the gathering."

"The less time for you to argue," he said with a rueful grin. "C'mon. Remember how much you hate snakes?"

She glared at his pitiful attempt at humor. "I'm going with you tonight."

"No."

"Yes."

"No."

"You can't stop me. I'm going to contact my hawk now, and I'll be with you and the others this evening." Annie spun away.

She made it all of three steps before Tombi caught up to her and placed a heavy hand on her shoulder. "How about a compromise?" he suggested.

She raised an eyebrow.

"I come with you now and stay by your side while you connect with your hawk. In turn, you'll agree to stay at the cabin this evening."

One step at a time. Get the flute and then renegotiate. "Okay. But stay at least a few feet away from me when I petition my guide. He'll be more likely to show up."

Annie had no idea if that were true, but Tombi's proximity made it impossible to concentrate on anything but the music of his heart.

He nodded and dipped forward in a mock bow. "I'm following you. Lead on."

Annie smiled to herself. Victory was won a battle at a time. She strolled to the path to the woods, Tombi close on her heels.

The temperature mercifully dipped several degrees under the canopy of trees. Annie located a fallen log and sat on the makeshift bench. Tombi backed off a few feet and stood, watching.

"Don't stare. You're making me nervous," Annie complained.

Tombi gave a long-suffering sigh. "I'll be over here." He gestured at a tree a few feet behind him. "No farther."

"Fine."

Annie deliberately turned her back on Tombi and drew

three deep, calming breaths. She let down the shields Tombi had taught her to erect and fully opened her senses. Wind whistled in the treetops, twigs crunched with the scurrying of small animals, the swell of an ocean wave breaking from far, far away, the hum of insects, Tombi's heartbeat. Annie drew the cinnamon stick sprinkled with frankincense essential oil from her mojo bag and inhaled. She held it between her palms as she pressed them together into the prayer position.

"I beseech thee, hawk," she whispered. "Your will is your own, your heart wild and free to roam the bayou. But if possible, I need your help. By the power of the universe that created you to fly and me to walk on land, I ask that you appear."

She paused and cocked her head to the side, straining to hear its presence above. A cold chill chased down her spine. What if Hanan had managed to free himself of the hawk's talons and kill it?

No. Surely she would have heard or felt some sign of such a catastrophe. Annie tried again.

"Please, help. We need that flute. Just this one favor is all I ask. With the flute we can stop Nalusa and contain the birds of the night—*ishkitini*—that prey upon you, as well. In the name of all the holy saints, please, come. Amen."

She kept her eyes pressed shut, hardly daring to breathe. Every second that ticked increased her agitation, and her fingers stroked the soft feathers braided in her hair. Annie crumpled the cinnamon stick in her hand and held it to her nose. The sweet spice odor calmed her mind, allowing her to focus. She pictured her hawk, flying high above the oaks and pines, wings spread majestically, eyes sharp and probing, searching below. Seeking, seeking. In its left talon, its gnarly claws clutched the thin reed—the flute that held their hope and safety. Salvation. How very fragile and small it appeared in the sky. So much rested on such a fragile instrument.

Have faith.

Grandma Tia's voice commanded—pristine and visceral—cutting through the static of the cacophony and doubt swirling through her mind.

That's all ya got to do, child. Faith moves the mountains and makes all things possible. Yer stronger than ya know. Make me proud.

If only her grandma were sitting beside her, holding her hand. She could do it then.

But Grandma Tia was miles away. This was something she had to do alone. Something sacred and holy between her and the hawk.

"I'm waiting," she whispered. "For as long as it takes, I'll wait for you."

The beating of wings roared above, loud as a hovering helicopter. Annie looked up. Her hawk screeched and flew close, so close its rapid heartbeat fluttered in her ears, and she heard the wind rustle its feathers. The flute was clamped in its hooked beak.

Annie tentatively held out a trembling hand. The hawk was upon her; she smelled the dusty scent of its skin beneath the feathers, felt its hot breath on her face. She wanted to run, wanted to tell it to give the flute to Tombi, but to do so would betray its trust, would repudiate the their bond.

She sank her heels into the red clay, determined to stay rooted.

The hollowed tube thudded onto her opened palm, and she curled her fingers on the warmed wood...

And nearly dropped it when the hawk took flight, disappearing in a loud roar, as suddenly as it had first appeared. Annie clutched the flute to her chest, watching in humbled awe as the hawk became a speck of brown in the darkened sky and then became one with the shadows. Would she ever see him again?

"Thank you," she whispered.

Tombi stepped in front of her, waiting for her to gather her emotions. "Your hawk came through. I'll be damned."

"No. You'll be saved."

He laid his dark hands over her own. The flute pulsed like a living creature. Joyful notes teased her mind; the Choctaw artifact knew it had come home once again.

"This belongs to you," she said, placing the flute between his fingers.

Tombi lowered his head and rested his forehead on hers. The moment was as sacred and precious as a wedding kiss, a vow of love, the promise of a future. All the things that could now be theirs.

He pulled away. "It's time. Thanks to you, we have a chance."

"More than a chance. You can't lose now."

"We won't." He squared his shoulders and took her hand. "Wait until the others see this. Tonight's ritual will be one of celebration."

Sparks of fire crackled and swirled upward, whipped by the Gulf breeze. The scent of burning oak, salty air and purifying sage signaled the welcoming of the full moon, sights and sounds he'd experienced since he was a young boy. The murmurs of his people were solemn and hushed, even more so than usual. Not finding Hanan had been a blow to their confidence.

Tombi came to an abrupt halt. "Wait."

Annie skidded to a stop beside him. "What's wrong?"

"Nothing. Thanks to you." Tombi pressed the flute into her hands. "You should be the one to carry this in."

She shook her head and tried to hand it back. "I don't care—"

"No argument." He took long strides away from her, emerging from the wooded path and into the field, Annie trailing behind.

The murmur of voices halted as they all stared at their approach. Annie hung back, and Tombi motioned her forward.

"We've got great news," he declared.

Tallulah broke from the group. "Did you find Hanan?" she asked, peering behind his shoulders.

"Even better news." He turned to Annie. "Show them."

Hesitantly, she raised the flute.

"The ancient instrument that will help us defeat Nalusa has been returned to us."

Tallulah was the first in line to celebrate. She eyed it critically and then faced Annie. Her throat worked. "Thank you," she said gruffly. She threw her arms around Annie and hugged her.

Tombi grinned at the round *oh* of astonishment on Annie's face.

"—knew she could do it."

"—never doubted her—"

"Tonight we win—"

"—Hanan is dead meat."

One by one, every hunter shook Annie's hand. Pride swelled Tombi's heart at her humble acceptance of their tributes. She'd won them over, had become one of them.

And had won his heart, as well. If they defeated Nalusa this evening... No. Tombi gritted his teeth. Tonight was all about the battle. Nalusa and his shadows would pay for the deaths of his parents, for Tallulah's suffering, for the suffering he'd caused everyone in the bayou. He would *not* be distracted from his destiny and duty.

Mela, the drummer, began beating the hand drum. Its rhythm was a call for celebration. Chulah and Pisa took Annie by either hand and led her to the fire. Tombi gathered with the others, and they encircled the bonfire piled with dried sage. The drumming stopped. Through the smoke and heat waves, he saw that all eyes were on him, awaiting the signal to begin. He raised his right arm, and the drumming began, slow and measured. Each put their right hand on the back of the hunter in front of them and stepped forward on their left foot, then slowly dragged their right foot beside the other and stomped.

The tempo increased, then slowed back down to its original pace, his signal to begin the antiphonal chorus. Tombi released two war cries and sang an old, old song calling upon the sun for power. After every stanza, the hunters repeated the verse until the song had been sung three times through.

He looked back at Annie and winked. She had a look of dazed excitement. This full-moon ritual was undoubtedly more colorful and exciting than the paper-burning ritual she and her grandmother shared.

"Enough," he said. "Let's save our energy for capturing Nalusa."

A large cheer erupted.

"You each know your assignments. Release as many wisps' souls as possible, and then at the first note of the flute, we attack."

Chulah raised a fist. "Tonight it ends!"

Tombi waited until the resulting cheering died down. "We have every reason to be confident, but don't take anything for granted. Even in a weakened condition, Nalusa is powerful and cunning," he cautioned. "Plus, Hanan may still be out there. So be on the lookout."

He stared each hunter in the face, and they nodded

grimly. Childhood faces of friends he'd played stickball with, had wrestled with, gone to school with since kindergarten. "Courage and luck be with you, my friends."

In groups of twos and threes they disappeared into the darkness of the woods, until it was just Annie and him standing by the dwindling fire. Silently, she handed him the flute, and he carefully placed it in his backpack.

"I'll put out the fire, and then I want you to stay inside the cabin until I return. Don't open the door for anyone."

Annie lifted her chin. "I'm going with you."

Why was he not surprised? "No. You've done more than enough." He dragged over a bucket of sand by one of the tents and threw it on the fire.

Annie grabbed another one, her small body bent over double from lifting the fifty pounds. "I want to be with you."

"You would be a distraction," he argued, relieving her of the bucket and tossing it on the dying embers.

Which was partly true, but the thought of Nalusa sinking his fangs into Annie would destroy his soul like a battalion of shadows couldn't. If she didn't want to save herself, at least she'd listen to reason about hindering his safety.

She opened her mouth, as if to offer more objections, but he kissed her—hard and swift. If all else failed, he had to know that Annie lived on, that his life had been worth something, that he had helped her control her gift.

Annie loved him, but he'd held a bit of himself back, and she knew it. If he died, he wanted her to move on and find someone who could give her all of himself. Someone who could put her happiness first.

Tombi told her none of this.

He ended the kiss. The longer he waited, the more difficult the parting.

"Go inside," he said gruffly.

She shook her head.

"Please."

Annie bit her lip. "Maybe I could help if you take me with you."

"No. I would be looking out for you and not focusing on anything else."

"If you're sure—"

"Very. Go." He stepped back and crossed his arms. "I'll watch until you get inside."

With a sigh, she nodded and walked slowly back to the cabin.

Her silhouette appeared in the den window, and she pressed her face against the glass.

He longed to go to her, to the warmth and light of the cabin. But his duty was clear, and he would not stray. Tombi turned away and headed into the inky blackness of the bayou swamp.

Annie restlessly paced the cabin; burning some energy moderately helped manage the terror. She'd done everything she could do, lit incense, prayed at her makeshift altar and called Grandma Tia and asked her to do the same. She stared out the window, willing Tombi to materialize from out of the darkness, to walk across the field and back into her arms. Alive and safe and victorious.

Nothing but night's black veil. She drew the curtain and started to turn when a speck of light appeared in her peripheral vision. Annie stared again into the night.

A blue-green orb skittered to within a few feet of the window. Its shaped wavered and flickered like a candle in the wind; the green color pulsed rapidly within its core.

High-pitched wailing assaulted her ears. She recognized that voice.

Bo.

Tombi was in danger. Annie flew to the door and ran down the porch stairs. "What's happened?"

"You must come. Quick. Bring your herbs."

"Is it Tombi?" she asked, already rushing back up to the door.

"No." She could have sworn she heard sobbing. "It's Tallulah. Hurry."

Relief washed over her, followed by a tinge of guilt. She didn't want anybody hurt or killed. Annie grabbed her pocketbook and went to her altar, stuffing in everything available: candles, herbs, essential oils, Florida water, tea.

Back out the door she followed the flickering, agitated wisp that held Bo's soul. Even without the light, she could locate Bo from the grief-stricken melody that flowed out of him like a mighty river. On and on she stumbled through the swamp until a stitch cramped her side, and each breath felt like inhaling flames of fire.

Annie stopped and leaned against an oak, trying to catch her breath.

"Almost there," Bo urged.

Reluctantly, she straightened and pressed on.

Another few feet and Annie heard a low moan of pain.

"Here. Help her!" The wisp pulsed in and out with agitation above a cypress, and then its light faded away. Underneath, Tallulah cowered, hands clutching her temples.

She rushed over and dropped to her knees. "Tallulah, it's me, Annie. What happened to you?"

Eyes fogged with pain looked up at her in confusion. "Wh-what are you doing here? Dangerous. I sense a wisp is nearby."

"We're safe for the moment. Where are you hurt?" Annie pushed Tallulah's hair from her face, searching for blood or a wound.

Tallulah placed a hand on the back of her skull. "Here."

Annie felt the baseball-sized knot. "How did this happen?"

"Felled by my own weapon," she said bitterly. "I shot a wisp, and one of the *ishkitini* grabbed my stone and threw it back at me." She whimpered as Annie probed the damage. "Strange. That's never happened before." She stopped and drew a shaky breath. "Wasn't…expecting it."

"Nalusa and his shadows grow stronger," Bo said.

Tallulah stilled. "Did you hear something? Or did this blow to the head make me crazy?"

Annie scrambled in her bag and pulled out a bottle of water. She added a tincture of willow bark. "This might help the pain," she said gently.

Tallulah lifted the bottle to her lips and drank greedily.

"Is she going to be okay?" Bo asked anxiously.

"I hear something again." Tallulah straightened. "I swear it sounded like… Bo? Are you out there? Can you hear me?"

The wisp glowed and flickered before them.

"Tallulah. My love."

Wonder clouded Tallulah's eyes. "Bo! I can hear you." Tears ran down her face. "I've missed you so much. Come back to me."

"If only I could."

Bo's voice was filled with such sadness, Annie felt her own eyes fill with tears. She couldn't imagine how awful it would be if something were to happen to her love.

"But it's time to let go of the past," Bo said. "For better or worse, the battle ends tonight. Before it starts, I need you to do one thing for me."

"Whatever you want," Tallulah promised at once.

"Release me. There's nothing more I can do to help."

"But…if I release your spirit, I'll never be near you again."

"I'll still be with you. I'll be there when the birds sing at morning's awakening, when the wind lifts the hair from the back of your neck during the noonday heat, and when the stars glow in the heavens at night, I'll be watching over you."

Tallulah wept, and Annie cried, too, for the gentle man who had been Tombi's best friend and who had been taken so young and had been so in love.

"And I'll look for you and remember you. Always." Tallulah dried her eyes and struggled to her feet, a rock in her hands.

Annie turned her back. The moment was too intimate and personal to witness.

A whoosh of sound and the air shimmered with a splintering of light, until one lone glow remained. It hovered a few seconds and then sped up into the heavens.

It was done.

"I thought he'd never leave."

Tallulah spun around, but Annie absorbed the shock in the pit of her stomach. She turned slowly, as if her body was weighted by cement blocks. As if some small part of her mind had known this was inevitable.

Hanan, sporting a grotesque, bloodied scar across his forehead, gripped a leather belt in front of him, snapping it open and shut, the sound a riptide in Annie's ears as she imagined the strap cutting into her flesh.

"Run, Annie," Tallulah demanded.

"No." Annie stepped close to Hanan. She had her hawk and her hoodoo, while Tallulah was only armed with a bag of rocks.

Hanan roughly pulled her tight against his body and jerked her so she faced forward; the bite of the belt choked into her neck until she could barely breathe. "Leave or I'll kill her now," he warned.

"You son of a bitch," Tallulah snarled. "I can't believe I ever—"

"Screwed me?" Hanan asked, amusement lacing his words. "You quite enjoyed it. Over and over again. Remember?"

An *ishkitini* screeched nearby. Annie lifted a hand and signaled for Tallulah to go. Pain erupted as Hanan twisted her neck, so fiercely Annie heard sinew and tendon pop from deep within. She whimpered.

"Stay and watch your friend suffer," he spat. "The *ishkitini* will do much worse to you."

Tallulah scowled at Hanan and turned to Annie. "I'll get help," she vowed.

Annie stared at the promise in Tallulah's eyes until the acorn-brown pupils disappeared and blurred into the stygian darkness.

The night was alive with the drone of stinging insects, the thrashing of tree limbs, a rumble of distant ocean waves and the rasping breath of her captor hot in her ears. Through the symphony of terror, she heard her own heart thump as violently as a trapped rabbit's quivering.

She'd never felt so utterly alone.

Chapter 19

The eerie shrieks of the *ishkitini* prickled the flesh on Tombi's forearms, yet he continued on, ever deeper into the woods, until the air became dense with a suffocating miasma, which meant wisps were nearby.

Lots of them.

Above the treetops, flocks of *ishkitini* shadowed the full moon. Will-o'-the-wisps, *Hashok Okwa Hui'ga*, lit the ground in a ghostly festival of lights, outnumbering his hunters by a large margin.

An overwhelming despair threatened to slow his steps, but Tombi pushed on, heading for the sacred land of his ancestors. Nalusa knew he was in a compromised position and had gathered all his forces to even the fight.

He pictured Annie, remembered his sister and friends who were circling around the edge of the wisps, coming together to encircle Nalusa and his shadow beings. He threw back his shoulders and fingered the backpack straps holding the flute. He took comfort in possessing the ultimate weapon and that Annie was safe in his cabin.

Another fifty feet to go until reaching the sacred land border. The wisps sensed the danger; they darted across the swamp erratically, moaning with the souls of the trapped spirits. The squall of misery that combated the *ishkitini* screeching. Tombi drew a deep breath and focused on the human footsteps advancing along with him. All was according to plan.

He plunged forward until he was a good ten feet inside his ancestral land. It was time. Attack the wisps now, and free as many spirits as possible before playing the flute and confronting Nalusa. If he did it too early, the shadow king would cower behind his following. And Tombi wanted the chance to wrestle him, one on one. Tombi cawed, mimicking a crow.

And ran. All of the tribe rushed inward, compressing the circle's circumference. They threw rocks, careful not to throw strong enough to hit one another. A few wisps escaped, light blinking upward, the inner hearts glowing and pulsing. If they defeated Nalusa, they would do a cleanup operation later to find and free the remaining trapped souls. But if Nalusa won, the poor souls would be trapped forever, roaming the swamps with the parasitic wisps controlling their movements. Tombi doubted any of them had Bo's incredible will and strength to briefly take control of the wisps and communicate with the outside world.

Puffs of smoke erupted from the glowing wisp hearts—like a million sparklers waving in the sea breeze. The sparkles burned out, and the souls coalesced into pure white light that spiraled upward. If Annie were here, she could detect a symphony. At least, that was how Tombi imagined it would be—utter joy at the sudden freedom.

The screeching above intensified. A great horned owl flew directly at him, eyes aglow with murderous intent. There was no time to grab another stone and fend him off. Tombi clutched the dagger in his left hand, his own eyes focused on the owl's breast, its most vulnerable place, housing its beating heart.

The owl would scratch first, before his knife could strike, and it would be a vicious slice into flesh, or worse, it could rip out his eyes. A quick glance around, and he saw the *ishkitini* bearing down on them all. Damn birds. To be defeated by these winged creatures would be humiliating.

A burst of light appeared between him and the owl. Tombi blinked and threw his right hand over his eyes to protect himself from the blinding conflagration.

It was a trapped spirit who, instead of flying up and away, had remained.

A loud screech of pain rent the night air. A smell of burned feathers and singed animal flesh clogged his nose and throat. Tombi crouched low and removed his arm from his eyes. The *ishkitini* lay before him—dead.

The lone light rocketed up and away, chasing its freedom with the others released. All around him, his tribe took aim and fired at the advancing *ishkitini*. Nearly a third of them were taken down, and the rest turned tail.

Tombi smiled in grim satisfaction. The tribe moved closer until they formed a tight circle. A few of the men were bleeding, but all looked well. Yet…

"Where's Tallulah?" he asked, fear thickening his tongue.

Chulah stepped forward, his face haggard. "No one's seen her in over an hour."

"Go find her," he ordered.

His friend nodded and left the circle, eager to ease his mind. *She's okay. She can defend herself.* Tombi respected her defense abilities and sharp mind. He couldn't worry about his twin until Nalusa was defeated.

They would never have a better time than this moment. Two of the hunters quickly gathered twigs and started a bonfire in the center of the circle. Each of them threw bundles of sage on the flames, the pungent scent that helped counter evil and allow the holy to enter.

Tombi dug the flute out of his backpack and blew on it, beginning an ancient song of victory. The notes drifted, pure and compelling, filling him with purpose and resolve.

A rustle shook the underbrush a few yards away, and the grinding metal whir began, drowning out the flute music. Tombi stopped playing. A whiff of decay permeated the land. Tombi's heart tripped, and all his senses heightened. His friends turned and stared, and they waited as one for Nalusa to appear.

Dark shadows melded into the form of a tall, thin man who stepped into their vision. He had small pointed ears and red, glowing eyes that sought Tombi.

"So you've got the flute," Nalusa said in a voice that rumbled like thunder. "But you are still no match for me."

"We'll see about that. Seems all your help has disappeared." Tombi lifted his hand, ready to signal for his friends to begin the attack.

"That doesn't mean I am without power. I have something you want. Something you consider precious."

Tombi hesitated, arm held midair. His heart skittered up to his throat. Nalusa had his sister. What else could it be? Unless…

Another rustle from behind a clump of cypress trees, and more dark shadows emerged. Two of them. A blond male and a slight woman with a familiar shock of brown hair curling down to her hips.

"Annie!" Tombi's hand dropped to his side, and a

numbed shock bolted through his body like a current. His fingers loosened, and the flute began to slip. He fisted both hands, and the cane reed almost snapped in two pieces while he willed his mind to catch up to his racing heart. *Not Annie. Not Annie. Please, not Annie.*

Nalusa's deep-throated laugh jangled through the bayou. "Ready to make a deal? The flute for your girlfriend."

"Don't do it, Tombi!" Annie pleaded. "This is your chance."

Hanan jerked the leather strap, and Annie's knees crumpled, face contorted in agony.

No. What mattered most was no longer revenge. It was love. He would fight Nalusa not just for his sister's ruined life or the tribe that was his family now. Not for his dead friend and not for the greater good of humanity, but he would fight to save Annie. He'd do whatever necessary to keep her safe.

She was his world.

"How about this," Tombi said, slipping the backpack off his shoulders and letting it drop to the ground. "Have Hanan release Annie, and we battle for the flute. Just you and I."

Nalusa ran a hand over his long, pointed face, ears twitching and teeny eyes surveying Tombi.

"I'm a mere human," Tombi goaded. "This shouldn't be hard for you."

"You are more than a puny mortal." A fine drizzle of spit foamed at the corners of his thin lips. He pointed a finger at Hanan. "Release the girl."

Hanan scowled but took a step backward.

Damn traitor. If he defeated Nalusa tonight, he'd show no mercy dealing with Hanan later. Annie took great gulps of air, and Tombi winced at her suffering.

He stepped toward Nalusa, fists raised, and they commenced circling one another—watchful, with deadly intent, gauging their first moves. By the bonfire's light, Tombi saw that Nalusa's face was largely featureless, with only a shadowy patch of skin where a nose and cheekbones should appear. His flesh was black, but patterned copper designs shimmered on his skin in the firelight, making him appear half human, half snake. Even though the eyes were human-shaped, the red embers of his pupils burned with the misery of a thousand souls.

Tombi stared harder. Did he see human faces contorting in misery within those red eyes? He took a deep breath. *Focus. I can't let him invade my mind, or I've lost before the fight has begun.*

Nalusa struck first, swinging a right hook, aimed at Tombi's face.

Tombi ducked at the last possible second and put out a foot to trip Nalusa. The soul-eater danced away and regained his balance.

"Not bad," he muttered. "You've been training for this fight for years, haven't you?"

Tombi didn't respond, waiting for Nalusa to show a moment's loss of concentration before he tried to volley a series of punches.

Melancholy roiled over him in waves. A bitter miasma invaded his lungs, his heart. Fighting seemed…too hopeless, too futile. Who was he to think he could battle the Shadow King? He stiffened his spine and shook off the dreary thoughts.

Go for the neck. According to ancient lore, if Nalusa had a weakness, it was this one part of his anatomy.

Nalusa lunged, swinging wildly with his right fist. Tombi pushed at the advancing arm, spinning and hammering Nalusa in the back of the neck with his right elbow. Numbness shot through his right arm. A stinger injury. The

Shadow King's neck muscles were as heavy as cement, muscular and flexible beneath a wall of sinewy muscle.

So much for ancient legend.

Nalusa staggered, but at once regained his balance and threw a few fake jabs, obviously trying to find a weakness in Tombi's defense. Tombi stayed alert. He wanted to shake the numbed right arm and get the blood flowing, but to do so would clue in Nalusa on his injury. He couldn't let that happen.

Time for a little testing of his own. He threw a fake punch but overcommitted, leaving the one side of his body open and vulnerable. Pain exploded in his right hip, and he was thrown to the ground from a vicious kick. Didn't take Nalusa but a nanosecond to react to an opportunity. Tombi rolled a couple of yards and leaped back to his feet, body semi-crouched and fists up in the defensive position.

That had been close, a near thing. It was believed that if Nalusa grabbed a man, there was no escape. His strength was equal to a thirty-foot boa that could constrict and crush muscle and bone.

Nalusa advanced and delivered a barrage of left and right punches. Tombi's quick reflexes deflected each one, but the assault still weakened his strength. His hip ached, and his right arm still tingled. No doubt his enemy realized this and was toying with him like a broken-winged bird being bitch-slapped by a hungry cat.

At last, Nalusa seemed to grow impatient. He scowled and drew his arm back and then forward, ready to deliver a killing blow.

Tombi turned to the side at the last possible second, which left his opponent startled and off balance.

There would never be a better chance.

He gathered all his strength and power and kicked Nalusa in the head, knocking him to the ground.

Nalusa stood and slowly smiled. "No one has ever lasted more than a minute fighting me. Finally, I have a worthy opponent."

Despair again threatened to engulf Tombi's mind. He'd delivered his best move, a kick that would have killed any man. Yet, his enemy shook it off. Nothing had worked. Not the sacred relics in his medicine bag, not Annie's charms and not his years of training for this fight.

Annie's scream ripped the air. Ripped his heart.

Tombi spun around, ready to rush to her defense. A giant hand clamped on his left shoulder bore down, guiding him to face forward again.

Scalding pain ripped the front of his chest, and the scent of blood assaulted his nose. His blood. Dazed, he glanced down and saw shredded flesh. How had this happened?

Nalusa laughed and licked a bloody finger that sported long, razor fingernails as lethal as the *ishkitini*'s talons. "Mmm…delicious."

Chills prickled his arms and chased down his spine. He'd been warned that Nalusa's saliva was poisonous, no matter what form he appeared in. Now that venom was invading his bloodstream, would spread to every inch of his body. He had to stop this. Had to get to Annie. In desperation, he opened the medicine bag belted at his waist and removed a blessed bottle of tannic acid mixed with spring water from their sacred land.

He poured it over his lacerated chest, praying for the best.

The pain stopped immediately. Tombi tossed the empty bottle aside. "Fight's not over yet."

Nalusa's eyes flashed, the banked fires of his pupils flamed. Enraged, he swooped down and grabbed a large branch and charged.

The loss of blood had left him dizzy, but Tombi clamped

his jaw shut and stiffened his shoulders. If he failed tonight, he'd have to trust that his friends would carry on the fight against evil. That Annie would go on to live a long and happy life. That his death held some meaning and purpose.

Shrill screams echoed in Annie's brain like the death throes of a wild cat in a canyon. Only the raw burning at the back of her throat clued her in that it was her own voice.

Blood. So much blood. It seeped and oozed from Tombi's chest in crimson ribbons. She'd tried to scream a warning, but all she'd done was make it worse for Tombi.

"It's almost over now, bitch."

A thousand needles of fire prickled the back of her scalp as Hanan jerked her to her feet.

"And we can continue where I left off last time." His arm went around her stomach, and Hanan shoved her against his hard body. "But this time, it's going to hurt so bad," he whispered in her ear. "You are going to pay for what that hawk did to me. It will be long and painful, and when I'm through with your body, I'll kill you."

"You're crazy."

Hanan took one of her arms and pinned it behind her back. "Shut up and enjoy the show. Tombi was a fool not to join Nalusa. He's paying for it now."

Annie's gaze swept the ring of warriors and their grim, set faces. Couldn't they see Tombi needed help? Damn their pride and honor. *I have to do something.*

Annie closed her eyes and took long, shuddering breaths, willing the noise and the smells and Hanan's painful grasp to fade. She pictured herself falling down a long, dark tunnel, falling, falling...to a safe, quiet space where none could intrude. *Help me, Grandma Tia. I beseech the saints and all that is holy and good, be with me. Help me escape Hanan and help Tombi. Don't allow evil to soil this sacred land and destroy the one I love. I ask for a sign.*

A strong cadence, a marching music, lifted her out of the tunnel, speeding Annie back to present reality. Tallulah was near.

A thud, like the sound of a cracked egg, vibrated along her spine. Hanan's arm dropped, and he fell backward.

Annie whirled around and instinctively cowered.

Tallulah shoved Hanan's back with her foot, and he rolled lifelessly beneath her. "Good riddance," she muttered.

"Forget him. Tombi needs our help." Annie tugged at Tallulah's shirt, desperate to save Tombi.

Tallulah shook her head. "No. I was behind the trees and heard the deal. Nalusa and Tombi, one on one. We wait."

"To hell with that." Annie turned, but Tallulah grabbed her arm and held her.

"No. My brother must win it on his own merit. You can't dishonor him and our people."

Annie's eyes sought Tombi's, looked for some reassurance that he could win.

Tombi staggered like a drunken sailor; blood ran in rivulets down his chest. It didn't look as if he could win anything in his condition.

Annie sank to her knees and prayed. *One more request. By the power of all the elements and roots and all the magic of the bayou and the saints...protect my love. Shield his mind and body with a golden aura that Nalusa cannot penetrate.*

She hardly dared open her eyes, afraid of what she might find. If Tombi died...the sun would set on her happiness. Once, her only wish was silence, but Tombi had helped her achieve so much more, had opened her eyes to love and possibility and what it meant to live a life of courage and honor.

Be brave now. Be there for him if the end is truly near. Annie took a deep breath, preparing for the worst, and opened her eyes.

Light as vivid as marigolds surrounded Tombi's body. Her spell had worked like nothing she'd ever before even thought to attempt. Awe and hope flushed out the pit of dread she'd fallen into.

Nalusa snarled and bared his teeth; the grinding noise of metal whirred from within his thin body, sounding like the wailing of thousands of souls trapped in hell. His eyes flashed, red and crackling like fire.

Music as pure as harps and flutes played a symphony from Tombi's golden aura.

Nalusa thrust his right hand at Tombi, attempting to cut into his flesh once more. The long, gnarly fingers extended and sizzled upon contact with the light. Nalusa screamed and jerked his hand to his chest, as if he'd been burned.

Tombi's brows knit, and he turned, seeking understanding. Annie scrambled to her feet, and he gazed directly at her and nodded. *Thank you*, he mouthed.

Before she could respond, Tombi whirled back around to face Nalusa and charged, throwing his weight onto Nalusa. They fell to the ground, Tombi on top. His hands encircled Nalusa's neck, and his thumbs bore down into the soul-eater's windpipe.

She couldn't watch. Annie looked down at the ground. The metal grinding noise slowed, decreased in volume. And stopped.

Was he dead?

From behind, Tallulah cheered, and the other hunters joined in. Tallulah put a hand on her shoulder and gave a little shove. "You can open your eyes now. It's over. Did you have something to do with that light?"

Annie opened her eyes. Nalusa had been reduced in size until his height only reached Tombi's hips. A thick cord was knotted around his neck, and Tombi, whose aura had dimmed until all that remained was the suggestion of a yellow haze, held the end of the rope.

"I…I thought Nalusa was dead. What's happening?"

"You can't kill Nalusa Falaya. Not completely. All you can do is contain his power." Tallulah pumped a fist in the air. "And we've done it!"

Tombi held up a hand and silenced the cheers. A hush settled over the bayou, as profound as the windless calm before a hurricane. Tombi jerked on the rope and led Nalusa forward; the hunters fell in behind the two.

"C'mon," Tallulah urged.

Mystified, Annie tagged along.

Tombi broke out in song. His rich, deep baritone formed Choctaw words she couldn't understand. He'd sing a chorus or two, and then the hunters would repeat the same lyric back, like a church reading.

All singing stopped abruptly as Tombi approached a gigantic oak that looked as eternal as the land itself. The circumference of the tree must have been at least six feet, and its trunk and branches seemed to extend forever to the sky.

"Please, let me go," Nalusa whined like a toddler. "I promise to be good. Really. I won't cause any more trouble." His voice was high-pitched and scratchy.

Tombi shook his head. "You cannot be trusted. Time to return to your home." He picked up Nalusa and stuffed him into the large hollowed-out hole in the tree.

Nalusa screamed and kicked, but he was no match for Tombi. He disappeared into the hole with a long wail that lingered and echoed through the bayou.

A single coral ray from the rising sun cracked open the sky, and birds began chirping.

Real birds, normal birds. Not the piercing shrieks of the *ishkitini*. Their voices were like a blessing and benediction, nature's omen of the triumph of good over evil. A great weariness settled in Annie's bones as the pump of adrenaline crashed, recognizing Tombi was out of danger and her work was done.

Tombi retrieved the ancient flute from his jeans pocket and blew on it three times—short, staccato bursts. He raised both arms, lifting the flute skyward. "Let peace return to Bayou La Siryna. May Nalusa Falaya and his power over the shadow beings be forever constrained to this ancient tree until the end of time. May our ancestors look upon us now with favor, and may the sun's warming shine bless our work here today. We ask in the name of all that is holy and right and just."

"Ikahli. Amen," Tallulah muttered at Annie's side.

Tombi lowered his arms and placed the flute inside the hollowed oak and turned to them. "It's over," he said simply. "Finally. Thank you, my friends." He nodded at his sister. "I see we are all one again." A shadow crossed his face. "Except for Bo."

Tallulah spoke up. "Bo's spirit was released tonight. He's at peace." Her voice broke slightly at the end, and Chulah made his way to her, encircling her waist with an arm.

Annie smiled at his act of caring. Surely one day Tallulah would recognize he loved her, and she could move on from her grief.

"But there is still one thing left to do," Tombi declared.

The hunters looked at one another quizzically.

Tombi marched to where Annie stood and took her hands in hers. "I owe you my life. *We* owe you our lives.

Without you, this wouldn't have been possible. At last, I can tell you what is in my heart."

He dropped to one knee, and Annie gasped.

"I love you, Annie Matthews. Will you marry me?"

Chapter 20

"The Blood Moon of October is a-comin' tonight. Yer life will never be the same," Tia Henrietta announced, sprinkling herbs and roots into a mojo bag. Despite the dour words, a broad smile chased away the deep hollows in her face. "Bet you won't be burnin' no slips of paper at midnight, prayin' for the Good Lord to remove yer hearin' gift."

"I have everything I want." Annie patted her grandma's hand, still frail from her recent ordeal, but once again adorned with rings in an explosion of crystal colors. "It's good to have you home again. You concentrate on getting your strength back."

Tia sniffed. "I'm fine now I'm back home. And I intend to be around a long, long time."

"Your heart—"

"Is fine," Tia interrupted. A flush darkened her cheeks, and she dropped her gaze to the mojo bag. "Never nuthin' wrong with it in the first place."

"Wh-what are you saying?" Annie stammered.

"Now, don't you be givin' me that look. I had to get you down here and to visit longer than a few weeks. A little fib never hurt nobody."

"Little fib?" Her spine stiffened, and she took a step back. "How could you lie to me like that? I was worried sick about you."

Tia Henrietta grabbed Annie's hand. "Don't get yer dander up. I had a vision you were needed in Bayou La Siryna and that you would learn to appreciate yer special gift." Tia's lips trembled. "Yer all I have in the world."

Annie softened at the admission. It wasn't easy for her grandma to swallow her pride. And until a few weeks ago, Grandma Tia was all she truly had in the world, as well. How could she be angry when this morning she was right where she was meant to be, surrounded by love? She bent down and kissed the top of Tia's head. "I'm glad you're all right. But no more secrets between us. Okay?"

"Deal." Tia resumed her work, and the ethereal scent of crushed rose petals filled the den. "I intend to be around to see my great-grandchildren one day."

Annie rolled her eyes. "We're not in any hurry for that. I'm going to the kitchen to see if Tallulah needs any help."

Cozy kitchen smells replaced the herbal scents from the den. She watched Tallulah transfer hoecakes from an iron skillet to a plate on the counter, and marched over.

"Mmm." Annie spread butter on a cake and bit in. Creamy sweetness melded with the crispy fried corn bread in an explosion of awesomeness.

Tallulah shot her a sideways glance, a smile tugging her lips. "Heard y'all wouldn't be doing one of your witchy ceremonies tonight at the full moon. Good thing my brother will be keeping you busy until dawn."

Warmth flooded Annie's cheeks, and she almost choked

on a bit of hoecake. Hastily, she poured a glass of sweet tea and took a long swallow.

A sharp ping bounced against the front door.

Annie grinned. "Is that—"

"It is."

Annie put down her glass and turned toward the front door.

"Not so fast." Tallulah tugged at her sleeve. "Our custom is to make the groom wait. He can't think you're too eager."

Annie groaned. "Really? Or is this some sibling thing where you take any opportunity to tease and torment each other?"

"He's too arrogant for his own good," she said, laughing. "I try to take him down a notch when the opportunity arises."

A barrage of thuds assaulted the door.

"What's all that racket?" Tia called from the den.

"Don't worry, I've got it," Annie said, rushing to the front porch. She jerked open the door and blinked. Tombi stood on the steps—tall and dark and long black hair glistening in the sun. In honor of the occasion, he wore a colorfully beaded leather vest and had two narrow braids by the sides of his face with crow and eagle feathers woven in the plaits.

Every time she saw him, her heart rang to know that this magnificent man was hers. Crazy Annie had struck gold.

"About time," he muttered.

Tallulah smiled as she walked up. "Impatient, Tombi?"

"Very," he answered shortly.

The heat from his eyes warmed Annie to the core. He longed to make love again as much as she did, to spend the night together and wake up in the same bed come morning. Ever since Grandma Tia had returned from the hospital three weeks ago, she'd insisted her granddaughter return to the cottage. Arguing about her old-fashioned notions of living together before marriage had been fruitless.

Annie gave him a quick hug. "It won't be long now," she whispered in his ear. He squeezed her in a bear hug, and she laughed and pushed at his chest.

He stepped back with obvious reluctance. "You look beautiful," he said gruffly.

She ran a hand down the front of the vanilla, lacy dress that flowed down to her ankles. Grandma Tia had sewn it with much love and skill. Annie had woven fresh flowers into the bodice and made a matching floral garland for her hair. Like Tombi, she'd also braided two thin strips by her face and threaded in a few of the feathers Tombi's hunters had given her after her ordeal with Hanan.

"Thank you," she said shyly. She bent and picked up one of the smooth, tumbled pebbles Tombi had thrown at the door. "So this is the heralded messenger of love?"

He grinned and gave a mock bow. "A token of my affection."

"You accept it, and there's no going back," Tallulah warned with a snicker.

"I'll keep it forever." Annie stared straight at Tombi as she spoke. Their ancient custom for a man to make an overture to a woman by tossing a pebble her way filled Annie with whimsical delight. She'd honor this stone as much as she did her engagement ring.

Grandma Tia's voice rang out from the den. "That you, Tombi? Come in," she ordered.

Tallulah took off her apron. "I'm going to gather with the rest of the guests outside." She stood on her tiptoes and brushed Tombi's cheek with a swift kiss. "You've got a good woman there," she whispered, before slipping out the door.

Annie took his strong hand in her own, and they entered the den.

"For you," Tombi said, holding out a beaded leather pouch to Tia. "It's filled with natural cures and relics and blessed by our medicine man. He claims it will help strengthen your weak heart."

Annie suppressed a snort. Barely.

Grandma Tia gave her a sharp stare before nodding to Tombi. "Thank you. Please, sit down."

They sat together on the edge of the sofa, across from Tia.

"I have something for you, as well." Tia placed a small red felt mojo bag in his hands.

Tombi held it to his nose and sniffed. "What's in here?"

"Juniper berries, for passion and stamina. You know, in the bedroom."

"Grandma!" Annie blushed, mortified. As if Tombi needed that. He'd kill her if he had any more passion and stamina.

Tombi winked at her.

But, oh, what a glorious way to die.

"I take it this means we have your blessing," he said drily. "Thank you for the gift. I'll be sure to put it to good use."

"You have something for me, too?" Annie asked, trying to turn the conversation.

Tia produced a pink mojo bag tied with lavender ribbon and bulging with her grandma's garden goodies. "I fed this here gris-gris with a bit o' everything while I anointed it with my special marriage oil and recited verses from Song of Solomon. There's catnip to captivate, red clover flowers fer a prosperous marriage, lavender fer romance and harmony, rose petals fer luck, and some juniper berries fer your passion to match Tombi's."

"Sounds like you covered all the bases." Annie suppressed a smile. "Including having the ceremony during the full-moon phase."

"Ain't no use takin' chances." She fixed Tombi with a stern look of warning. "You best take good care of my Annie-girl."

"Yes, ma'am." He reached for Tia, his strong fingers closing over her frail hand. "I promise."

She grinned. "Well, don't tell me. Tell it to the preacher." Tia waved a hand. "Shoo."

Tombi rose and squeezed Annie's shoulder. "I'll be outside waiting for you."

It wouldn't be long now. Annie stood and nervously adjusted the garland in her hair. At the door, Tombi paused and gave her another slow, sexy wink that made her knees turn to jelly.

"Go on now," Tia chuckled.

The front door clicked shut, and Annie paced the pine floorboards. Tia stood watch at the window.

"It's time," Grandma shouted. "Go!"

Annie took a deep breath.

"I'll be joining the rest of the folks out there." She kissed Annie's forehead. "Yer Tombi's a good man. Now git going."

No more waiting. No more lonely nights. No more unlovable Crazy Annie. Excitement bubbled inside. She couldn't wait another moment.

Annie burst out the front door and into the warm sunlight. They were all there. Off to one side of the field stood Tallulah, Miss Verbena, dozens of Grandma Tia's friends and customers, Chulah and all of the former shadow hunters.

And Tombi. Looking as handsome and sexy as she'd ever seen him. Chulah stood at his side, holding his arms.

Tallulah broke from the pack and waved her arms at Annie. "Run!"

She bounded down the porch steps and hit the ground running, conscious of all eyes upon her. No simple wedding march would do for this occasion. She bunched a fistful of the ankle-length dress and ran through the field, feet pounding red clay. No high heels, but the dainty white sandals were an impediment nonetheless. Her heart pumped stronger, truer, in a joyful celebration of love and life. Halfway across the field, she spared a glance over her shoulder.

Unleashed from his friends, Tombi began his chase. Long, loping strides that could easily outpace her. That wouldn't do at all. Annie kicked off the sandals and pumped her legs faster. According to their custom, if he captured her too quickly, it meant either her love was weak or she was uneager to mate.

Neither was true.

Her lungs filled to bursting, and her labored breath echoed in her ears, loud as an oncoming freight train. Had she run far enough and hard enough? Annie eased up slightly at the slight hitch in her right side.

For the first time in her life, she wasn't really running away *from* anything but *to* something. For every step alone in the field, Tombi would match it and then, at last, overtake her. That was, if he truly loved her and wanted to claim her forever.

Only ten feet away, a line of ripened blackberry vines edged the woods where the fattened deer grazed within. The Choctaw called this the Hunter's Moon season, a time of celebrating the harvest and taking stock of provisions for the coming winter. An auspicious time for a wedding. From far away, friends and family shouted their encouragement for Tombi to hurry and claim his bride.

So why hadn't he swept her up yet? He should have

caught her by now. If he loved her and wanted her forever, then why—

The soles of her feet vibrated with the pounding of his footsteps from behind. A great whoosh of air, and Annie was upended, caught up in strong arms that braced her securely under her back and legs. She shrieked and wrapped her arms around his neck.

Tombi's normally somber face was transformed by a triumphant smile. "I've got you now," he said, and the low baritone of his voice strummed against her chest, thrilling her with its promise of complete possession.

"Only because I let you catch me." Best not to let him get too smug. Annie traced his lips with her fingers, marveling at the depth of their love.

"Kiss her!" Chulah shouted.

Amid the whistles and catcalls, Tombi pressed his mouth against hers. A passionate kiss with the promise of more to come. Annie opened her mouth, welcoming him in, deeper.

The harsh sound of beating wings penetrated her haze of passion. Dread tightened her lungs. Had the *ishkitini* returned? She broke away from Tombi and gasped at the sight of a large brown bird swooping down, pale eyes piercing her soul.

Her hawk.

"Thank you," she whispered, weak with profound relief at the recognition. Without her spirit animal, this day wouldn't have been possible. "Thanks for everything."

The hawk slowed, flew closer. Close enough that Annie was able to reach out a hand and brush it against the reddish-brown feathers of his breast. The hawk's heart pulsed beneath her fingers, fast, proud, strong.

And then it was gone. Left in an explosion of movement as abruptly as it had first appeared.

"I was afraid the birds of the night were back," Annie admitted. Tears blurred the edges of the tree limbs and turning leaves as she raised her head, searching for her animal spirit. "I wonder if I'll ever see my hawk again."

"The *ishkitini* can never harm us again. Nalusa's no longer a threat," Tombi assured her.

"And what about my hawk?"

"An animal spirit is yours for life." He planted a tender kiss on her forehead. "Just as I am yours for life."

He carried her in his arms the few remaining yards left to cross in the open field. More good-natured cheering erupted from the gathered witnesses, and Annie laid her head against his broad chest, perfectly at peace.

They reached the forest, a place none of them had reason to fear anymore. Tombi slowly set her back on her feet, and her body brushed the strong, hard length of him. Desire coursed through Annie, pooling at her core. Forever wasn't long enough to love this man and be loved by him.

He took her hand and raised their joined arms. According to custom, this signaled to everyone that they would complete the journey of life equally yoked as husband and wife.

Together.

* * * * *

MILLS & BOON®

n o c t u r n e™

AN EXHILARATING UNDERWORLD OF DARK DESIRES

A sneak peek at next month's titles...

In stores from 10th March 2016:

- **Her Werewolf Hero** – Michele Hauf
- **Immortal Redeemed** – Linda Thomas-Sundstrom

MILLS & BOON®

Why not subscribe?
Never miss a title and save money too!

Here's what's available to you if you join the exclusive **Mills & Boon® Book Club** today:

✦ *Titles up to a month ahead of the shops*
✦ *Amazing discounts*
✦ *Free P&P*
✦ *Earn Bonus Book points that can be redeemed against other titles and gifts*
✦ *Choose from monthly or pre-paid plans*

Still want more?
Well, if you join today, we'll even give you
50% OFF your first parcel!

So visit **www.millsandboon.co.uk/subs**
to be a part of this exclusive Book Club!

MILLS & BOON®

Why shop at millsandboon.co.uk?

Each year, thousands of romance readers find their perfect read at millsandboon.co.uk. That's because we're passionate about bringing you the very best romantic fiction. Here are some of the advantages of shopping at www.millsandboon.co.uk:

* **Get new books first**—you'll be able to buy your favourite books one month before they hit the shops

* **Get exclusive discounts**—you'll also be able to buy our specially created monthly collections, with up to 50% off the RRP

* **Find your favourite authors**—latest news, interviews and new releases for all your favourite authors and series on our website, plus ideas for what to try next

* **Join in**—once you've bought your favourite books, don't forget to register with us to rate, review and join in the discussions

Visit **www.millsandboon.co.uk**
for all this and more today!